I0709353

Devil's Track

Detective Mahoney Series

Julie Hiner

Killers and Demons

Devil's Track © 2023 Julie Hiner

All rights reserved. No part of this publication may be reproduced, stored in a retrieval system, or transmitted, in any form or in any means – by electronic, mechanical, photocopying, recording or otherwise – without prior written permission. All events, locations and characters are either fictional or used in a fictional way, as products of the author's imagination.

First Printing in 2023

Publisher: Julie Hiner

KillersAndDemons.com

Editing by: Taija Morgan

Bio Photo by: Aune Photo

Cover Design: 100 Covers

ISBN: 978-1-7389176-0-0

First Edition

To the wild rock gods of the late 90s.
To all those who seek spiritual enlightenment.
To all those who are wrongly accused.

Contents

Kill or Be killed

Chapter 1

The Cecil

June 1993

Stella Mahoney had a burning desire to sink into the seedy underbelly of her beloved city. *Calgary.* Her birth town. The place she hadn't returned to since her father's funeral.

A clang rang out through the thick night air as a bottle rolled down the dark alleyway. A couple wiry-yet-rough-looking men leaned against a wall beside a dumpster. The ends of their cigarettes blazed red as they inhaled deep drags. Their eyes violated Stella as she passed them, eating her up, devouring her sensuality, tasting the last drops of sweet innocence clinging to her.

She was sixteen, yet she knew she didn't look it. It had been four years since her father had been murdered, and she'd aged a lifetime since then.

Only twelve years old when he died, she had no choice but to comply when her mother forced her away, putting miles between her and the city that had consumed her father. Her mother had spouted a million reasons to whisk her off to a place with beaches and sunshine. Stella knew the truth. Her mother needed to get herself away from all the memories. The long, lonely nights at home, waiting, wondering when, or if, he would walk through the door. Her mother accused him of abandoning them.

The way Stella saw it, *they* had abandoned *him*.

He had no choice. Her detective dad had chased corpses and hunted human monsters because he *needed* to. He was the one who put his own life on the line to save innocent victims. He was the one who stopped a sick man with a taste for blood from taking another young girl. A girl just like Stella.

Her heavy boots hit the oily pavement with wet thuds. A streetlamp buzzed at the end of the alleyway, flickering, trying to stay alive for lone passengers.

Chatter crawled from around the corner. Signs of civilization in this seedy pit, deep in the belly of the downtown core. Stella followed it. She wanted to see, to feel, to taste the places her father had left his essence in, putting the pieces together, solving gruesome murders, hunting killers. She was thrilled for the first time in a while when her mother had expressed a desire to stay connected with friends she'd left behind. Stella had put on a show for her mother's friends, smiling and being polite for the entire day. When they finally returned to the hotel, her mother popped a couple sleeping pills and chugged several glasses of wine. Stella knew the memories were too much. They'd visited all the places her mother and father used to hang out, before he was a detective, when he called her mother *Bea*. Stella could still hear the soft snore from her mother's side of the room as she'd made her sneaky departure.

Stella walked along Riverfront Avenue, the dark river snaking beside the pathway, the moon glimmering off its sheer surface. She'd gone into a couple joints where they welcomed her pretty face and ignored the hint of how young she was. None of the places felt raw enough to saturate her need to feel the darkest pit of this city.

After crossing the centre line of the core into the east end, the population along the pathway increased in numbers. Those discarded from society clung to their few belongings, curling into themselves along the riverbank, seeking precious moments of rest where they could leave the reality of their broken lives.

When a flashing neon sign came into view, perched high on an old brick building, Stella turned from the river and walked toward it. Purple-blue flickers called her to *The Cecil*.

Two blocks from the buzzing sign, she'd cut through an alleyway to avoid a clutter of rough and tattered-looking patrons sharing smokes outside a run-down establishment.

Now, eager to escape the eyes of the two men visually devouring her, she quickened her pace and followed the sound of drunken voices. Slurs and hoots indicated the entrance to this *Cecil* must be around the corner.

She reached the end of the alley and turned toward the noise. The buzzing sign cast a violet glow over the pavement and the clutter of people outside sharing stories and substances to heighten the mood. A muscular man in a biker jacket whistled at her.

A woman with a tight perm and shiny golden heels punched him in the shoulder. "Can it, Tito."

Stella hesitated. What was this place? The building stretched out to the right, a sign indicating a hotel lobby. *Lounge* pulsed from a second lit sign over the doorway behind the crowd. She wove through the clusters of people and walked through the door.

The place must have been a high-class joint in some other decade. A long bar, accentuated with brass fixings and a marble countertop, ran along the left side of the lounge. Mini chandeliers dotted the ceiling. Stella imagined they had once sparkled like collections of diamonds. Now they forced out a meek glow.

Clusters of patrons were scattered throughout the lounge. Women in cheap, tight getups, attempting to look fancy, draped themselves over poorly dressed men who looked like they'd already lived a lifetime.

Stella walked up to the bar, finding a seat between two empty stools. She hoisted herself up, smoothed her stray strawberry-blonde locks with the palms of her hands, and pulled her leather jacket tighter over her chest.

A lean man—muscles rippling down his bare arms, black tank top clinging to his pectorals—approached from the other side of the bar. He looked at her. "You here for a drink?" His rough voice spoke of years of inhaling toxic substances. His dark hair feathered around his shoulders. Wind and time wrinkled his chiselled face.

"Bourbon. Straight up," she said, leaning into the bar, slipping her jacket away from her chest.

The bartender eyed her exposed skin for the briefest of seconds. He looked her in the eye. "Hefty order for a young lady. I'll get your drink. You just be careful in here."

"You got it." She winked at him.

He smirked, then turned to tend to her order.

She swivelled in her stool and scanned the crowd. The place was bustling. The crowd was not high class. The air, drenched in sweat and desperation, hung like a heavy cloak.

A woman in heels teetered beside a pool table, the drink in her hand splashing onto the green cloth. Her hair, thick with hairspray, clung to the carefully crafted contours she'd moulded it into, despite her erratic movements. Her skirt, plastered to her body, barely covered the essentials. She babbled as several greasy-looking men in jean jackets and leather pretended to listen, getting hard-ons as they caught glimpses beneath her skirt.

Was she a hooker? Or was this her fancy night out?

Tingles of excitement rose through Stella's insides. This was the type of place she'd been craving. A historical nugget in the seedy underbelly of the city she longed to be in. These were the type of people she loved to watch. The ones who had lived life. Faced their fears. Been outcasts, stomped on, forgotten, and broken.

She wondered if The Cecil had been as shady back when her dad lived in this town. One of the few cities in the prairie province, Calgary, an oil town, sat smack in the middle of Alberta, up in cold Canada. He'd made his departure four years ago. He'd chased a killer out east. He'd never returned home. She could still hear his voice over the phoneline, the night he chose to leave her forever.

Bea would have a full-on meltdown if she knew Stella was in here.

The bartender returned with her drink. She smiled at him, then took a long swig of the bourbon. It reached caramel-laced fingers over the back of her tongue and left a trace of numb as it slid down her throat.

"Aren't you young to be such an experienced bourbon drinker?" the feather-haired man asked.

"I'm older than you think. I'm cursed with a baby face." She smiled slyly. Did he buy it?

"Sure," he said, his eyes skeptical.

"What is this place?" she asked.

"The historic *Cecil Hotel*. Been around since 1912. Used to be a high-class stop for businessmen. Now…" He scanned the room. "A spot for cheap drinks and rooms by the hour. City's talked about bulldozing it for years. But then where would all these people go?" He grinned.

Stella nodded as she took another long swig of the bourbon.

A ruckus in the corner caught their attention. Two men at the beginnings of a brawl lunged at each other.

"Ben. Ross. Cool it," the bartender yelled across the room.

The two men stopped and walked their separate ways.

The bartender looked at her. "Be careful. This place is known for nightly murders."

"Whatever. I'm fine." Stella sipped the bourbon.

"Listen. I'll get you another drink. On the house. If you get out of here right after."

Free bourbon. But a shortened show. What the hell. She'd seen enough. And she needed to get back before her mother's pill-and-wine coma wore off. "Sure."

After her second bourbon, Stella kept her promise to the bartender and made her exit. The night air scraped icy fingers over her cheeks as she left the sweaty heat of The Cecil.

A pair of smokers huddled close together, looking lost in love, or substance. Their eyes glazed over as they whispered to each other, passing a joint back and forth.

Stella pulled her leather jacket close around her. Coastal evenings were much milder and more forgiving. She walked briskly back the way she came, seeking the shortest path to the river walkway that would lead her to the west side and the fancy hotel with the river view.

The alley she'd come up before was empty. Her boots thudded along the pavement as she hastened her pace. The streetlamp at the edge of the alley flickered. As Stella approached the dumpster, the light buzzed loudly behind her, then flashed out. She blinked, adjusting her vision. The outline of the dumpster appeared. She continued her aggressive pace.

"Well, well…what we got here?" A man stepped out in front of her from behind the dumpster. His greasy hair stuck to his face. Saliva oozed over his cracked lower lip as he rubbed his dirt-caked hands together.

"Get out of my way," Stella spat.

The man stepped in close, suddenly, as he slid a gun from his belt. He touched the barrel against her cheek. "Nah." His face hovered inches from hers, wafting hot, sour puffs of whisky into her nostrils.

She swallowed against bile-laced bourbon surging up her throat. Eyeballing the gun against her cheekbone, she sized it up as a Ruger P97. She stood still, staring the man in the eyes.

A shadow loomed behind him. Arms rushed down, clenched fists whamming the back of the man's neck. The gun slipped from his grip, clattering over the pavement.

Stella jumped back.

Her greasy-haired attacker whirled around, pulling a knife from inside his jacket. He thrust the knife at the shadowed figure, slicing the blade through the air. The figure jerked back.

Stella scanned the ground—the gun was nestled next to the dumpster. She lunged for it.

The greasy-haired man ran at his attacker. The man braced himself. Feathered hair fell over his shoulders. Muscles rippled under his black tank top.

It was the bartender from The Cecil.

Stella's attacker raised his knife and ran at the bartender. The bartender kicked his leg out. Boot connected with gut. As the attacker hunched over, his blade sliced downward. The blade ripped into the bartender's shin and stuck in place as he fell back onto the pavement.

Greasy hair fell over his eyes as the attacker clutched his stomach.

Stella's hands trembled as she raised the gun, gripping it tightly. The hammer was already cocked. She walked up behind the attacker, hovered over him, and touched the trigger with her finger.

"Don't move," she growled between gritted teeth. Her heart pattered as quick as a hummingbird's.

Silence hung over them. No one moved. The world stopped.

The attacker jumped to his feet, spinning to face her. She stared into his eyes. He stepped toward her, forcing her to cower back.

Pop cans lined in a row along a fence flashed through her mind, reminding her of all her secret target practices with her father.

Reaching his hand toward her throat, the attacker lurched at her.

It was him or her.

Stella pulled the trigger. A blast shattered the silence. The bullet whizzed, hot smoke through cold air. It pierced the attacker's flesh and plunged straight into his heart. Scarlet splattered through the air. A gush of hot blood poured from the hole. The attacker clutched his chest, fell to his knees, skin ripping against pavement as he hit the ground.

The bartender groaned, a couple feet away. He gripped the knife sticking from his shin and pulled it out. Blood soaked through his jeans. He got to his feet. Yanking his tank top off, he tied it tightly around his shin before walking up to her. The gun was still aimed straight ahead, shaking in Stella's grip.

"You can lower the gun," he said.

"Yeah," she whispered. She dropped her arms slowly. *Holy shit.* What would Bea say now?

The bartender took her hand, gently released the gun from her grip, and pulled out a white towel hanging from the back of his jeans. "You're one hell of a shot."

Steadying her breath, Stella found her voice. "I...my dad...he taught me." She pictured herself pulling the trigger, over and over, aiming at the same can until a bullet pierced its belly.

The bartender wiped down the gun, walked over to the dumpster, and tossed it in. A mushy thud rose from the depths of wet waste.

"What...what are you doing?" Stella croaked. Her mind whizzed with images. Dryness scratched her throat.

"Get out of here," he said.

"But..." She looked at the man lying face down on the pavement in a puddle of red.

"Just another nightly murder at The Cecil," he said.

She stared, her mouth open.

"It was you or him. Self-defence. Trust me, when the cops eventually get here, you'll be treated like all the other tightly clothed ladies who cling to The Cecil. You know the truth. Live it." He waved his hand, gesturing for her to scurry along.

Stella nodded, licking her dry lips. She took a step down the alley. Then another. She didn't look back.

Chapter 2

Flaming Night Terror

June 1993

A blazing fire shot sparks into the midnight sky. The bright glow from the moon overhead melded with red-fingered flames, licking the tips of black trees. The edge of the dense forest cut a dark silhouette into a tangerine background.

The tiny house at the edge of the forest burned. Its wooden floorboards charred and crackled. Its glass windows shattered into blazing shards. Its patchwork roof sizzled like hot coals. The fire grew, feeding off every splinter of wood, devouring the house.

Viviana huddled in the corner of her bedroom, clutching her shabby brown teddy bear. Her shoulders shook. Fire-red strands of hair stuck to her cheeks. Her sweat-soaked nightgown plastered her skin. She could barely see her bedroom door through a mix of tears and smoke.

The door burst open, sending a string of straw dolls hanging from the doorknob flying across the room. *My dolls.* She wanted to cry out, but her voice wouldn't come. It stuck in her thick saliva-coated throat like a clog of hair in a drain. She was so thirsty, yet her whole body was wet.

One of the straw dolls landed by her foot. She grabbed it, clutched it to her heart, hiding it behind her teddy bear.

Damaris appeared, standing in the doorway, a commanding figure with long, raven hair. Her midnight eyes searched through the smoke, landing on Viviana.

"Dami," Viviana cried, crawling across the room using both her knees and one hand. In her other hand, she clutched the bear and the doll.

The smoke pillowed into a cloud, concealing Damaris. Seized by a coughing fit, Viviana crumpled onto the floor; the bear and the doll fell from her hand. She gripped the carpet, heaving with dry coughs.

Damaris grabbed Viviana's arm. "Viv. Get up."

Viviana swallowed, wetting her throat enough to ease the coughing. She scanned the carpet. Her bear wasn't anywhere. The doll lay within reach. She grabbed it, then pushed herself up to her feet.

"We have to go," Dami yelled.

Viviana succumbed, letting Dami pull her by the arm, shielding her eyes from the smoke with her hand, still clutching the doll.

Through the doorway, the hallway filled with smoke escaping from the last bedroom. Their parents' bedroom. Viviana charged toward it.

Dami dug her fingers into Viviana's arm, stopping her. "No. We have to go."

"But, Mom, Dad. We have to get them," Viviana exclaimed. Her lower lip trembled. She clutched the doll harder, her knuckles turning white.

"Viv. I won't let you die," Dami said, holding her grip on Viviana's arm.

Viviana looked at her parents' bedroom door.

A loud crack echoed overhead. A wooden beam fell from the ceiling, blazing with fire, landing an inch from Viviana's foot. Sparks flew. One of them landed on Viviana's nightgown, igniting into a hot flame. Viviana's flesh burned beneath the thin material. She screamed. Dami ripped off her cloak and wrapped it around Viviana, suffocating her in a death-grip hug. The fire extinguished. Pain seared Viviana's skin.

Following Dami, Viviana clutched the doll, her fingers white and numb. She fumbled her way down the stairs. One of her slippers fell from her foot. Dami's fingers dug even harder into her skin, drawing a droplet of blood. The blood slithered down her hand in a stream of sweat.

They reached the front door. Dami yanked it open and thrust Viviana outside. The cold seized her, squeezing her lungs and running icy nails over her face and down her arms. Viviana gasped, trying to breathe in the freezing air. Dami grabbed her again and ran down the walkway, to the edge of the forest.

They stood, looking back at the house in silence. Loud crackles echoed through the quiet night as charred chunks flew through the air, streaming sparks in their wake.

"Mom and Dad," Viviana cried. Tears streamed down her cheeks, blurring the house.

Dami turned her till their eyes met. "Listen. Viv. Mom and Dad are gone."

"What do you mean?" Viviana's lower lip trembled. She clutched the doll in her trembling hand. Her fire-red hair stuck to her face. She tried to swipe it away, but her fingers stuck in mucous and tears.

"They're gone." Dami looked at her. "I went into their bedroom. It was too late."

"What do you *mean*?" Viviana pleaded.

"Someone killed them," Dami said.

"No." Viviana shook her head.

Sirens wailed.

"We have to go," Dami said. "We have to hide. They'll take us away."

Viviana shook her head. Her mind couldn't comprehend what was happening. Dami led her into the shelter of the forest. Viviana's mind whirled with a haze of images. She couldn't think.

Dami quickened her pace.

Viviana kicked off her one remaining slipper and pattered her bare feet over the soft dirt trail weaving through the forest, clutching the doll her mother had made in her hand, following her sister into the darkness of whatever lay beyond.

Savage Beat

Chapter 3

Savage Beat

July 16, 1999

The air dripped with savage energy and sweat. Guttural vibes vibrated through the air, clinging to the mad, tightly packed crowd pushing against the stage. Stella stood her ground. She made up in aura what she lacked in stature. Her first fierce heavy metal experience had been five years ago, when she'd turned seventeen. She knew how to navigate this crowd. She jostled along with the mob, eating up the manic meal being fed to them by the rock gods up on their pedestal.

The lead man screamed his last words into the microphone clutched in his hand. His sidekick guitarist sidled up next to him, arm swinging wildly, strumming out the last electric shots of their final track for the evening. The crowd erupted. The voltage screeched to max.

Stella relished in the wild energy, absorbing it through every pore. This was the one place that she could let go. That she could...*be.*

It's the music of the devil, people would say. *"How can you, such a sweet girl, listen to that loud and scary stuff?"* people would ask. She'd stopped sharing her musical taste with others. It was her choice. Her world. Her desire.

It wasn't the music of Satan. She knew the hand of the devil. She'd seen it, in the work of the sadistic monsters her father had died chasing. She knew where the devil resided. It wasn't in the savage vocals of a heavy-metal icon. It was in the core of the human beasts who took the life of innocent beings. Too young to die. Too innocent to be gutted like animals and left to bleed out.

The front man raised his hand. "We are Slayer. Thank you! Goodnight." The microphone went silent. The leather clad crew stomped off stage, chains swinging from their belts as they waved to their fans.

The crowd settled around Stella. Despite the open stadium and the rush of cold night air, the temperature was in overload. The air molecules dripped with moist heat. Strawberry-blonde curls stuck to Stella's forehead and the back of her neck. She pulled the elastic from her wrist and secured her long hair in a makeshift ponytail at the top of her head. The night was young. Slayer smashed their set. But, she wasn't here to see Slayer.

Stella unzipped a pocket in her leather jacket, pulled out a silver flask, uncapped it, and took a long swig. The sweet bourbon hit the back of her tongue. She let it linger before releasing it to drizzle down the back of her throat. She slid the flask back into her pocket, then settled into the rumbling crowd. The energy had calmed to a steady buzz. She was up at the front, where she belonged. Front row, floor. There was no other way to take in a lineup of live heavy metal. Lucky for her, she'd been able to secure front row VIP tickets to the biggest metal music fest to hit the Thunderbird Stadium. It wasn't luck, exactly. She'd done enough favours for members of several of the bands playing. She'd cashed in her tally of good deeds. Here she was. Not exactly here to see the bands she'd done good deeds for. She was here to see Mr. Zombie. Rob. She wondered what people called him. Robert? Robbie? Robbo? Or King Zombie. That's what she'd call him, if she got to meet him. If she made the right moves from her front-row perch, she just might. Her insides blazed at the thought.

Rumbling from the back of the stage caused a surge in the crowd. It wouldn't be long now. The act she was here to devour would be looming over her. Her arms sizzled. Her brain buzzed. She couldn't wait. Another swig from her flask flushed warmth down her throat to the pit of her belly. She shook her head at the small baggie filled with white powder exchanging hands. Friendly offerings between fellow metal heads. The buzz of the live music was her high. The surge in drugs available in the party scene didn't tempt her. The sight of white powder only produced a jolt of sadness within her.

A flash of her dad in an underground bar, in a back room, sniffing powder off a table, numbing the pain of the bloody slash in the side of his gut. She couldn't explain the image throbbing in the back of her mind. Her dad had traces of cocaine in his system, but his body was found inside his car outside the mansion of Saul Ripper. The last killer he'd hunted.

Stella shook the thoughts from her mind. She took another swig of bourbon, then readied herself for the moment she'd been waiting for. She hadn't agreed to take time off and flown out to the big city of Vancouver to spend her time mourning the past. She was here to ride the high of the energy vibrating from a metal god. She was here to drink it in. To drink him in, if possible.

A single electric strum vibrated across the air. The crowd erupted. Several more strums followed. The crowd couldn't contain themselves. Stella stood strong, at the very front, looking up over the lip of the stage. Every particle of her being sizzled.

There he was. Walking across the stage, raising his microphone. Before his face was revealed by the bright stage lights, his voice—deep, strong, gruff—released the pent-up energy of a being that must have been holding it in for far too long. Lyrics of burning witches seeped from his soul. Stella smiled. He'd started with her favourite track. *Dragula.* A true work of metal madness. The track that had topped the charts. The one she consumed, repeatedly, never getting enough to reach oversaturation.

He crept across the stage into the manic energy of the wild crowd.

His face came into view, gleaming under the bright lights. In full glory, his painted white face with dark eyes shot another jolt of excitement through Stella's core.

The Zombie God approached the edge of the stage. Stella stared straight up into his eyes as they wandered over the crowd. His gaze found hers. They paused. Locked in a stare as his mouth moved, Stella succumbed to a moment, swept into a silent tunnel at the pit of a raging concert. The savage world around her became a complete blur. His voice screamed louder. His eyes moved on. The world came alive around her again in a single violent jolt. She continued to stare, letting her body go wild with the rest of the crowd.

Her head banged through the sweat-infused air. The elastic fell. Her hair flung in all directions. The track ended. The crowd went crazy. Stella screamed with all her might, releasing years of rage and pain. The hurt little girl within surfaced, screeching her song.

Chapter 4

Groupie Hotel

A buzzing awoke Stella. She opened one eye and peered at her surroundings. Scantily clad bodies cluttered the room, sprawled in awkward positions over the bed, the floor, the couch. The buzzing persisted. Stella opened her other eye. Something vibrated in the pocket of the pants she was wearing. She slid her hand into the pocket and pulled out her murder phone, the one that buzzed when a corpse was found and she was called. Her excellent performance as an officer had earned her a detective's badge at the ripe age of twenty-two. The price was the invasion of her privacy any time of day or night.

She sat up, scanning her body. Somehow she was clothed. She grabbed her sweater, balled up beside her, then crept out of the room. She closed the door quietly behind her, showing respect for the rest of the metal-fest party clan. They had a lot to sleep off.

The phone had stopped buzzing. Just as she was about to redial, it lit up again.

She cleared her throat. "Mahoney here." Her ability to fake alertness surprised her.

"Stella. Get on a plane. Get home," Detective Sutton, her boss, barked from the other end.

"New case?" She walked down the hotel hallway, scanning the chipped walls and battered doors.

"Yeah. I know. I gave you a couple days off. Suddenly I'm short staffed," Sutton said.

"I'll jump on the next flight." Stella swallowed a burst of bourbon-laced bile.

"Good. I'll get Peggy to send you the location. Go right to the scene."

"Gotcha."

Sutton hung up without a goodbye. She chuckled. He was so damn uptight. All the time. Maybe he should get out once in a while. Blow off some steam. It sure worked for her.

She continued walking down the hallway, trying to recall which way her room was. She turned a corner. There it was. The room at the end of the hall. Number 166. Images of the evening flooded her mind as she found her key and took stock of her room. After a quick gather of the clothes strewn over the room, she threw them in her backpack and headed for the door. There were regular flights between the big city and her hometown of Calgary. A quick one-hour ride through the air would land her on her feet. She'd skitter off to the crime scene. She yawned just thinking about it. Probably just another boring murder. Someone in the victim's close circle of friends. The husband. Or the boyfriend. Whatever. Toward the murder she went.

Chapter 5

Just Another Murder

Tires squealed as Stella pulled a hard right into the parking lot of the low-rate apartment complex. She slid her blue Sunfire into a free spot, next to Sutton's glossy blue Chevy pickup. He'd called her six hours ago. Peggy had her ticket home booked and waiting for her at the airport. Her Sunfire had been waiting for her in the overnight parking when she landed. She'd managed a good twenty-minute nap on the plane until the kid behind her decided to start kicking her seat. Despite the glare she'd shot back at the mother of the kicking child, the constant pounding of sneakered feet had continued in a steady rhythm.

Stella scanned her reflection in the rear-view mirror. It wasn't a complete tragedy. But it wasn't great either. Likely her appearance was not up to Sutton's clean-cut standards. *Fuck him.* He's the one who pulled her from her metal-infused vacay. Hell, he was the one who had forced her to take the time off in the first place. He'd told her she was too much like her father, never taking a break. The department required it. *Blah, blah, blah. Whatever.* She'd followed orders. She was here.

She tied her hair back in a low bun at the base of her neck. She scrubbed underneath her eyes with her fingertips, removing some of the smeared black liner and silvery shadow that had migrated in her party-infused sleep. Snatching up her black leather coat from the passenger seat, she opened the door and sprung into the chill air. Summer. It was supposed to be. It was chilly as fuck for summer. That was the Canadian prairies for you.

Slamming the door, she walked toward the apartment complex as she slid the coat over her arms and pulled it around her chest. Without time to go home before coming to the scene, she was clad in her concert attire. Black leather pants. Matching tank. She'd left the gem-studded belt and leather bracelets in her pack in the car. The coat was long and ample to make her look at least a tad professional. Or so she thought.

She scanned the complex. Police tape blocked off the entrance to a unit on the second floor. Taking the stairs two at a time, she approached the scene at the top. She ducked under the tape and into the apartment. A cloud of rot descended upon her. She choked back the greasy egg-and-cheese sandwich she'd wolfed back on her drive to the scene. Steadying her senses, she got a hold of herself and charged into the room. Sutton was in the corner, barking orders to two latex-gloved techies. They looked like clones in plastic goggles and jackets with iridescent lettering declaring them the CST squad. The taller of the two held a camera in his hand.

They nodded their heads, then turned and walked toward a door appearing to lead to a bathroom.

Sutton turned to her. "Stella." He looked at his watch. "That was fast."

"I pack light. And Pegs had a ticket waiting for me." She crossed her arms and nodded at the door the techies had gone through. "Body in the bathroom?"

Sutton nodded. "Yeah. Bathtub. It's like a horror movie in there. Blood. Lots of blood."

"The victim?"

"Woman. Twenty-seven years old." Sutton slipped a notepad from his jacket pocket and flipped through it. "Cindy Rider. Lived in this delight of a home with her husband, Roy."

"Let me guess, Roy isn't around."

"Nope." Sutton flipped his notepad shut. "Last seen three days ago, leaving the building. Smell got the neighbours wondering. Landlord found her. Called it in." Sutton sniffed the air. "Jesus, Stella. You smell like a party in a cheap motel."

Stella smirked. "That's 'cause you called me from my party in a cheap motel."

"You look like hell."

"Thanks."

"Seriously, Stella, you gotta get your act together."

"Seriously, Sutton. You gotta lay off. You told me to take time off. Then you called me in. Told me to get my ass here. So I did." She glared.

Sutton sighed. "Fine." He looked toward the bathroom. "I need you here. I'm down two detectives. One of them is at the hospital, with his daughter. Other flew out east to his mother's funeral."

"Well, I'm here. As foul as you find my stench." Stella smiled wide.

Sutton grinned. "Yeah. Fine. When they're done in the bathroom, scour it."

"Done."

"Then go home and take a goddamn shower." Sutton grimaced.

"Done."

"Then go see Blackwood."

"Blackwood? Isn't liaison with the medical examiner the prime investigator's glorious job?" Stella asked.

"Yeah. Was. She doesn't like me. She might be more amiable with you. She was chummy with your dad, you know." Sutton looked at her.

"She was?" Stella's neck tingled. She'd only seen Blackwood in passing at the occasional scene. She knew her dad had worked with her. She didn't know how close they'd been.

"She was. Maybe she'll be friendly with you, since you're a Mahoney." Sutton turned to leave. "Gotta get back to HQ. Scour the bathroom. Get cleaned up. Drop in on Blackwood. She should be well into processing the body by now."

"Got it." Stella moved toward the bedroom to put the pieces of a grisly act together.

Chapter 6

Itching Flesh

Twinkling diamond stars scattered over the denim sky. The moon, high and bright, lit the dirt pathway snaking through the forest. The white bark on the tall birch trees stuck out against the gloomy night background.

A chill in the air swept over Viviana's face and through her insides. She shivered. Pulling a purple scarf tighter around her neck, she scrambled to catch up to Dami.

"Hurry up," Dami called from ahead. Her long, flowing raven hair and cloak melded into one, fluttering behind her in the breeze.

Viviana ran to catch up. Her fire-red hair danced in the wind. Leaves crunched under her boots. She knew it was time for the ceremony. The Ritual. Part of a series of little services they held in memory of the ones who had taught them their beliefs, their ways. Tonight, they would honour the ones Viviana had loved more than anything on this earth. Their parents.

A circular clearing appeared ahead, perfectly carved into the forest, a border of birch shielding the enclave. Dami was already fast at work on the preparations.

Viviana paused at the opening to the sphere of grass, watching Dami lay out the ceremonial items. Dami preferred her full name—Damaris. The dominant woman. A name in religious history, in memory of an Athenian woman who was converted to Christianity by St. Paul. Their father had given the name to their firstborn daughter the moment he laid eyes on her. He used to tell the story, excitement dancing in his eyes.

"C'mon, Viv. Are you going to stand there daydreaming all night, or are you going to help me?" Her sister looked up at her now with a certain sweetness in her gaze.

"Yes. Sorry." Viviana knelt on the soft grass and reached for a bag. Dami had been so patient with her over the years, and she overlooked the shorter version of her name that Viviana loved to use. It reminded Viviana of the way their mother used to talk to them.

"We need to hurry. It's nearly time." Dami hustled, doublechecking the position of the Palo Santo candles spread around a knife placed in the centre. Set at the top of the handle of the knife was an amulet of amethyst, a sign of wisdom and a protector from intoxication.

Viviana rustled through her bag and pulled out the salvia apiana. Dami insisted they only use the white sage in their ceremonies, that it had a stronger purging effect.

Dami fished in the folds of her cloak, retrieving her special lighter. It was silver and engraved with the daisy protector symbol. It had been a gift from their father, and Dami never went anywhere without it. Dami ran her fingers along the smooth silver. Chills trickled down Viviana's arms. The chills turned to sparks, tiny hot pokers pricking her skin. A flash of flame burst through her thoughts.

Dami snatched the sage from her. "I'll do it."

Dami stood and walked around the circle of candles, lighting each one. Golden-red flames licked the night air. A soft glow ebbed through the enclosure.

Viviana watched the flame, reaching from the lighter into the night. Hot fingers heated the cold air, transforming particles into dangerous pokers, igniting the wicks, sending heat over the wax, melting it, morphing it forever.

Dami flicked the cover over the lighter, extinguishing the flame. She looked up at the waning moon. "Perfect. It's time to shed and release."

She lit the sage, waiting till a burst of flame crackled the ends, then held it out in front of her. She blew a single breath over the tiny fire. It extinguished into a plume of smoke, weaving up through the night sky. Dami placed the smouldering sage in the centre of the ring of candles, beside the knife. She sat down on the grass, pulled her knees in toward her, and rested her chin on them. She clicked the lighter open, holding it in front of her, and flicked the flame to life. *On.* Burning hot. *Off.* Cold air. *On.* Searing the sky. *Off.* Cool relief.

Viviana sat, transfixed, watching the flame flicker on and off. The searing heat blazing one moment, extinguished the next. She studied her sister's wide eyes, alive with fascination, staring at the flame.

Viviana looked into the orange core of the flame. An itch trickled up her arm. She slipped her hand under the sleeve of her cloak, crawling her fingers up her skin, finding the rough, distorted patch. She stared at the flame. Her distorted skin itched. She scratched at her burned flesh. She scratched at the memory captured bright and clear in her mind. She clawed harder, scraping the itch away. She slashed at the flames burning in her mind, willing them to leave her forever.

"Viv." Dami's hand rested on her arm, eyes finding hers. Her sister had the soft expression of concern rarely exposed by her dominant and vile demeanour.

Viviana slid her hand from her cloak. "It itches."

"Use your power." Dami tapped Viviana's temple with her fingertip. "It's all in your mind. It's all energy. The energy you choose to manifest." She smiled, scarlet lips stretching her smooth, pale skin.

Viviana relaxed her shoulders and closed her eyes. She took a few deep breaths and cleared the hot flames and destructive thoughts from her mind. The cold night air cleansed her as she breathed in long and slow.

Viviana opened her eyes. Dami stood, sliding the lighter into her pocket and staring up at the moon. The moon glimmered. It seemed to shift, as if clicking into place. Dami smiled. "It's time."

Chapter 7

Lonely Apartment

Stella turned the key in the lock. She opened the door. Musty air with a tinge of loneliness swept over her. She scanned the small apartment she called home. Her heart heaved. She was expecting to forget about her life for a couple days while dousing herself in metal and booze. She sighed, walked into the apartment, and closed the door.

Her keys clinked against the small glass bowl she tossed them into. It was red. It was chipped. She'd found it in her father's apartment when she and her mother were removing all of his belongings. It was quaint. Didn't quite belong with the rest of the décor, or rather, the lack thereof. She'd grabbed it and claimed it as her own.

She walked down the hall into the main living space. Tall shelves lined the walls filled with collections of music. The CD collection she'd built occupied the shelves along the wall to the right. The LPs that had been her father's were lined up precisely in the shelves along the furthest wall at the back of the room. His record player was perched in the corner of the room where the two walls met. Her shiny silver CD player sat next to it. They were contradicting setups, of different decades. One represented her own life. The other symbolized the life of a man she felt connected to despite the rare times she was within close physical proximity to him. She'd spent endless hours listening to his music, seeking to know him. Seeking to bond with him in his afterlife.

She selected a CD from her collection, one with a muscular front man painted on the cover of the case. His long hair wild. His muscles bulging. His demon-painted face savage. Perfect. She could dowse herself in memories of last night's concert, and the afterparty with the star of the hour, while she got herself cleaned up to Sutton's standards.

She inserted the CD into the player, selected a track, then pressed play. Closing her eyes, she lost herself for a moment in the high-octane riff thrumming from the player. The raw voice sang of shrieking lips and ragged tongues, drowning her in ecstatic memories. She often had a craving for *Superbeast* after a high-voltage show. King Zombie shimmered through her mind. He had been savage on stage. Off stage, an intense masculinity had seeped from him.

She sighed. Time to get moving.

The scene at the shitty apartment complex had been textbook. A broken lamp. A shattered bulb. A mess of sheets. Drops of blood leading to the bathroom. It appeared that whoever had murdered Cindy had been in the bedroom with her. There had been a struggle. She was dragged to the bathroom, thrown in the tub, and bludgeoned to death.

The blood was ample. Spattered everywhere. The techies had lifted prints in the blood spattered across the baby-blue tiles lining the walls around the tub. Apparently, Roy, Cindy's husband, had a record. If the lifted prints matched his, the case would be closed.

Stella walked into her bedroom, stripped off her clothes, then meandered into the bathroom. She turned on the hot water in the shower and examined herself in the mirror. Steam filtered through the small space. She looked pale. Tired. She'd have to find a jolt of energy to deal with the standard, textbook murder case. Just another day. Just another body.

When she'd pursued a position on the homicide unit, she'd thought she'd be hunting down killers of another calibre. Like the ones her father chased. So far, it had been a string of humdrum cases. Killers who struck once, then were done. Killers who didn't clean up after themselves. Average people, run down by life, losing their shit. Their emotions got the better of them, turning them into one-time killers. When it was over, they panicked and fled. They never got far. Wham, bam, they found themselves behind bars, questioning what they had done.

Steam filled the bathroom, clouding her reflection. She stepped into the shower, tilted her makeup-stained face up to the warmth of the water, and let it wash away the thrill of her metal vacation cut short.

The small things in life. That's all she got. The occasional moment where she was swept away in the thrill of the wild, able to pretend she wasn't a rookie detective, trying to follow the rules, bored with the same case over and over. Trying to pretend that she'd moved on from the death of her father. Trying to pretend she didn't want more than anything to make him proud. To follow in his footsteps. As ridiculous and cheesy at it sounded. Trying to convince herself it would all work out, while avoiding the silence of lonely moments that threatened to expose what was festering inside of her. Pain. Hurt. Fear.

Chapter 8

Bathtub Bludgeoning

Stella flashed her badge and a smile to the silver-haired woman behind the desk. The woman smiled back, buzzing open a door. Stella walked in and followed a long hall to a room at the end. The room where she would meet—for the first time, one on one—the corpse expert who had more face-to-face time with Stella's dad than Stella had.

Nerves jiggled in the pit of her gut. Stella took a deep breath in, held it, then exhaled. No time for nerves.

She straightened her pressed, button-up shirt. Smirking, she thought of how impressed Sutton would be that she'd chosen an adult shirt. Maybe he wouldn't even notice. Maybe she went to all this effort for nothing. Whatever. She was here.

Down the long hall she went. She approached a sturdy-looking door, checked the number, and pushed it open. It was heavy. A whoosh of cold air swept over her. The room was dark and quiet. A bright bulb glared from the far corner.

A woman with long, dark hair, wearing a white lab coat, leaned over a steel slab. It looked as though she was engrossed in her examination of a body. Likely the victim Stella was here to get an update on. Poor Cindy, bludgeoned to death, likely by Roy, supposedly the love of her life.

Stella walked over to the corner. The woman looked up from her work.

She smiled. "Can I help you?"

"Detective Mahoney. From homicide. I'm here to check on the victim from the apartment." Stella extended her hand.

"Medical Examiner Blackwood." Blackwood extended her hand in return. "Sutton informed me you'd be coming by." She chuckled. "I don't think he likes me."

Stella nodded. "He said the same thing about you."

"Really?" Blackwood raised an eyebrow. The bright light gleamed off a silver strand amidst her hair. "I think perhaps he and I have...different styles. I was used to working with your dad."

"My dad was different from Sutton?"

"Yeah." Blackwood grinned. "Quite."

Stella pondered what that meant. She had no idea what her dad would have been like from the perspective of a medical examiner. She only knew what she read about his cases. In papers. In old case files. The only hint of personality she had was what she could read from him over the phone or during his brief visits.

"You need an update. For Sutton," Blackwood broke the silence.

"Uh, yes. That's why I'm here." Stella swallowed. A ball of doubt roiled in her stomach.

"Listen, this feels awkward." Blackwood snapped off her latex gloves and grabbed a fresh pair.

"Yeah, it does. It's just...I've heard you worked a lot with my dad."

"I did. We worked cases together. A few of them were real serious."

"That's it? You only worked together?"

Blackwood crossed her arms. "Yeah. That's it. But you already know that, don't you?"

"When I walked in here, I figured my dad would probably go for someone like you. But...you're more likely to fuck me, aren't you?" Stella's mouth pulled into a thin line.

"You're too young. And I don't mix murder and sex."

Touché. This woman could hold her own. "You worked well together?"

"We did. Your dad was direct. Didn't play games. Always wanted to get to the bottom of things. Expose the truth. Catch the bad guy. But you know that." Blackwood raised an eyebrow.

"I guess I do," Stella said.

Blackwood snapped a latex glove over each hand. "Why don't we get you that update." She turned to the body on the slab.

"Sounds good." Stella sidled up next to Blackwood.

The woman who had been found in the bathtub in her rundown apartment, soaked in a bath of her own blood, now lay clean, pale, and shining under the bright overhead lights. It amazed Stella how the gore could be so easily washed away. As if the events that had led this woman to be here on this steel slab had never happened. Stella wondered who would miss this woman. She wondered where Roy was.

"Ready for some blunt-force trauma facts?" Blackwood said.

"Shoot." Stella snapped open her notepad.

"COD appears to be just that. Blunt-force trauma. To the head. The skull has been smashed in several places. Six, to be exact. Fact one. When multiple forces are applied in succession, each successive contusion causes a higher level of damage than the previous. Fact two. The level of force applied to the skull was high. Based on the cracking of the skull, even the first blow was likely enough to kill her. Fact three. Each of the following blows, again based on the shape and depth of the cracks in the skull, appear to be at least equal in strength to the first blow." Blackwood paused, pointing at an exposed portion of skull. The flesh torn away, clumps of hair missing. "As you can see, the force was enough to rip away the skin and the hair. Thus exposing the skull. Thus allowing direct examination of the resulting fractures."

Jeebus. "This guy didn't tire easily." Stella shook her head.

"That, Detective Mahoney, is up to you to decide. I'll give you the medical facts. You'll do the conjecturing as to how these facts came to be on our dead woman here." Blackwood crossed her arms.

Stella smirked. She liked Blackwood. "But, COD is blunt-force trauma."

"Fairly safe to say so, yes. As you can see, the rest of her body is almost untarnished. Some bruising, on her upper right arm, here." Blackwood pointed to the pallid arm marked above the elbow with deep purple and sickly yellow. "Shape of the bruising indicates she was likely grabbed and pulled. Hard. Appears the victim had died a couple days before she was found. The bruising would have to be quite deep to display this colouring."

"Bruising doesn't stop, postmortem?" Stella asked.

"No. It continues, at least for a few hours. It appears that whoever grabbed her, grabbed hard. The bruising progressed rapidly. To get this colour, it would likely take five or six hours. The bruising would have stopped a few hours postmortem. So, she would have had to have been killed a few hours after being grabbed, at most. Most likely the struggle ensued, didn't last too long, then she was hit on the head, repeatedly, then bled out."

Stella scribbled in her notebook. "COD seems pretty straight forward then."

"Unless I find anything else, it's a logical conclusion."

"Any indication of who did this? Any trace left behind?"

"Prints. On her arm, where the bruising is. I lifted them, sent them off to the lab."

"There were prints on the blood in the tub," Stella said.

"Double the prints."

"This guy was messy. My gut says it's Roy," Stella said.

"Roy?"

"The husband. Who has apparently vanished since his wife's accident in the tub."

"Oh. Yeah. It's not looking good for Roy. Even if the ones in the tub belong to the victim, I don't see how the ones on her arm could be hers. It's extremely unlikely someone would be able to grab their own arm hard enough to cause this level of bruising," Blackwood said.

Stella snapped her notebook shut. "Anything else?"

"No. This is straightforward. Not a lot to process. Like I said, her body is quite untouched. Just the bruising and the smashed-in skull. The blood must have all come from her head," Blackwood said. "You got a cell number? I can keep you posted."

"That'd be great." She tore a page from her notepad, wrote the number to her murder phone down and handed it to Blackwood. She sighed.

"You okay, Mahoney?"

Stella snorted. "How come you're cool calling me Mahoney?"

"You mean because Sutton can't?"

"Yeah. And he's not the only one."

Blackwood crossed her arms, pausing. "Well, your dad always called me Blackwood. He didn't have a hard time applying the last-name rule to me, even though most of the personnel on a murder investigation are men. Guess I feel like I should pay it forward. Besides...things aren't easy for you, are they?" She smiled. "Figured I could cut you a break."

"Thanks." Stella turned to leave, then paused. "Have you worked on a lot of *real* cases, you know, like the ones you worked on with my dad? Real serial killers."

"Before I came here, I worked on some doozies. Real humdingers."

"Don't you get bored? I mean, don't you miss those real cases? Stopping serious murderers?"

"No. Not really." Blackwood lowered her plastic goggles. "You be careful what you wish for, Mahoney. Stuff like that never leaves you. It sticks. In your mind."

"That's what happened to my dad, isn't it?"

"No one knows for sure what happened to your dad. But, if I were to guess, then yes. I would say the images were a lot to take." Blackwood smiled.

"Thanks." Stella turned and walked through the morgue door, playing an imaginary film through her head, creating her version of her father as he sought to catch a killer.

Chapter 9

HQ and Jake

Stella pulled her blue Sunfire into a parking spot close to the front door of HQ. A pink hue glowed over the horizon. The sun was on its way to bed. Stella wished she could be. Her metal-infused party of the night before was catching up with her. Her plan had been to spend the day in her cozy bed, listening to CDs, after her late-afternoon flight home. She even had Captain Chow's paper menu by her bedside, ready for her order of ginger beef and sizzling rice with shrimp. There was nothing better than a bowl piled high with MSG-infused Western-style Chinese takeout after a night of savage groupie-style partying.

She walked through the shiny glass doors and past the front entrance.

"How are you, dear?" Peggy smiled. Her lips were always so red. Like a ripe cherry.

"Pegs. I'm fine."

"You look tired. That was rough of Sutton to call you back from the vacation he told you to take." Peggy's blonde bob framed her face.

"Yeah, well. Whatever. I'm here." Stella smiled.

"I'll put on a fresh pot for you in the war room, if you'd like."

"Thanks, Pegs."

Stella walked down the narrow hallway to the messy cubicles cluttered together. She grimaced. It was like a pigpen in here. Sutton complained about her appearance. Her smell. Yet, the other detectives couldn't keep their workspaces clean for a second. At least she had an excuse. She was off duty. The rest of them, they were pigs on duty. All the time.

She rolled her eyes and walked over to her desk. She heard typing coming from the far corner. Jake's light was on. Swell. Maybe he could help her put this boring case of the bathtub bludgeoning to bed. Then she could crash for the night. And maybe even half the day tomorrow. Sutton owed her the time off he'd stolen. Didn't he?

She threw her leather coat over her chair and walked over to Jake's desk. There he was, immersed in his work, typing some complex search into his high-end computer. He was good at finding stuff on the World Wide Web. She walked up behind him. *Netscape* was open on one of his screens. Letters appeared in a search pane as he typed away.

"Jakey," she said.

Jake jumped. He looked up at her, halting his typing. "Yikes. You scared me. Thought you were off to meet your rock zombie hero."

"I was. I did. Hell of a metal fest. Hell of a night."

"Shouldn't you be home in bed with Chinese takeout?" Jake slid his thick black glasses further up the bridge of his nose.

"I should. Sutton put me on a case. I flew back this morning."

"A case? Oh...the one with the bloody woman in the bathtub?"

"Yeah. Should be easy to close. Can you help me?" She smiled wide, pleading with her eyes.

"Love to."

"I need to find this Roy." She flipped open her notepad. "Roy Rider. Unit 8, Cherry Blossom Village, Marlborough Close N.E."

"Is Roy responsible for the bloody body in the bathtub?" Jake typed away. Chocolate locks of hair slipped over his glasses. He blew them away.

"Most likely. He's our number-one suspect. He's the husband of the bloody carnage. Went missing right around the time of the bludgeoning. Prints were found in the tub and on the woman's arm. I'm waiting on a match. In the meantime..."

"You'd like to find Roy."

"Yes. I'd like to have a chat with him. Maybe push him a little. He might do the right thing. Come clean." Stella smirked.

"Sutton know you're on this path?" Jake shot her a look.

"Meh. Will be. We're meeting up in fifteen. You know the drill. He'll run the show. Make it look like it's his idea to get Roy in while we're scouring for any other potential leads. I'll agree, then have him in here pronto, on the boss' command." Stella leaned over Jake's shoulder.

"You're breathing on me. Didn't you brush your teeth after your metal party? Geez." Jake brushed the shoulder of his emerald-green sweater vest.

"Well, sooorry." Stella stood back. She breathed into her cupped palm and sniffed. Yikes. She did smell like the afterparty she'd crept out of in the shitty motel room this morning.

"Here." Jake pointed to a black screen lined with green letters.

Stella squinted at the neon gibberish. "What's this? What about your fancy Netscape there?"

"That's for the World Wide Web. The commercial version of interconnected web pages for the general public." He pointed back to the neon green and black. "This is the interface we use to search the databases that the general public does not have access to."

Stella rolled her eyes. "Whatever. What does it mean?"

"A credit card issued to Cindy Rider was used. Two hours ago. At Motel Town."

"That group of shitty motels by the Denny's?"

"That's the one."

"Roy must be treating himself to a night out, using his dead wife's account."

"Right. Well, looks like Roy went to the liquor store, attached to the Super 8." He continued typing, scanning more results as they appeared. "Oh, and look at this. He checked himself in."

"Swell. You're a wiz." She tousled Jake's soft locks.

He blushed but didn't pull away. "Yeah. I am. And you're lucky I'm so nice to you."

"Meh. You love me. Besides. It's your job." She smiled, then made her way to the war room, prepping for the golden greeting she was anticipating from Sutton.

Chapter 10

Nestled in Bed

The voice of the Zombie King filled the entire room. Screeching lyrics of burning witches, ditches, weakness, and bleeding clawed through the cozy bedroom. Stella twirled a pair of cheap wooden chopsticks around sauce-drenched noodles, digging them into the takeout box. She slurped in the noodles and sauce, licking her lips, then settled back into a stack of fluffy pillows nestled behind her head. She sang along to the metal god with a mouthful of sticky noodles. Flashes of his face, inches from hers, were still fresh in her mind. The only thing better than a manic night were the lingering memories afterward.

The light from a streetlamp filled her room with a soft glow. As soon as the bathtub bludgeoning had been put to bed, she'd sped home in her Sunfire and set herself up for a luxurious evening of hiding from the world. She'd turned off the lamp on her bedside table, turned up the volume on the CD player, and popped open both takeout boxes delivered from Captain Chow's.

She'd been up for thirty-six hours since Sutton had summoned her home from the party motel. After a quick rundown with Sutton, she'd found Roy at the Super 8. She'd been assigned a patrol as her backup, as all other detectives were unavailable. Sutton ignored her protests when she claimed a patrol would only slow her down. She put up with the patrol. He behaved well, taking her orders and standing behind her as she pounded on the door to room 325—the room at the Super 8 that Roy had checked into with Cindy's credit card.

Roy didn't last long in the interrogation room, with nothing to drink and Stella looming over him. He was a mess the moment she cuffed him. Clearly, he was not an experienced murderer. She broke him down. He cried. He confessed. He was locked away. The print results would seal the deal when they came in.

Sutton had agreed to give Stella the day off he'd stolen. Murder pending, of course.

After washing away the smell of the concert, the afterparty, and thirty-six hours of chasing down a novice murderer, she'd settled in for the night.

The voice of King Zombie heightened with the chorus, a rough guitar riff and pounding beat weaving together in the background. She closed her eyes, pictured his face, and relived the afterparty one more time.

Chapter 11

Spiritual Enlightenment

The moon cast glimmers off a small stream trickling over a mini staircase of stones. The water was so clear, it was transparent. The polished stones beneath were exposed and shone in green, silver, and earthy browns.

Viviana perched on a soft, moss-covered rock, resting her bare feet on the edge of the stream. She loved this place. She wished she could bring Dami here. A pulse of guilt tugged at her heart. She never hid anything from Dami. But this place was a small sanctuary carved into earth by nature herself. It was untouched. It was pure. It had the perfect energy for spiritual enlightenment.

The darkness in Dami's aura had heightened lately. It had always been there. Viviana had seen it in Dami's eyes even when they were children. But it had always been tamed. Like a second thought. Lately, it had become more dominant. Viviana could feel it seeping through Dami, pulsing a dark aura around her, poisoning the energies she emanated into others. Into the earth.

She couldn't bring Dami here. She was afraid of what would happen to this sacred space.

Viviana looked up at the moon. A chill crept through her as she thought of the things Dami had done, claiming it was their calling, their legacy, to avenge their parents' deaths. To purge the earth of the evil hunters who had extinguished their mother and father.

The moon pulsed, its glow sending shivers down Viviana's arms. She pulled her cloak tighter, wrapping her arms around herself. The moon had always been their guide, until Dami stopped following its cycles. Viviana looked at its celestial glow. It changed shape, transforming into a perfect triangle, a dark pupil within. T he *All-Seeing Eye.* The one her father had told her about. The one that watched them. The one that watched everyone. She could feel the cold judgment of the

All-Seeing Eye now, strongly present, watching her watching Dami as she chose which humans to extinguish.

Viviana couldn't understand how Dami could take a life. She'd seen signs of darkness in Dami when they were little girls, but their father had always been there to guide Dami toward the light. Viviana had wracked her brain, read and reread all the guidebooks of their coven, and dug through the teachings of her parents stored in her mind. Nothing in the ways of the coven that she knew had ever spoken of choosing—of *purging*.

Dami followed a different guide. She declared that they had been chosen to clean the earth of everything that threatened their way of life, their family, their coven, and all covens.

Flashes of the sacrifice Dami had made pulsed in her mind. The smell of broiling flesh stuck in her nostrils. The glow of the red-hot symbol of Satan burned through her thoughts.

Dami had talked, night after night, about sacrificing an evil human, making Viviana's ears bleed with fear. Viviana didn't know how much more she could take. Until Dami finally did it.

Viviana had stood and watched.

Since the moment they'd fled from their burning home, Dami had a hatred within her for the people responsible. A man and a woman, the couple that led the local church. Dami was sure they had lit the match that started the flame that consumed their house and killed their parents.

Dami had forced Viviana to run all night through the forest and to the next town. They found an abandoned shack on the edge of the woods where they squatted for the night. The next morning, Dami left, insisting that Viviana stay hidden. Dami didn't return until dark. She had food and water. The next day, they moved to the next town. The pattern began. The girls running under the cloak of night, Viviana hiding in abandoned houses all day, and Dami returning with supplies. Viviana didn't question. She wasn't sure she wanted to know what Dami had to do to keep them alive.

Dami told her that she'd seen papers, and that everyone thought they were dead. Heat reddened her face as she spoke of the leaders of the church and how they had vanished. Viviana wished she knew how to temper the darkness within Dami, now broiling to the surface in full rage. She wished she had the same powerful ability to guide Dami like her father had.

The sisters never stayed in one place for very long, yet they didn't stray too far from their hometown. Dami clung to the hope their parents' killers would return.

Finally, one night, Dami declared that they had to find a more permanent place to stay. She spoke of their father's sister, the aunt that lived on the other side of the country not far from the Rocky Mountains. Viviana had faint recollections of this mysterious aunt. After banishing her from the coven, their father had forbidden the girls to ever speak of his sister again. Now, with nowhere else to go, Viviana believed Dami that no matter how hard and long the journey was, getting to their aunt was their only hope.

When they finally made it to the house on the edge of the woods outside of Calgary, it took an instant hold on Dami. It was abandoned. Their aunt had passed away months earlier. Some kind of sorrow overtook Dami. The last thread of a family, someone who could take the weight off Dami's shoulders, was gone.

Something switched in Dami, and she became vengeful. She spoke of purging the world of evil people. One day, she hit a young vagrant over the head with a rock in the woods, tied him up in the basement, and burned his skin. Dami spent evenings in the basement, developing some sort of ritual, cooking her victim to d eath.

Viviana stood in stunned silence. She might as well have been holding that flame to his flesh. He was purged by her inaction.

Viviana swallowed hard and stared into the trickling stream. She slipped her hand into her pocket within the folds of her cloak and pulled out a little purple book etched with gold lettering. It had been a gift from her father, one of the few items Dami had managed to save from the fire. It was filled with lessons of reaching true spiritual enlightenment. She'd felt close to it, like it was within her reach, not that long ago. Now, she felt far away from it. Like something was pulling her the other way as she watched it vanish down a dark hole.

A tear trickled over her cheek. The chill air nipped at the droplet. She looked up at the moon again. It quivered. It was still there. It hadn't been swallowed by the All-Seeing Eye. There was still hope. She knew it. She could feel it washing over her in the soft glow of the moon.

She opened the book, flipping to the page that called to her now. Her red lips moved as she read aloud to the croaking frogs and the chirping crickets.

THE SEED OF SPIRITUAL ENLIGHTENMENT

The seed is the most important part of achieving spiritual enlightenment. The seed must be authentic. It must be protected. It must be fed.

A perfect seed is a heart with true intention. A soul of bright and positive energy. A mind clear of destructive thoughts.

If a seed is flawless, then its purity must be protected. The physical body is a house of protection. The body must be respected, the physical shell, the emotional being inside, and the spirituality of the mind.

Once the seed is pure and protected, it must be nourished to grow. To nourish your heart, mind, and soul, you must practice the ways of manifestation of clean and positive energies. You must choose the energy, plant it within, and manifest it into the world.

You, my child, were born with the purest seed within. You must protect it.

Love, your coven leader and father.

Tears trickled down her cheeks as Viviana closed the book and secured the golden band around it. She held it in her palms and looked at it. Energy swelled within her heart, flowing through her veins. Love, purity, and positive intentions fuelled this energy. The energy that was within her, that she longed to manifest, that she dreamed of infusing into her sister. At a moment like this, clear thoughts in her mind, she believed it was possible. Then the ball of doubt roiling in the pit of her belly would remind her she was in deep. Too far, perhaps, to turn back.

Two paths opened before her. One of spiritual enlightenment. The other of loyalty to the only family she had left.

Hunter

Chapter 12

Church

A breeze swept a scatter of dried and fallen leaves down the narrow street. Grey clouds stretched wispy fingers through the sky.

Viviana pulled her cloak tighter around her, fighting off a shiver.

She stood beside Damaris, on the edge of a sidewalk, looking up at a small chapel. It was less than magnificent. A humble building resembling an old house.

"How cute," Damaris said with a snark to her tone.

Viviana kind of thought it was. It looked welcoming, homey, like the small building their coven used to convene in.

"The leader should be arriving soon, alone. If she's sticking to her schedule," Damaris said.

"What do we do now?" Viviana asked, even though she knew.

Damaris sighed. She turned and glared at Viviana, her eyes taking on that angry hue that seemed so prevalent lately. "How many times do I have to tell you?"

"I just want to make sure I get it right." Viviana reached out and stroked Damaris' arm. "You said it had to be perfect."

Damaris' expression relaxed. "We wait until the leader comes." She slipped her hands into the folds of her cloak and pulled out a photo. "Madeleine. Her message to her followers is to *purify* themselves. To rid themselves of all evil in all areas of their lives." The woman in the photo smiled. Her long, sandy-blonde hair fell around her shoulders. She wore a prim button-up pink sweater. She looked innocent. Damaris put the photo away. "She's been poisoning her followers. Telling them people need to be purged from the earth. People like us." A demonic hue clouded Damaris' eyes.

Viviana shifted on her feet. She put her hand in her pockets beneath the folds of her cloak. She'd watched Madeleine spread her message, hiding in the crevices at the back of the church while Damaris had sat in the back row, taking it all in.

She'd heard this woman speak of purification, of ridding one's life of negative energy. But she didn't understand how it had been targeted at them. Or how it had been intended for the people of the congregation to go out and physically remove humans from the earth, the way Damaris had interpreted it.

Damaris grabbed her arm. "You remember the plan, right?"

"Yes. We watch her go in. Make sure no one sees us. We go and pretend we are new in town and interested in joining the church. We ask for a tour. When we get to a room with no windows, I pretend I'm not well and fall down. You panic. When she bends to check on me, you..." Viviana paused. Her hand wrapped around the straw doll in her pocket.

"I give her a dose of good old-fashioned witch poison." Damaris smirked. It was a smile Viviana hardly recognized. But she hardly recognized anything about Dami lately. "We carry her out to the van."

"Are you sure she's the right one?" Viviana blurted out.

"What? You heard what she said. People need to be purged. *We* need to be purged. She's just like *them*." Anger blazed behind Damaris' eyes. She spat her words out.

"Are you sure she was talking about us?" Viviana continued.

"Of course she was. Remove the evil. You know what these people think. *We* are the *evil*." The anger building in Damaris flushed her face.

"Yes." Viviana swallowed, grasping for another tactic. "Are you sure we need to *practice*? I mean...we could go back now... find them."

Damaris' face softened. "Yes. When we find them, it has to be *perfect*." She licked her lips. Darkness flashed across her eyes.

The wind picked up. Leaves scattered, dancing over the street in clusters, sending crinkles through the air. A chill crept through Viviana. What was *perfect*? Dami had taken her time *practicing* on the vagrant from the woods. When she was finally done, she'd declared that they needed to start a *cycle of purge*. Viviana had bit her lip, not wanting to ask questions that she wouldn't like the answers to. How many times would they have to act out this horrifying play before Dami was satisfied?

"Look. I think that's her." Damaris pointed down the street. A woman walked toward them, her sandy-blonde hair fluttering in the wind. The woman pulled a silk scarf tighter around her neck.

"We need to hide." Damaris pulled her arm, leading her behind an ample bush.

They crouched. Damaris watched the woman from small gaps in the shrubbery. Sweet honeysuckle wafted from small white flowers. Viviana breathed it in. It reminded her of a small dirt path she used to wander down, behind the little house at the edge of the forest. The house she wished with all her might she could be in now. But it was gone. All that was left was a charred skeleton of the wooden structure that had held it all together. They'd gone back. Once. Before fleeing to the other side of the country. Damaris wanted to find the people who burned their house. The people who burned their parents. But all they found was a carcass of the past.

"OK. She's in. Let's wait to make sure she's alone," Damaris said, focusing on an opening in the bush.

The cold chill from the wind clung to Viviana's bones, swirling through her. She shivered. She stroked the straw doll with her fingers, feeling her mother's soft red curls brush against her cheek as she hugged her. She could still smell the lavender clinging to her mother's sweater and hear her mother's voice telling her that *Viviana* meant *life.* That her fire hair was a symbol of *otherness.* Her ice-blue eyes were a sign of purity. That she was a rare gem.

Damaris nudged her. "Let's go."

Viviana succumbed to the pull that Damaris had on her. The chill from the wind wove to the pit of her belly and swelled into an icy ball. Nothing about this aligned with the guides within. Nothing about this resonated when she connected with the higher spirits. Nothing about this felt right. None of it made sense.

Every time she found her voice and questioned any of it, the anger within Damaris surfaced and the demon within her shone its eyes.

Without Damaris, she had no coven. No family. But, Damaris no longer seemed to be Damaris.

They walked briskly down the sidewalk, up the steps, and into the church. The warm, bright main entrance caressed her. Water colours and pastels hung on the walls. Soft piano music filled the space. This didn't feel like a place of evil.

The woman with the silk scarf appeared through a side doorway. "Welcome to *The Church of Life.*" She smiled.

Damaris smiled back. A smile Viviana only saw during the playing out of this script.

"I'm Madeleine Martin. Founder of the church," the woman said.

"I'm Nicole. This is my sister, Cynthia," Damaris said, her voice coated with sunshine.

"Can I help you?" Madeleine asked.

"Yes. We are new in town. We are looking for a new family," Damaris said.

"Well, we always welcome new members. Would you like a tour?"

"You aren't too busy, are you? Are you here alone?"

"I'm the only one here at the moment, but it's no trouble at all. I assure you," Madeleine said.

"Perfect." Damaris smiled.

They followed Madeleine into the main sanctuary. It was small, quaint, yet had a godly air about it. Triangular stained-glass windows cast red, orange, blue, and purple shapes over the floor and the wooden pews. The front stage, barely elevated, looked holy with golden cups lining a centre table and rectangular purple silk cloths hanging along the ceiling. A series of pipes were set into the left side of the back wall next to an organ perched in the corner. It felt spiritual. It felt like the aura that Viviana summoned up when she nestled next to the trickling stream in her secret enclave in the forest. Was Madeleine any different from her? Creating her sanctuary and speaking to her higher spirits?

They'd halted at the front. Viviana had tuned them out, not hearing a word they'd said.

"Where are you from?" Madeleine asked.

Damaris jumped in, "Oh, just a little town in the prairies. You probably haven't heard of it." Damaris blushed and put a hand to her heart.

How did she do it? Would Madeleine buy this act?

"Try me," Madeleine said.

Damaris answered, "Torch River."

"Oh. I guess you were right. I don't know where that is."

Nobody knew where it was. It didn't exist. Viviana smiled, attempting to hide her nerves. Images of Forestville, their hometown, floated through her mind. She wished they could be there now.

"Why don't we go to my office? I can give you all the information, in case you decide you want to join us for a service. Test us out." Madeleine smiled, leading the way through a side door.

The aura of the sanctuary pulled at Viviana. She felt rooted.

Damaris turned and glared at her. Viviana shuffled to catch up. On the other side of the doorway was a small, dark hall.

"Watch your step. I apologize for the lack of lighting. It's not far," Madeleine said.

Damaris grabbed Viviana's shoulder and hovered, her face a mere inch away. Hot, sour breath invaded Viviana's senses. She stared into demon eyes. Damaris had changed. Again.

"Now," Damaris breathed the hot words over her.

Damaris turned toward Madeleine.

The cold returned in the pit of Viviana's belly. It clutched at her insides. She froze in place.

Damaris turned and stared her down with an evil glare.

She gave in. She let out a loud gasp and crumpled to her knees.

"Cynthia," Damaris gasped, using her sister's latest alias as convincingly as if it were really her name.

Madeleine halted and turned.

Damaris leaned over Viviana, her face washed with concern. She winked, confirming the first act of the play was well underway.

Madeleine hovered behind Damaris. "Is she all right?"

"I'm not sure. She's pale. She's not responding." Panic rose in Damaris' voice.

Madeleine gently pushed her way to Viviana. "Let me take a look. I know first aid."

Damaris stepped aside.

Madeleine knelt down and placed a hand on Viviana's back. "Are you OK, dear? Can you hear me?"

She smelled like honeysuckle. The cold clutched Viviana's gut. Her insides roiled.

She looked into Madeleine's eyes.

Damaris loomed behind, arm raised high, needle gripped tightly in her hand. The demon had fully returned, looking hungrily at her prey. She brought her hand down.

The needle pierced the back of Madeleine's neck. Damaris pushed the plunger.

Madeleine gasped. Her hand swept the back of her neck, landing on the plunger. Disbelief washed her eyes. She fell forward, landing on Viviana. Honeysuckle filled the air. Viviana swallowed down the cold ball crawling up her throat. She stared her demon sister in the eye.

Chapter 13

Murder Collage

S tella stood, glass of bourbon in hand, staring at the intricate collage of crime scenes she had carefully constructed over the years. It took up most of the wall opposite from her shelves of CDs. Every serious serial killer to hit within the borders of the country over the last twenty-five years had a place in the gory, gruesome photo album spreading its evil fingers across the wall.

She'd looked at it so many times, she could picture every single photo and newspaper clipping with her eyes closed. It had been several days since she'd put the bathtub bludgeoning to bed, and she had nothing better to do.

Cases gone cold, here in Stella's beloved city, were brought back to life by clusters of photos bordering the main collage. Between investigations, Stella got bored. Restless. She'd taken to digging up files from cases that had stopped dead in their tracks. There were three that currently caught her attention. All young women, blonde, vagrants. As she'd scoured every detail, only one thing seemed consistent across the trio. His name was Stag. She'd been following him in her free time, gathering intel, trying to put together a strong enough case to re-open the investigation. It had proven to be more of a challenge than she'd expected.

She took a sip of bourbon and let her gaze wander.

At the very centre of the elaborate collage, a photo of what could only be described as a human vampire glimmered. He had been one of the worst to ever exist. He had plunged a knife into the gut of the one man who had truly loved her. Detective Mahoney. Jagger. Her father.

She had spoken to her father that very night. She could still hear his voice. She could still feel him from the other side of the country, over the phoneline. Far away. Distant. Lost.

Yet her hatred didn't burn for this human vampire. She looked at his face in the photo. Painted up like some freak of nature. Part human. Part vampire. Part glam demon. White lines streaked his cheeks. Purple shimmer glazed his eyelids. Dark black lined his parted lips. Whoever he had been, he wasn't the reason her father died. Leaving her alone.

Her gaze wandered, finding the photo she yearned to see. Again.

The face of a man who played games. Sergeant Tomlinson. The polished man in the pressed suit. Dressed to impress. Saying what he needed to get where he wanted to be. Ignoring the gut instincts, the knowledge, the experience of a detective called to duty, to leave his team, fly across the country, and dig up ghosts of the past. Without her father, the case never would have been solved. Tomlinson did everything in his power to stop her father from stopping a killer. It was Tomlinson who put that knife in the hands of the vampire. It was Tomlinson who slid that knife into her father's gut. If it hadn't been for Tomlinson, the investigation would have followed protocol. Logic. The righteous path. And her father would not have had to sacrifice himself to stop a human vampire.

An internal investigation had been launched against Tomlinson. His badge had been taken. Had it been enough? Stella wished she could truly make him pay. A life for a life. The idea throbbed in the back of her mind. She let it simmer, yet she didn't allow it to surface. To morph into action.

Maybe one day she would.

Chapter 14

Sacrifice

The dark basement glowed soft orange from the small flames atop a set of tall candles, forming a perfect circle around the human sacrifice.

Viviana stood in the corner. The cool of the concrete wall soothed her arms as she leaned against it. She wished she could tame the heat surging through her. The fire blazing in the pit of her belly. This felt wrong. She ran her fingers through her hair, securing strands behind each ear, revealing her face.

The woman in the centre of the flames trembled. Her arms tied behind her back, her sandy-blonde hair fell over her face, sticking to her wet cheeks. The heat from the room caused sweat to trickle down the woman's face, her neck, her arms, sticking her shirt to her breasts. Blood dropped onto the floor, falling from the slits cut into her wrists by the binds digging deeper each time she pulled her arms in a meek attempt to escape her fate.

The woman looked over at her. Their eyes met. The woman tried to speak through the white cloth tied over her mouth, suffocating her words. "Whff...mmmfff."

The woman's plea was incomprehensible. Viviana figured she was trying to plead for her safety. Inquiring as to what was going to happen to her, why they were doing this, and what she had done wrong.

What *had* she done wrong?

Creaking from the stairs jolted Viviana. Damaris descended the staircase, her hair flowing into her long, dark robe. Damaris' presence ebbed through the entire basement. The small flames on the tips of the candles flickered.

Damaris approached a CD player set atop a table beside two speakers. She clicked play. Chanting ebbed through the basement.

Viviana cringed.

Damaris walked toward the circle, looking directly at the woman in the centre as she pulled a glove over each of her hands.

The woman's eyes widened as she saw the woman in the cloak. Her hunter. Damaris. The dominant woman. The one Viviana had followed ever since they ran from the burning house into the safety of the forest.

Damaris raised her arms, her cloak falling behind her back. "It is time. For the purge." Her voice was confident, strong, commanding.

Viviana pushed herself from the safety of the wall and walked across the room to join her sister. It was really happening. Something cold grasped her insides. Like an icy claw, digging into her gut. She halted, hunching over. It was bad energy. The All-Seeing Eye flashed across her vision. Staring into her soul. Telling her she was walking down the wrong path.

Damaris turned to her. "What's wrong with you?" she demanded. "It's time. You aren't going to fail me now, are you?" Dami's glare pierced right into Viviana's heart.

Viviana stood tall. "No. I am here." She couldn't fail her sister, despite what her internal guides were telling her.

Her sister was all she had.

Viviana summoned her strength, forced the vision of the All-Seeing Eye from her mind, and walked up to Damaris. She looked up into the dark eyes of the sister she loved, the sister she followed, the sister she no longer knew.

Damaris looked back at her and smiled, slow and sleek. A demonic hue tainted her face, tinged her gaze, and seeped from her into the space between them.

"It is time." Damaris hissed.

Viviana clutched her hands together, pressing on her belly, easing the pain throbbing inside like a warning. She looked into Dami's evil eyes and responded, "Yes. It is time." She swallowed back a trickle of bile surging up her throat. It tasted foul and burned her insides like acid as she forced it down.

Damaris moved her lips to the words of the ritualistic chant vibrating through the room. She looked at the woman. "It is time. We purge *you.*" She slipped her amulet adorned knife from within the folds of her cloak, raised her hand, and pointed the shining silver blade straight toward the trembling woman.

Glints from the flickering flames shot off the blade. The woman trembled, tears soaking the gag in her mouth, drowning out her pleas for life.

The human sacrifice. Viviana wished she didn't know that this woman's name was Madeleine. That she had a life, a church, a congregation. Her own type of *family*. Just like the coven had been their family—hers and Dami's—growing up.

Dami continued to perform her ritual. "You have been deemed evil. The earth needs to be cleansed of you. You label others as Satanic worshippers. You seek to rid the earth of these evil beings. You lead people down your path, feeding them your lies, telling them that these evildoers must be removed from the earth." Dami pointed the end of the blade into the side of the woman's face. A droplet of blood burst from the fresh slit and slithered down the woman's wet skin.

Viviana shuddered. She swallowed against a sudden surge of hot stomach acid, boiling inside of her. The cold claw clutched at the pit of her belly. She pressed her hands harder against her stomach.

Dami moved the blade away from the woman's face and raised the knife in both hands toward the ceiling. She lowered her head. Her hair slipped over her face, from beneath her hood. She spoke low and deep. "You have deemed us as Satanic worshippers. My coven. My family. You have hunted us and extinguished us from this earth. It is time for you to be purged, for it is you who hunts, worships evil, and shall pay for your wrongdoings."

The woman's eyes grew wild. Her entire body trembled. Blood and sweat dripped in soft splats against the floor beneath her.

The flames of the candles flickered in unison. Dami lowered her knife, then bent and picked up a candle. She circled the woman, her prey, her sacrifice, like a lioness stalking its fresh kill. She chanted as she looked into the flame.

Viviana's mind went crazy with thoughts. She wanted to stop Dami. She wanted to look into her demonic eyes and plead with her until the sweet innocence she once had returned and sparkled bright, killing the demon within, giving her sister back to her. Sparing this woman.

The smell of burning flesh floated through the room. The sound of sizzling skin followed. Dami stood, holding the flame of the candle to the woman's arm. The flame licked the woman's flesh. The skin turned red, small wisps of smoke wafting off it. The skin broiled under the heat of the flame. The woman's scream, muffled beneath the cloth, drummed into Viviana's ears. Her mind whirled. She placed her palms over her ears, trying to drown out the sound of the woman suffering. She closed her eyes and willed the image of the burning flesh from her mind. She tried to smell something other than cooked human meat. The world whirled around her. She fell to her knees.

"Viviana. You will stand up now," Dami's voiced boomed through the thick imaginary wall erected between Viviana and the basement.

Viviana jumped, falling back onto the floor. She looked at Dami, glaring down at her, commanding her to stand and take part.

"Viviana. Did you hear me? This is our calling. You are my coven. My family. Your loyalty is imperative. We must cleanse the earth of the evil that took them. The ones we loved the most."

Viviana looked into Dami's eyes. She trembled. She forced herself to her feet.

"Very good." Dami walked back to the circle.

Viviana followed. She pressed her hands hard into her stomach, forcing away the pulsing dark ball, the warning that the path chosen at this moment was not the one for her. Not the one for spiritual enlightenment. Not the one to ease the glare of the All-Seeing Eye.

Viviana slipped her hand into the folds of her cloak, finding the straw doll her mother had made. The only piece of her mother she still had left. Clinging to it, to the past, to the way she knew she should follow, she stepped forth onto the path pulling her now. The path laid out by Damaris, her sister, the only part of her coven left standing and breathing, in flesh.

Viviana took a deep breath as something ripped through her, tearing her insides apart. She watched as Dami held the flame to the woman's leg, broiling the skin down her upper thigh, cooking it slowly, inducing the pain and suffering that had once been inflicted upon their parents.

Chapter 15

Nightcap

The alley was dark and damp. A steady dripping echoed through the heavy silence as drops of dirty water plunged from exposed pipes onto concrete. A blaze of red broke the darkness as Stella lit a cigarette and took a long drag. The heels of her boots ground against oily gravel scattered over the alley floor. The chains hanging from her belt jingled as she walked toward a black door.

She stared at the purple neon sign.

Her first experience with *The Cecil* had been six long years ago. The night she'd snuck out of the hotel room, her mother in a wine-and-pill-induced sleep. They'd come back to their once-beloved hometown. Stella had crept into the seedy underbelly of the city, driven by a desire to see, to feel, to *taste* the places where her father had hunted human monsters. To find the essence of her dead father. The night had taken a shocking turn. She'd killed, for the first time.

It was rare for her to think about it. She hated the feeling of hot blood trickling over her fingers and the raspy sound of the last breaths of life that lingered around her. *It was me or him,* she would remind herself.

Stella shook off the memory, then took her time finishing her cigarette. For the millionth time, she replayed her plan. She'd been following Stag for months. His real name was Stephen, but on the streets, he was known as Stag. If he was holed up in The Cecil, as she suspected, his bar tab would be tagged with Stag. It seemed to Stella that he'd left more than one body in his wake. She'd found three separate cold case files. Three young girls left in ditches near the city limits. Blonde. Homeless. Too much time between kills, and the ability of Stag to linger outside of the immediate circle of all three victims had left him off the suspect list. Since Stella had few hobbies when she wasn't on a case, she'd had ample time with fresh eyes to do a meticulous scan and put the pieces together.

Her father wouldn't have left this alone. Neither would she.

She took the last puff on her dwindling cigarette and stamped it out with the heel of her heavy boot. Sliding her hand under her long leather coat, around the back of her belt, she slid the knife she'd secured there out of its sheath. She brought it around and took a long look at the shiny blade. She ran her pointer along its edge and smiled. It gave her some sort of comfort to have it with her. She didn't intend to use it, yet she couldn't help thinking it was the perfect knife for gutting a Stag. It had been a lot harder than she thought to get three separate cold cases re-opened. She needed more intel. Something solid to crack the ice off the files.

Stella slid the knife back into its sheath, pulled the sides of her long leather coat around her chest, and exhaled. No more fucking around. It was time.

The black door let out an unoiled screech as she flung it open. She stepped inside. Instantly assaulted by a mix of cheap tequila, rot, and urine, she swallowed back a gag. She took a couple breaths, acclimatizing her senses. She took several long steps into the joint, taking note of every patron, their stance, their hands, their position in the bar, and their general demeanour. She needed to scout out the feisty ones in case of any trouble.

Chatter jolted Stella from her thoughts. She scanned the room. A couple men clad in borrowed clothes—probably from the local donation bin—leaned over the end of the bar, perched high on stools. Sitting at their thrones, throwing back shot after shot of the cheapest bourbon in town, clapping each other on the back as they solved the problems of the world of the lowlife.

In the corner, by a pool table, a scantily-clad, short, doughy woman physically rubbed herself against a scrawny, scraggly-haired man. Either they were soulmates, or she was trying to find a place to sleep for the night.

Stella walked up to the bar, found a stool in the centre, and hoisted herself up. The bartender looked at her from his perch on a cracking wooden stool in the corner, rolled his eyes, and sauntered over.

He glowered at her, his unkempt hair half covering his bloodshot eyes. "Yah?" He was a far cry from the chiseled, feather-haired bartender that had served her first drink in The Cecil.

"Bourbon. On the rocks." Stella slapped a bill on the bar. "Keep the change."

The bartender looked at the bill with surprise. He snatched it up, then turned. A sudden snap appeared in his step.

Stella re-examined the image of Stag forever etched into her mind.

Salt-and-pepper spikes of hair. His jawline, long, his mouth in a permanent sneer, revealing a couple sharp fang-like teeth exposed at the back. Stag. Stephen. Forty-two years old. No permanent address. He'd taken up residency at The Cecil. At least, that was the word on the street.

Stella settled in at the bar, sipping her bourbon slowly, scanning the room discreetly.

Anxiousness clawed through her gut. She knew she had to temper it. She'd been waiting for this night for a while. The boring times between murder cases had been eaten up with the extensive research she'd done to make sure her execution was perfect.

She occupied herself by watching the progression of the maybe-girlfriend maybe-prostitute fondle the wiry guy over by the pool table. The two cheap-bourbon drinkers at the end of the bar grew louder. Their appreciation for each other increased as they continued to solve all their problems, amazed at their own, and each other's, wit.

Giggling erupted from a side door leading to the hotel. A tall, blonde, shiny-skinned woman stepped through. Her tattered skirt barely covered the necessities. Her breasts bounced freely beneath a sheer tank top. It would have been a miracle if she'd come from outside in that getup. She must be staying in the hotel. Likely on Stag's bill. Her clothes and the wrinkles around her young eyes said that she needed any handout she could get.

Her companion entered behind her.

Stella took in a sudden breath. *Stag.* She looked back at the bar, taking renewed interest in her drink. Her ears perked. She tuned her senses toward the couple of interest.

Every ion in her body flared with heat. She wanted nothing more than to slip the knife from beneath her coat and lunge at the savage beast entering the bar. She knew better. She had fire within. Sometimes it was nearly impossible to tame. But she had to. She wanted to gut this Stag. The way to do that was get the magical piece of intel required to put him in a cage.

She sat, focused on her drink, clinging to every syllable uttered between Stag and his sexpot.

Chapter 16

Stalking

Stella's energy broiled. She'd been absorbing the progression of the evening—and the disgusting flirtation between Stag and a desperate young woman in a tattered miniskirt. Nursing her second bourbon as slowly as she could, she continued to blend in at the bar. Just another lonely patron.

Her cue came when Stag's beeper lit up, and he made for the black door to the alleyway. Stella waited a couple minutes, then shot back the rest of the bourbon in the stained glass. She casually slipped from the stool and exited. No one had paid her any attention while she was there. She doubted anyone would notice her stealth departure.

The cold air hit her lungs. She exhaled a puff of white breath. She scanned the alley—left, then right. *Dammit.* Where had Stag gone? She walked carefully across the asphalt, stepping with caution to mute any potential clicking of the heels of her boots.

She heard a voice. Deep. Gruff. Sounded like Stag. It was coming from the right, from behind a dumpster. Creeping across the alley, she made her way to the edge of the dumpster.

Two distinct voices argued from behind the pile of steaming garbage. Remnants of old food wafted through the air.

"Don't fuck with me," Stag's voice erupted.

"I'm not. I swear," a meek voice said, shaking with fear. "I wouldn't. Listen. I have a daughter. She's only ten. Please don't this."

Stella froze. She swallowed.

"Why would I give a fuck? You stole from me," Stag said.

"I didn't. I wouldn't. I know who you are. It wasn't me, I swear. I delivered the entire package. To the guy with the buzzcut. And the pierced eyebrow. Just like I was told. I swear. I didn't take anything. It was all there." The man sniffled. "Please. My daughter. She has no one."

An image of her father flashed through Stella's mind. Her dad. His voice. The last time she talked to him. The day he went away. Forever.

Stella crept around the dumpster.

Stag pressed the tip of a blade against the man's throat.

"Please. No." The man's shrill voice climbed an octave.

Stella wrapped her hand around the hilt of her knife and pulled it from her belt.

She sprung into action. She pounced from behind the corner of the dumpster, knife raised. A portly man, shirt askew, belly spilling over his belt, was wedged up against the alley wall. Surprise hijacked the pleading look in his eyes when he saw Stella.

Stella struck before Stag could turn around. The heavy handle of her knife hit the back of his neck. He fell to his knees.

"What the fuck?" Stag yelled. He turned, lunging for Stella's legs.

He caught her. She fell forward, hitting the pavement hard. The knife flew from her hands, clanking across the ground.

Stag stood, his legs shaking. He yanked a gun from his belt and pointed it at Stella. A whiff of sour whiskey and a flash of dirt-caked hands yanked her back six years. The night she stared down the barrel of a Ruger P97. Him or her.

She hoisted herself up on her elbows. Pain throbbed in her chin. She stared at the gun. It looked like a Glock 19. Standard. Easy to use. Maybe Stag was a poor shot. She contemplated her next move as she stared into Stag's eyes.

Stag glared back. "Who the fuck are you?"

"No one. Just walking by."

"And you thought you'd be some goddamn hero?"

Stella smiled slyly.

"What the hell you smiling at?"

"Nothing."

"Nothing? You know who I am?"

"Can't say I do."

Stag pushed the barrel of the gun against Stella's throat.

A shadow loomed over Stag. Something hard came down on the back of his head.

Stag went down. The gun flew from his hand and slid across the pavement.

The portly man stood, his hands trembling as he clutched a bloody rock.

Stella scrambled to her feet, ran to her knife and picked it up. She walked over to Stag. He was face down on the pavement. She rolled him over with her boot. Part of his skull had been caved in by the rock, blood spilling rapidly from the wound.

He looked her in the eye. "You...bitch." His eyes rolled into the back of his head. His wheezing gurgle eased as the life left his body.

The man, still holding the rock, looked down at Stag. "Oh my god. Is he...is he dead?"

Stella crouched down and pressed her fingers against Stag's throat. She looked up at the man. "Yeah."

"This is bad. Real bad. I didn't mean to kill him. You...you saved me. I...I have a daughter. I was only trying to get us out of this."

"It was self-defence."

"You don't understand. I was part of a drug deal. Big one. I was desperate. I never should have done it." The man dropped the rock. It hit the pavement with a wet thud. "Miss...I can't go to jail. My daughter. I'm all she has."

Stella scanned the empty alleyway. A flicker of the feather-haired bartender appeared. She could hear him telling her to get out of here. It was just another murder at The Cecil.

"Go home to your daughter." Stella sheathed her knife, then wiped Stag's neck with her shirt where she's pressed her fingertips to test his pulse.

"But, won't the police come?"

Stella stood. "Here? Sure. Eventually. Check the paper. In a couple of days. It'll be tagged as another routine night at The Cecil."

The man nodded in stunned silence.

"Take the rock, throw it in the river."

The man grabbed the bloody rock, then stumbled away.

Stella turned and walked down the alley, heels crunching on oily gravel, hoping that she was right.

Burned/Alive

Chapter 17

Murder Calls

Clattering cut through the quiet of the small room. Buzzing followed. From beneath a puffy quilt fort of solitude, Stella stirred. The buzzing increased, followed by a clack. Stella removed the covers from her head and looked over at her nightstand. Her murder phone was active, buzzing and bouncing across the nightstand. Apparently the latest and greatest in cell phone technology; it was a pain in the ass. The only strand of hope it offered was the chance to work on a real case, and to prove she was the detective that her father had been.

Stella moaned, snatched up the phone, and answered the call. "Mahoney." She yawned into the bunched-up quilt.

"Stella. Sutton here. I need you on scene."

Stella rolled her eyes. "Where?" *It's Mahoney. Not Stella.*

"On the bad side of downtown."

Ha. I'm already on the bad side of town. "Sure."

"Across from Queen's Park Cemetery."

"Got it." Stella looked out the window at the orange-pink glow peeking through the curtains.

"I'll meet you there. Pronto."

"Got it, *boss.*" Stella smiled to herself. She'd heard that he hated being called boss. Apparently, it had been a label applied to her father, and he still had a hard time taking it as his own. She was confident she had placed just the right amount of emphasis to get under his skin.

Stella dropped her phone onto the end table and rolled out of bed. She shuffled out to the main room, put on a pot of dark roast to percolate, then perused her music collection. She was sure this was a *just another body, just another day,* kind of situation. The portly man, holding the bloody rock with trembling hands, flickered through her mind. A stop for a paper would be required. Confirmation that last night was just another murder at The Cecil was imperative.

She selected a Led Zeppelin cover from her father's vintage LPs. As she dropped the needle, she relished in the wailings of Robert Plant, telling her she was gonna sweat and gonna move. The rock gods left behind by her dad may have been from a different time, but the raw, electric energy they seeped had at least an inkling of similarity to her metal icons.

Chapter 18

Outside the Cemetery

The pink-orange hue of the sunrise had turned to a blood-orange drip over a cyan background. Stella steered her blue Sunfire through the empty downtown streets at high speed. She loved the view from this side of the core. Her apartment, nestled between a perfect view of the Bow River and the looming downtown towers, blended into the belly of the city. It was perched a few blocks over the line between the steady stream of people in suits and the messier humans cast aside by society. She preferred the messy side of things.

It hadn't taken her to long to whip her Sunfire down the empty veins leaving the heart of the city and plunging further into...how had Sutton put it? *The wrong side of town.*

Stella eased up the gas and pulled to the edge of the Queen's Park Cemetery. It was generally quiet in this part of town. She sometimes walked the sidewalks bordering the rows upon rows of charcoal headstones etched with names that family members couldn't let go of. Other than the occasional mourner, the groomed grass squares tended to be empty.

She spotted the concrete archway declaring the formal entranceway to the cemetery. She pulled up front and slid her Sunfire behind Sutton's glossy blue Chevy. She emerged from the car and pulled her leather coat tight around her. The morning chill had a bite to it, even on a summer day.

A lonely aura wafted from the deserted cemetery. Shadows stretched from the walls housing rows of urns like dark figures keeping watch. The thick silence shielded the place from the rest of the world like a cloak.

"Stella," Sutton's voice shattered the moment.

Stella turned to look across the street from the cemetery entrance. She waved, then walked toward the scene. Sutton stood close to an officer looking up at...*it.*

Stella's pace slowed as she caught her breath.

Adrenaline shot through her veins. The blood vessels in her neck pulsed.

This was it. The case she'd been dreaming of.

As she approached, the scene came into focus. It was like nothing she had ever seen. In person. She'd scoured plenty of photos of the worst murder scenes across the country. They were pinned in gruesome collages all over her apartment wall. Her research. Her obsession. To understand the minds of these sick humans. She thought of them as a different breed.

The details of the scene came into view. It was the skin. A loose cloth hung around parts of the body, most of its skin exposed. Sickly pink-red ridges riddled the flesh, bunching up into grotesque contours. Like it had been sizzled under high heat. The disfigured flesh ran all down the body's arms, thighs, legs, feet. It was grisly.

The body was human. It had to be. What else could it be? But in its state, it looked animalistic. The size indicated an adult. Bulges of burnt flesh hung from the chest, partially exposed from beneath the cloth. It appeared to be a woman. The hair. It was a wild mess of tangled knots, sprouting from the head.

Nailed somehow to a long spike, solidly perched into the ground, the body loomed over them. Appearing as though it were floating in the air.

Here she was, in this moment that she'd been waiting for. Dreaming of. To be hunting a killer of this calibre. As she got closer to the scene, she had no doubt this had to be to work of someone who had killed before and would kill again.

Chapter 19

Killer Scene

Stella spotted a woman examining the body. A silver streak in the woman's long, dark hair glared under the first rays of morning sun. *Medical Examiner Blackwood.* She sighed a breath of relief. Her first experience with her had been smooth—relatively. Blackwood was smart, thorough, and easy to deal with. The body loomed over them, perched high, suspended in time.

Stella worked her way up the hill, staring at the body. The skin all along the arms and legs was reddish pink, bunched into folds of distorted contours. Like it had been broiled. A loose cloth wrapped crudely around the body hung in folds, half concealing it. The midsection was exposed. Stella could swear she saw some kind of mark burned into the flesh.

Stella approached Sutton. "Boss."

Sutton turned. "Stella. Good hustle."

I live on this side of town. "No problem."

"This is serious," Sutton said.

"Never seen anything like it," an unfamiliar officer spoke, his voice meek.

"Stella, Officer Benton. Officer Benton, this is Detective Stella Mahoney," Sutton said.

Wow. You do know my last name. Stella nodded at the officer.

"Benton was first on scene," Sutton said.

"I was on my usual patrol. Sometimes the teenagers hang out in the cemetery. Figure no one will find them here," Benton said.

"What's with the skin?" Stella asked.

"It looks burned. But not charred," Sutton said.

"Like someone cooked it to perfection," Stella said. "A controlled burn."

Sutton nodded. "What do you think of the clothing?"

Stella looked up and down the body. "No idea. It's weird. Just a cloth...and it's intact. Probably draped over the body, after the burning." Stella narrowed her eyes. "There's some kind of mark on the abdomen. Maybe we can pull the cloth back and look."

"No," Sutton barked. "Let Blackwood do it."

Always by the book. Stella shook her head.

Sutton stroked a green rabbit foot hanging from his belt.

She'd heard it was some sort of good-luck thing. Helped him tune into his gut instincts. "Maybe your gnarly claw of a dead animal can tell us something." She smirked.

Sutton glared. "For fuck's sake, Stella." His face flushed. "You're always complaining about how *boring* all the cases are. I called *you* in on this one. Give you something real to chomp on. I mean, *look* at it." Sutton pointed up at the burned body. "Isn't this *real* enough for you?"

Stella put up her hands. "OK. I was only kidding around."

"Well cut it out. Take a closer look. Talk to Blackwood. Don't touch anything till she's done. Benton and I will set up the perimeter. Techies should be done soon." Sutton pointed at several personnel donned in jackets branded *CST,* scattered across the park with cameras in hand.

"Got it, boss." Stella nodded. She walked toward Blackwood.

Blackwood was standing close to the body, examining the abdomen.

"Blackwood," Stella greeted.

Blackwood turned. "Detective Mahoney. Good to see you again."

"You, too."

"Sutton's got you liaising with me?" Blackwood asked.

"Yeah."

"Guess my continued *dislike* for him is working." Blackwood smirked. "Look at this." Blackwood reached out a gloved hand and lifted the flowing cloth from the body's abdomen.

The flesh was cooked, similar to the skin on the arms and legs. Reddish-pink skin contorted into bunched protrusions of flesh. The very centre of the body's stomach stood out. A symbol was seared into the skin, leaving a charred, blackened mark.

"Geez," Stella said.

"Real humdinger," Blackwood said. "I've seen messages left by killers. Never seen a body branded like this."

"You think it's a message?" Stella asked.

"Definitely. It's some sort of symbol."

They both stared at the strange symbol. The face of a wild animal stared back at them. Evil seeped from its eyes. Its head melded into a five-pointed star, its horns pushing against the two peak points. A snake curled around the star, closing it inside a circle. Strange symbols sat atop each of the five points.

"What the fuck," Stella spoke.

"Yeah. You know what it means?"

"No clue," Stella said. "What kind of animal is that?"

"I don't know. Those might be horns. Maybe some kind of goat." Blackwood sighed. "Why do these creeps have to leave such weird, cryptic messages?"

"You've really had to do this before? Decipher strange messages?"

"Oh yeah." Blackwood nodded. "First case I worked on with your dad. Killer carved his messages into the flesh of the victims." She looked at the body. "I've got to get this body out of here. I can't process anything else with it hanging like this. I need to get it back to my lab. You take a look. See if that gut of yours tells you anything."

"My gut?"

"You're a Mahoney, aren't ya?" Blackwood raised an eyebrow.

"Yeah."

"Well, your dad had a strong gut instinct. It's what helped him catch killers. I assumed you must have it too. I mean..." Blackwood paused.

"What?"

"Well, it's just that you have a similar demeanour. You clench your jaw, just like he did, when he was pondering something. All you need a is five-'o'-clock shadow to stroke." Blackwood winked, then turned and walked down the hill toward a medic vehicle.

Stella slid her fingers across her jawline, thinking of her father's face. He'd had a strong jaw. Sturdy. And he *did* clench his jaw when he was thinking.

She shook off the memory and went to work absorbing the gruesome corpse hanging before her. Why would someone cook the skin like this? What did the symbol mean? The victim was broiled and branded, hung and left. On display.

Stella walked around the back of the body, examining the long wooden pole protruding from the ground, holding the body in the air. The wood was smooth, polished, clean. Uncharred. Why would the body be burned, then hung on this stake?

The face of a metal god flashed through Stella's mind. Screaming lyrics of burning witches.

She snapped her attention back to the smooth, wooden pole.

That was it. It was like a staged burning at the stake. Heat swelled in the pit of her belly. Right? Or was it? Was she on to something? Or was her mind cluttered with metal music?

Sutton walked up behind her. "What you got?"

"I was looking at the wood. Wondering why it wasn't burned. It's like some sort of staged burning at the stake," Stella said.

"What?" Sutton asked.

"Yeah. Like burning a witch at the stake," Stella said.

"What do you know about witchcraft?" Sutton asked.

"Not much. Just...bits from song lyrics."

"Work with Jake. Find out what kind of wood this is, and what the hell this symbol means. And become the department expert on witchcraft," Sutton said.

"Got it, boss."

"And follow up with Blackwood after she gets the body to the lab. She doesn't like me. You two seem to work well together. She always did like a Mahoney."

"Done." Stella smiled to herself. She suspected Blackwood didn't really mind Sutton. But she knew how to sway the selection of who was on her team.

Sutton started to walk away.

"Hey, boss?" Stella said.

"Yeah."

"Why are you so eager to explore the first idea I came up with?"

"Figure you must have the Mahoney instinct." He walked away.

Stella stood, looking up at the broiled and branded body hanging over her. She wondered what message the person who did this was sending to them. The heat in the pit of her gut blazed stronger. She wondered if she really did have the same gut instinct her father had, or if her erratic behaviour at metal concerts was leaving her mind cluttered with images that would lead her down a wild path.

Her brain buzzed. Electric energy vibrated through her. She had wanted this. Needed this. Now that it was here, the case she'd been waiting for, the energy surging through her seethed a tinge of darkness. Wasn't this the type of case that had led her father down a dark path with no way out?

Chapter 20

Black Book

Stella sat in the driver's seat of her Sunfire. The engine rumbled. Heavy percussion belted from the small black speakers mounted in the doors. A bluesy riff with a rock edge echoed through the car. A classic rock god of the past questioned her. Based on the wear and tear of her father's LP, he'd listened to *When the Levee Breaks* many times. Playing from the tape deck in her car, something about this track made her feel as though he was sitting next to her now.

She leaned over, opened the dash, and pulled out a black book. She sunk back into the seat, slid off the elastic holding the book shut, and opened it. Staring at the first page, the words drifted off the paper. *To my Stella. Words to live by. Love, Dad.*

The writing was rough. His penmanship always had been. The black lettering dripped off the page into her soul, just like it did every time she opened the small book he had left behind. Just for her.

She flipped the pages, finding the section on *Listen to Your Instincts*.

She'd read the entire book from beginning to end, over and over. The words about a gut instinct had stuck with her, but she'd been confused about their true meaning. Until now. The people who had known him the best, Blackwood and Sutton, had both revealed the meaning behind the term. At least in her father's world.

She read the section silently to herself again now, sitting in her Sunfire across the street from the most brutal murder scene she'd ever witnessed.

Life Lesson 8 - Listen to Your Instincts
A Mahoney has a feeling in the pit of their gut.
A tingling. A kind of...knowing.
I know you have this, Stella.

I've seen it in you, even as a young girl.

I heard it in your voice over the phone, when you questioned me.

I saw it in your eyes when you looked at me.

Stella, my girl.

You do not have to share your instinct with anyone else.

You can keep it as your own.

But, you must, you must *listen to it.*

You may need to find a way to follow it within the...rules around you.

But following it is something you must do.

Listen to your gut, my sweet girl.

Stella snapped the book shut and pulled the elastic around it. She wiped the tears trickling down her face. Tingles surged in the pit of her belly.

Chapter 21

Purge

The sun pushed warm rays through the tall pines. Clear water trickled along the side of the soft dirt path. Citrus and pine filled the air. It was a new day. A new beginning. Time to purge.

Viviana strolled along the pathway, relishing in the time she had free from Damaris' grasp. Here, alone, in the arms of nature, a freedom swept through her, elevated her, filled her with hope.

This was where she felt the closest to the spiritual enlightenment her father had spoke of. This is where the All-Seeing Eye wasn't staring down at her in cold judgment.

She skipped along the path, drinking in the fresh air, the bird songs, the aroma of nature. She took deep breaths until she felt high.

Coming to an offshoot, she veered off the path and down a rocky, narrow trail. Within moments, she was perched up on the soft moss-covered rock that was her stool. Her being settled. Everything within her calmed.

She breathed in long and deep, and closed her eyes. She held nature's air inside her, then released it slowly. Purified, she opened her eyes and pulled her ceremonial items from the folds in her cloak. She placed them in a row along the edge of a smooth rock. The purple book etched in gold with all the secrets to spiritual enlightenment written on its pages by her father. They'd only made it halfway through before he was taken. Her knife, engraved with multiple daisy symbols, intertwined and weaving up the handle, to ward off the hunters that claimed her happy coven was evil. An amulet of clear quartz set at the top of the handle, a protective stone for amplification of psychic ability. A small purple candle in a glass enclosure. And a lighter. Not a special one. Just a cheap plastic Bic that she would throw away after her ceremony. She couldn't carry a lighter—or any source of fire—with her for any amount of time. She would feel it burning her, singeing her charred flesh.

The rough patch of skin on her arm itched. She ignored it.

Not now. Now it was time to purify herself of the evil she had taken part in. Gone along with. No. She shook her head. She had chosen to succumb to Damaris' command. It was her doing just as much as it was her sister's.

She picked up the lighter. A bird cawed from overhead. She looked up. A large crow perched on a birch branch above. A sign. There was always a sign.

She returned her focus to the lighter. She snapped the wheel. A flame burst from the tip. She cringed. An itch tingled over the distorted patch of skin on her arm. She stared at the flame. The itch intensified into a slight burn. She hovered the flame over the candle wick. It lit. She released the wheel on the lighter and tossed it on the rock. The itch and the burn eased. The flame on the candle burned bright. Orange spice wafted from the melting wax.

Viviana forced her gaze from the flame, focusing on the warmth and the aroma from the candle.

She opened the purple book and found the page she needed.

Purge.

Purging has been misconstrued by many theories and religions. We must trust in the spiritual interpreters rooted from our inner guides.

True purging, for the spiritually enlightened, is a cleansing of the soul. It is a release from any wrongdoing we have committed. It is a literal washing of the negative energy within that has led us astray.

It is an internal bath.

We can choose at any time the energy we have within ourselves, that we manifest and share with the world.

To purge, light your Palo Santo candle, sacrifice a droplet of your life essence, and seek healing from the higher spirits.

Viviana put the book aside.

She reached for the candle, bringing it close to her face. The flame warmed her skin. She stared into the red-orange fingers reaching into the air.

A woman flashed through her mind. Trembling. Bound and bleeding. In a sphere of flame. She pushed the image away.

"I light my path with my fire. I seek its energy and its guidance." She put the candle back onto the rock, ignoring the slight itch that crawled over the rough patch on her arm.

She reached for her knife. She ran her fingers down its ivory handle, over each daisy protector symbol, infusing her skin with their shielding essence. She ran her pointer down the blade, to the tip.

Another flash of the woman. Madeleine. Muffled pleas suffocating against a tight white cloth, gagging her, choking her, taking away her life.

Closing her eyes, she chanted softly, "I sacrifice my life essence. I give my life to the higher spirits, as a sacrifice, in seeking purity of heart, soul, and mind. In seeking purification. In seeking spiritual enlightenment."

She opened her eyes, pointed the end of the blade into her palm, and sliced a small cut. She turned her hand over and released a few droplets of blood into the clear stream. With her cloak, she wiped her palm and the blade of her knife. She paused to look at the quartz amulet on the handle, then placed it back on the rock.

A light electrified her eyes. The image of Madeleine burned bright, searing her brain. The blood. The tears. The trembling. The fear. The burning. The smell of burning flesh.

Viviana closed her eyes tightly, wrenching her brain. She spoke loud and clear.

"I seek healing from the higher spirits. I seek guidance from the higher spirits. I light my path with my fire. I give of my life essence. I seek guidance. Show me the way."

The image of Madeleine disintegrated.

Viviana opened her eyes, taking in her natural sanctuary as if for the first time.

The flame flickered. The orange spice intensified. Viviana closed her eyes and leaned her head back, turning her face to the sky.

The wind, nature's breath, swept over her, like a deep sigh. The creek trickled louder. The birds sang in unison. The crow cawed once then flew away.

Chapter 22

Witchcraft

The after-work bustle of commuters streamed from the downtown core onto the main artery of the city. Stella wove her Sunfire back and forth, trying to make her way through the thick line of traffic. *Fuck it.* She grabbed the red-and-blue flasher from behind her seat, rolled down the window, and set the light on the roof of the car. She flicked the switch. Lights flashed. The siren blipped. Enough drivers made meek attempts to manoeuvre through the tightly packed rush-hour traffic that Stella was able to slide her Sunfire onto the far-right shoulder and make her way to the next exit. She'd take the back roads through the run-down neighbourhoods. She should have done that in the first place. Where was her gut instinct when she left the cemetery?

She flicked the siren off, but left the light flashing. She didn't want any trouble, should she be slightly over the fifty-kilometre speed limit in the residential areas. This area of town was more industrial than residential, anyways, on the north side of the river and far enough east that the neighbourhoods were far from clean cut or fancy. She blasted through narrow streets, weaving her way further north.

She reached homicide headquarters. Good ol' HQ. Her shoulders relaxed. Her mind eased. She needed to get moving. She needed a lead. Before sundown. She had to get somewhere with the broiled skin and stake of wood. And she had to pay a visit to Blackwood. All before the team convened.

Blackwood. Stella pictured her muscular body, the contours under her hiking pants. She seemed so prepared. So practical. Her sturdy boots, her hefty pack, like she was ready for anything. Stella wondered what Blackwood had seen. Where she'd been. What kind of bodies she'd processed. What kind of scenes she'd been plunged into, before she came here. Stella was sure Blackwood had worked down south, across the border. Where some of the worst serial killers in the seventies and eighties had conducted their work. She wondered if Blackwood had been part of any high-profile cases there. And what it had been like to dissect the work of a breed of killer that many never met.

Maybe, if she continued to *work well* with Blackwood, she'd be able to grill her. After this case was over. She snorted. Other than Jake, Blackwood was the only one she seemed to get along with. No one else on the homicide unit, or on the perimeter of it, wanted to work with Stella. No one. But Stella wanted it that way. Right? She kept telling herself that. Yet, deep down there was an inkling that it might not *work* for *her*. If she truly did want to be the homicide detective that her father would be proud of. She shook her head and the thought away. That type of thinking would get her nowhere. She needed to be the tough Stella. Show no fear. Reveal nothing. That was the way she needed to be. It had worked so far.

She pulled her Sunfire into an open spot facing the glass doors of HQ. The sun hung low in the sky, blasting its last rays over the tall glass doors. They'd been at the scene across from the cemetery all day. A strong need pulled at her—to get somewhere before the day was over. She stood from the car, breathing in the first hint of evening chill.

She blasted through the doors, nodding at Pegs on her way. Pegs nodded back, phone nestled between her blonde bob and her ear. The red lipstick lining her lips was as perfect as ever.

She went straight to Jake's desk.

"Jakey." She stood close to his chair.

"Stella. I've missed you." He didn't look up from his typing.

"Stop being sarcastic." She pouted.

"I'm not. I assure you." He turned and shot her a grin. The dimple in his cheek appeared.

Too cute. "Listen. I need help. *Your* help."

"You've been at a scene all day, I hear," Jake said.

"Yup. I need a lead. You're my answer."

"Shoot." Jake typed a few commands. Several open windows on the screen vanished. He rolled his chair over to the far end of his desk and clicked on another keyboard. A second screen came to life. A black screen with a single flashing square.

"The scene was elaborate. There's some weird shit I need to look into." *Where to start?*

Jake looked up. "Go on."

"Wood. There was a long wooden pole. Over six feet tall. Smooth. Polished. I need to know what kind of wood it was."

"Sure. If you give me something." Jake smirked. "Colour?"

"Light. Like pine." Stella dug into the pocket of her leather jacket and retrieved a stack of photos. She laid them out on Jake's desk.

"Sweet Jesus." He sat back in his chair, staring at the photos.

"Yeah. It was quite the scene. Look, here's a closeup of the wood."

Jake pursed his lips. "The wood looks standard. Not a strong lead."

"OK, so it's a long shot. But you're a computer wiz. Can't you work your magic? I find it hard to believe *you* can't narrow down where a stick like this would be purchased?" Stella pleaded with her voice and her eyes.

"I can give it a go," Jake said.

"The symbol." Stella shuffled the photos and pulled one forward on the desk.

"Double sweet Jesus." Jake slid his glasses off and wiped his eyes.

"Yeah. I know. It's...*gross.* As you would say. I *need* you to look at the symbol."

"OK." Jake slid his glasses back on and stared at the symbol burned into the abdomen of the dead body. "Wow. That's distinct. I can probably find something on that." He narrowed his eyes. "Is that lettering?"

"Yeah. There seems to be some sort of letter or symbol at each of the five points." Stella pulled another photo forward, zoomed in on the points and the strange letters.

"Why couldn't you have shown me *that* one? At least you can't tell it's on a body," Jake asked, exasperated.

"Oh man up. Really." Stella rolled her eyes.

"Now *this* is something. This is a good search item. This might lead us somewhere." Jake nodded. A chocolate curl fell over his right eye. He brushed it away and looked up at Stella. "Anything else?"

"Witchcraft."

"What?" Jake raised an eyebrow.

"I need to know about witchcraft. Look at this." Stella pointed at one of the photos.

"I'd rather not." Jake started typing.

Stella nudged his shoulder. "C'mon. You work for the *homicide department.*"

"Yeah. As an *analyst.* Digging through wads of data," Jake said.

"C'mon. We need to solve a murder here," Stella said.

Jake sighed, stopped typing, and examined the photo. "Fine. Show me. What?"

"The long stick. The body was attached to it. The skin was burned. The stake isn't burned at all. I think it's some kind of staging of a burning at the stake."

"So, you want me to look into the history of burning witches at the stake?" Jake said.

"Yeah." Stella nodded.

"Fine." Jake started typing.

"Thank you, Jakey." Stella smiled.

"Oh, my pleasure," he said. "You know, you're the only one who makes me look at these photos."

"No, I'm not." She tousled his hair.

He pulled away. "No. But the others only do it when it's absolutely *necessary.* You could have described your theory without making me look at a burned body." He shuddered.

"It's good for you. You need to toughen up." She smirked.

"No, I don't. I'm perfectly happy sitting here with my computer solving all your problems for you." He smiled.

"Whatever." She started to walk away, then paused. "Hey. Can you tell me the story?"

Jake stopped typing. "Again? I thought you were in a hurry for this stuff?"

"You've already got a search running. I can see it. By the time you tell me the story, the results will be in." She smiled, looking into his eyes.

"Fine." He turned to face her. "I was working at the paper. It was late. I was the only one in the office. Except for the editor-in-chief, Mr. Hammington." He stopped.

"Go on," Stella pleaded.

"The elevator dinged. A man walked into the office. Muscular. Sturdy. Five-o'clock shadow. Tweed overcoat and charcoal hat—almost like a fedora, but not quite. He stormed across the office. Didn't even see me. He went right up to Mr. Hammington's office and knocked on the door. Hard. The nameplate came loose and swayed back and forth." Jake chuckled.

"Then?" Stella crouched, her eyes wide.

"Mr. Hammington opened the door. He's portly. Short. He always had this ridiculous-looking thick black moustache. He looked up at the sturdy man. You could see fear in Hammington's eyes before the man at his door even spoke. The man was harsh with him from the get-go and forced his way into the office. The door closed. I heard them. The man told Mr. Hammington he was Detective Mahoney with Homicide. He demanded to know who wrote an article that mentioned him. He demanded to know how they could print stuff that wasn't officially shared by the homicide public relations. He demanded to know how Hammington could run his paper like this. That he had caused another murder." Jake paused. "It got crazy behind that door. Loud." He smiled. "I always wished I could have seen Hammington's face. Having someone breathe down *his* neck for a change." The dimple amplified. "The detective wanted some searches. On subscribers. Hammington gave him the runaround. Telling him he needed the proper paperwork and such." Jake shrugged. "Guess it was true, but Hammington was *not* co-operative." Jake paused.

"And then what?" Stella looked up at him from her crouched position. She swallowed, taking it all in. Trying to conjure up images of the story. Creating her own mini movie in her mind.

"Detective Mahoney stormed out of that office. I'm sure Mr. Hammington didn't know what had hit him." Jake smiled wide. His dimple swelled.

"Then you spoke to the detective," Stella said.

Jake looked at her. "Yes. I did. I told him I could help. He said, 'Oh, you heard that?' I told him it wasn't quiet. I told him I could get the search he wanted going since I'd be the one to do it anyways. He gave me the info, and his card. Hammington came out of his office. Nearly had a cow." Jake laughed. "Detective stood up to him. Then he departed."

"And?" Stella's eyes grew wide with anticipation.

"I knew I liked him. The minute I saw him. I *really* knew I liked him. The minute I talked to him."

The computer blipped. Jake shot a glance at it. Stella stood up. A tear glistened in the corner of her eye. She swiped it away fiercely before Jake could see it. She leaned in over Jake's shoulder. "What's up?"

"Got something for you. I *knew* that symbol was a hot lead." Jake read the streams of text flashing across the black screen in neon-green letters. "Here." He pointed.

"Now *you're* making *me* look at something I don't want to." She sneered.

"Funny. The symbol. It's from an album cover," Jake said.

"You mean, music?" Stella asked.

"I mean music. This should be right up your alley. Satanic death music. Isn't that your forte?"

"Very funny. What album?" She poked his shoulder and nodded at the screen.

Jake rolled his chair back over to the other computer and typed. A much-easier-to-decipher screen appeared. A box with images popped onto the screen, housing a series of sentences. An image appeared. A red album cover with the same symbol perched in the centre, coloured in black. In heavy black lettering over the top of the album cover, the words *The Satanic Mass* hovered.

"The Satanic Mass?" Stella asked.

"Figured it must be some sort of death metal thing," Jake said.

"C'mon, man. You know heavy metal *is not* Satanic." She glared at him. "And metal calms the mind."

"Really?" He looked up at her.

"Really. There's research behind it. The way tones can be placed together to impact the brain."

"Whatever you say." He turned back to the computer.

"So, what is this album?" She asked.

"I don't know. It was the first hit on the symbol." Jake tapped at the keyboard, zooming in on the image. "It's not quite the same. This one has a circle around the star. The one you showed me has a snake."

Stella shuffled through the photos she'd forced Jake to look at. "Hmmm. I see it."

Jake rolled back to the other computer. His fingers flew over the keys. Another series of neon green letters scrolled down the screen. "Got a match. The symbol, with the circle, first appeared on the cover of *The Satanic Mass*. The album you see up there." He pointed back to the other, easier to read, screen. "In 1968. Later, on the cover of *The Satanic Bible*. Whatever that is. In 1969." Jake typed some more. He leaned into the screen. "It's the Sigil of the Baphomet. The head of a goat transfixed upon a reversed pentagram. The symbols at each of the points are Hebrew. They spell 'Leviathan.'"

Stella clenched her jaw. "So, what? The killer worships Satan? Didn't witches worship Satan?"

"No idea." Jake shook his head as he continued typing. "Leviathan. Means sea snake."

"What does that have to do with a burnt body hanging from a stake?"

"Don't know. But there's a snake wrapped around the symbol on your victim. Let me start by finding you a copy of this album." He rolled back to the easier-to-decipher computer and typed away.

Stella watched the screen as images flashed. The searching halted. An album cover appeared again, on the screen. *Hot Wax* flashed across the top of the screen.

"Hot Wax?" Stella asked. "That's on 10th Street."

Jake looked at the screen, scrolling through the text. "Yeah. You know it?"

"Best place to get old stuff. LPs. Cassettes."

"Well, there doesn't appear to be any copies of this weirdo Satanic Mass album in the city. But, your Hot Wax has a copy of the Devil's Track. Exact symbol from your photo on the front. Snake and all."

"Doubt it's a coincidence." Stella turned.

"Well, you're welcome," Jake said sarcastically.

"Jake. Thank you. But I gotta go get that album."

"I could call and warn them that Detective Stella Mahoney is about to rock their world."

"Very funny," she called over her shoulder. Tingles shot through her gut. This had to lead to somewhere.

Chapter 23

Slimeball and Satanic Album

The door to *Hot Wax* creaked as Stella pulled it open. Tilted crooked on rusty hinges, it fought against the frame as she yanked it shut. Several peels of sickly yellow paint fluttered onto the dust-coated floor.

Must and stale body odour coated the space. The room was narrow, filled with long rows of albums organized by genre. An ancient cash register perched on a rickety counter at the end of the room. A greasy-looking young man sitting behind the counter, feet up next to the register, looked up from a copy of *Rolling Stone*, raised an eyebrow, then commenced his reading.

The track blasting shakily from cheap speakers ended. The next one started. Stella nodded her head in approval. The slow thrum of the heavy guitar riff weaving with the bad-ass bass pulled her in. *Electric Funeral.* Black Sabbath would always be in her top ten. She could still vividly picture the metal god performing this, days before, at her concert getaway. His sweat-drenched dark hair stuck to his pale flesh as he bobbed his head in time to the deep beat.

She scanned the rows of used albums. Pawned by unappreciative owners, unaware of the gems they had. Or discarded in haste for a few bucks to secure their next fix. Or a bottle of cheap booze.

Stella walked along the narrow edge of the store, scanning the labels on the ends of the rows. Pop. Nah. No one in their right mind would categorize the Devil's Track as pop. Rap. *Nah.* Hip-hop. *Nada.* R&B. *Nope.* She scanned every genre label written in crude handwriting on cheap neon-yellow paper. Nothing fit. To her.

The metal section called. It was the only logical choice for most. Most assumed metal was Satanic. She walked down the aisle, looking for the section marked D.

She found it. She leaned over and shuffled through the D section, pulling at long plastic casings and leaning them against the front of the shelf. The band names dripped in vibrant letters down the cases.

Depths of Evil, Dark Suffrage, Death's Sorrow.

There it was. Wiped clean of dust. A single copy of the *Devil's Track* housed in a plastic case. She slid it from the aisle and pushed at the row of CDs. They clicked back into place.

She walked to the other end of the room. Halfway to the unenthusiastic register attendant, the track ended. A high-voltage riff squealed. Words of the cold brush of death grazed her ears. Slayer. *Dead Skin Mask.* The greasy employee may not care about his appearance or his customers, but he had solid taste in music.

He looked up, rolled his eyes, then tossed his magazine aside. After a loud sigh, he stood, wiping his hands on his stained jeans, leaving streaks of sweat.

"That all?" he asked.

"Yeah. Is this the only copy you have?" Stella inquired.

The employee grabbed the case and stared at it. "Yup."

"You sure?"

The employee slapped his sweaty palms onto the computer. His greasy curls swung over his forehead. "Listen, lady, I've worked here five years. I do all the inventory. Never seen this album before. I would remember. It's creepy as fuck."

"You listened to it?"

"Yeah." He set the CD on the counter and punched keys on the register. "I check every used CD. Make sure there are no scratches. And I was curious." He flipped the CD case over and pointed at the back. "Says here it was produced by the Poison Sisters. Never heard of the studio." The register dinged. "That'll be 4.99."

Stella slipped her wallet out of her coat pocket and fished for a five.

"Didn't know what section to put it in. Felt wrong to put something so blatantly evil into the metal section. But...didn't know where to put it." Greasy Hair thrummed the counter with his fingers.

"You're a metal fan?"

"Yeah."

"Me, too." Stella slid a ten across the counter.

"Really? You look too...clean." Greasy Guy smiled. He pulled her change from the register then slid it across the counter.

Stella reached for the change. Greasy Boy slapped his sweaty hand over hers. She froze.

"Say, how 'bout you go see Raging Ruffage with me. Tonight. At the Republik. I got two VIP tickets." He massaged her hand with his oily fingers.

In one swift motion, Stella slipped her hand from his slimy grasp, grabbed his wrist, and flipped his arm over.

He shrieked in pain. "OK. I'm sorry. Please let go. Please." Sweat trickled down his puffy cheeks.

Stella eased her grip, still twisting his wrist. "I need info. Record of who pawned this."

"Listen, lady, I want to help, but I can't just give out info of our sellers." Sweat poured down his face.

Stella let go of his wrist. He pulled his hand back, rubbing circles into his wrist with his other hand.

Stella pulled out her badge, snapped it open and slapped it onto the counter. "I need the sales record."

Greasy Boy raised his left eyebrow. "You're a cop? That's hot." He licked his chapped upper lip.

Stella lunged toward the counter.

Greasy Boy jumped back, raising his hands. "OK. OK." He shook his head. "I'll get the record. Contact info is required, if the seller wants to collect. You always this aggressive when looking for info?"

"I'm not always dealing with a slimeball."

Grease Ball pouted. "Harsh." He turned to a small computer on the other end of the counter. He pushed a button. The computer hummed. "It'll take a minute."

Stella grabbed the change still sitting on the counter and put it in her wallet. She shoved her wallet and her badge back into their respective pockets in her leather coat. She stared at Grease Ball.

He shifted on his feet, watching the humming computer. "I remember the guy."

"The one who pawned the album?"

"Yeah. Real shifty. Acted all nervous. I just assumed he was itching for a fix. I mean, we get a lot of desperate sellers in here needing a quick buck."

"What did he look like?" Stella asked.

"Five nine. Skinny. Long, blond hair. Looked like he needed a shower."

Stella choked back a chuckle. This grease ball was telling her that the pawner needed a shower? Sutton's face popped in her head, telling her to go home and take a shower. *Guess we all have our moments.*

The computer blipped. "We have life," Grease Ball exclaimed. His fingers fell over the keys as he typed. A grey square flashed onto the screen, housing a name and an address.

He turned the counter toward her. "I knew it. Like I said, I remembered him. I'd never seen this album before. I was curious. Asked him where he got it. Couldn't understand him. He was all mumbles and twitches."

Stella slipped her notepad out, flipped to a fresh page and jotted down the info. *Cletus Dynkin. Marbank Drive.* Other side of town. Deep in the northeast.

She snapped her notebook shut. "You said you listened to it."

He turned the computer back into place. "Yeah. Weird as shit."

"What did it sound like?"

"Strangest thing I ever heard. Not music. Definitely not metal. Deep chanting. No instruments. Couldn't understand all the words. Some other language. It creeped me out. I only got a couple minutes in. Usually, I check the whole thing. For scratches. I couldn't do it. I felt..." He stopped and looked across the room at nothing.

"What?"

He didn't respond.

Stella slapped the counter.

He jumped.

"What?" he asked.

"What did you feel? When you listened to it?" She lifted the CD and flashed it in front of his face.

"Uh...weird. Cold. Like something was crawling through me." His face flushed. "I sound cuckoo."

"No. You don't. Thanks. You were a big help." Stella grabbed the CD and turned. She walked toward the door.

"How about those VIP tickets?"

She spun on her heel. He shot her a cheesy smile.

"Not in this lifetime." She stomped toward the door.

Chapter 24

Morgue

The hallway, dimly lit, seemed darker than last time. Stella reached the lab where Blackwood processed bodies. She leaned into the heavy door. A whoosh of cold air swept through her.

The lab was dark. Light shone from the far corner. Blackwood's corner. Stella followed it.

Blackwood, engrossed in her work, leaned over the body stretched out over a steel slab. The single silver strand stood out from her hair, glimmering under the bright light.

Stella warned of her approach. "Blackwood."

Blackwood looked up. "Mahoney." She smiled. Her almond-shaped eyes exuded warmth from behind large, plastic goggles. "You ready for some postmortem facts?"

"Shoot." She flipped her notebook open.

Blackwood shuffled closer to the body. It didn't look much different than it had hanging from a stake on display, across from the cemetery. Nothing could wash away the reddish-pink tone the flesh had taken on. The skin was permanently distorted into disfigured folds and contours. The symbol burned into the flesh for all eternity. Stella stared at it. The five-pointed star pulled at her.

"Skin fact one," Blackwood said.

Stella snapped from her reverie.

"The skin, along the arms and legs, has suffered third-degree burns. Based on the colouration and shape. Skin fact two. Based on this assessment, the skin was burned, off and on, over the course of hours. Skin fact three, the heat source was likely an open flame. Initial scan of the colouration and folds leads to that preliminary conclusion. I've sent off a sample of the epidermis for analysis. We might get a more conclusive determination of heat source." Blackwood took a deep breath.

Stella looked up from her rapid notetaking.

"Skin fact four. The severity of the burns lead to suspicion that internal damage was done. Examination of the internals indicated that the heat had reached the majority of the internal organs with little dissipation. Essentially, the victim was slowly burned until they died. Could have been from shock, the heat exposure, or even organ damage."

"Cooked to death," Stella said. Burned. At the stake. Without the stake. "Helluva way to die."

"Humdinger." Blackwood looked at her notes. "Toxicology. Traces of phenolic compounds. I think it has something to do with fermentation. Maybe it's some sort of alcohol. Also traces of alkaloid."

"Cocaine?" An image of her father flashed through Stella's mind.

"Maybe. Not enough to determine the source. Based on the amount in the bloodstream, I'd say it was enough to take the victim on a wild ride. Not enough to kill her. Hopefully it was enough to numb the pain."

Stella paused from taking notes. "Got an ID?"

"No. We're still trying to determine who she is. May have to go through dental records," Blackwood said.

Stella scanned the body. The cloth that had partially covered it at the scene was now removed. The burned flesh was fully exposed.

"Ready for some DNA info?" Blackwood asked.

"Yeah." Stella looked away from the burned flesh, at Blackwood.

"DNA fact one. Several types are present. Blood. Prints. Saliva. DNA fact two. All DNA belongs to one person. DNA fact three. The profile matches that of the internal fluids taken from the body." Blackwood scanned her notebook, then set it down.

"So, all DNA found belongs to the victim," Stella said.

"That is the logical conclusion," Blackwood said.

"So, what? There was a struggle? The victim's blood and saliva got all over everything," Stella said.

"If there was a struggle, there is no sign of it. Nothing under the nails. No scratches. Or cuts. No bruises. Of course, over half the skin is badly burned. Thus, there could be indications that we can't see." Blackwood paused. "There is usually some indication by the nails, which are miraculously intact."

"She was beaten. Couldn't fight back. Possibly drugged. Maybe tied down."

"Likely. Welts around her wrists. Cut in some places." Blackwood pursed her lips.

"This isn't a first kill, is it?" Stella asked.

"Based on everything I've seen, no," Blackwood said. "The cloth that was covering the body was clean. Must have been put over the body after the burning. Standard material. Not a good lead."

Stella bit her lip. "We need something strong here."

"Symbol." Blackwood checked her notes. "Skin facts. COD. DNA facts. Toxicology. Final piece of the puzzle, for now, is this symbol." Blackwood shuffled over to the body and stared at the burned circle.

Stella followed. The five-pointed star pulled at her.

"The flesh within the area of the symbol suffered third-degree burns. Symbol fact two. The flesh within the area of the symbol was burned for a matter of minutes. Less time. The heat didn't reach the internals underneath," Blackwood said.

"Like a brand. What would do this? Metal?" Stella asked.

"Symbol fact three. Traces of metal fragments were found embedded in a sample of the epidermis sent in for analysis." Blackwood flipped through her notes.

"The way that symbol is charred into the skin, it looks like a brand," Stella said.

"The analysis on the metal fragments indicates a high level of titanium."

"Is titanium used in brands?" Stella rubbed her chin.

"I don't know. And I've ventured too far across the line between fact and investigation for one day. This is where you make inferences and open up paths. This is where I stick to processing dead parts, analysis, and facts." Blackwood crossed her arms and narrowed her eyes.

"I wonder what a cattle brand is made of. And how do you customize something like this? Blacksmiths? Do they still exist?" Stella blurted.

Blackwood smiled.

"OK. Anything else?" Stella blushed.

"No. But I'll let you know if there is," Blackwood said.

"Great." Stella stole another glance at the five-pointed star.

"Weird. Isn't it?" Blackwood said.

"I got a lead on the symbol. It's on the album cover of the *Devil's Track*. I snagged a copy and got the name of the pawner from the salesclerk." Stella smirked.

"Ah. You've got the Mahoney charm."

"What?" Stella swallowed. How much like her dad was she?

"He was good at charming information out of leads." Blackwood smiled. "You know, the worst cases I worked on with your dad had some weird symbols and messages."

"Really?" Images of photos plastered to her apartment wall flashed through Stella's mind. Messages cut into the flesh of dead bodies. A swirling vortex branded into skin. She wasn't ready to reveal her extensive research of the cases that tied Blackwood to her father.

"Some weirdo stuff. Your dad always figured it out. Him and his team."

Team. Yeah, he had a good team. All she had was Jake.

"Use your team. Might be more promising than you think," Blackwood said.

"Thanks. I gotta go." Stella turned. Tingles shot through the pit of her belly. Team. Input. Seek. None of it was on her path. She wondered if she was more solo than her father had ever been.

Chapter 25

Parker

The small room suffocated Stella with a barrage of detective body odour and stale coffee. Jake was perched in the corner, computer set up on a small table, coffee pot perking away on a table to his right. No one else had arrived yet.

She walked over to Jake. "Jakey."

Jake looked up from his mad typing. His sun-coloured sweater vest gleamed under the bright overhead lights. "Hi, Stella. Did the ME give you anything?"

"Yeah. Hey what's with the sweater? My eyes are burning." She smirked.

"Ha. Very funny." He glared. A chocolate curl fell over his right eye. He brushed it away.

"Blackwood is smart. And fast. She was already deep into processing the skin tissue and the symbol burnt into the abdomen. Turns out you can determine how long skin was broiled for, and how long ago the cooking started." Stella raised an eyebrow.

"Gross." Jake frowned.

Stella reached over and tousled Jake's soft curls. "Meh. You're just a weak-stomached geek."

Jake smiled. "You know it."

"Hey team," Sutton called from the doorway. He walked briskly up to the front of the room.

"Hey boss," Stella greeted.

"Detective Sutton," Jake said.

Sutton slapped a stack of files on the long table running down the centre of the room. He walked toward the back corner where Jake and Stella lingered. "That coffee fresh?"

"Yeah. Doesn't taste like it. But it is," Jake answered.

"Perfect. I love the taste of stale coffee. It's in my detective veins." Sutton smirked. Steam rose from the Styrofoam cup in his hand as he poured it full of coffee.

Stella chuckled.

Someone knocked on the door.

They all turned.

A muscular, average-height young man stood dressed in a freshly pressed, crisp white shirt, and navy-blue suit jacket and jeans. His wrinkle-free, olive-coloured skin shone under the bright lights. "Detective Sutton?" He poked his head in the room.

"Ah. Detective Parker. Come in."

Detective Parker walked toward the group.

Sutton pointed at Stella. "Detective Stella Mahoney, meet Detective Gavin Parker."

Stella raised an eyebrow, scanning the detective up and down. He looked slightly older than her, but not by much. *Who is this clean-cut rookie?* She extended her arm. "Detective."

Parker returned her shake.

His shake was firm. Confident. His smile appeared genuine. No one could be this perfect. As she released her hand from his, cologne infused the air. She knew that one. Versace. *Blue Jeans.* She was sure of it. There was his first strike.

"Parker? Like Peter Parker?" Stella smirked.

Jake giggled.

"I'm sorry?" Detective Parker inquired.

"You're not gonna slip into a phonebooth on the way to a scene and change into your superhero suit, are you?"

Parker smiled. "You never know."

Sutton intervened. "Stella." He glared at her. "Sorry, Detective, it seems we have a class clown on our team."

Parker shrugged. "All good. Not like it's the first time I heard that one." He shot Stella a look that said *touché.*

Sutton walked to the front. "All right. Enough. We have a murder to solve. You two can work out your partner dynamics later."

"Partner?" Stella blurted out the question before her mind could comprehend her own reaction.

"Yeah. Parker and Mahoney. Newest detective team in town. Just in time for the worst murder to hit since…well…since that damn stepfather-son duo." Sutton walked up to the cream-coloured wall lining the left side of the room. A series of photos lined the fresh coat of paint, held in place with cheap plastic brightly coloured tacks.

Partner. Stella's brain seized around the words. What the flying fuck just happened? She thought she'd be solo. She'd made it pretty clear how much she disliked working with others. And she'd been sure as hell that no one around here wanted to work with her. Just how she wanted it. She'd had a clear plan. Work with Blackwood and Jake. Follow Sutton's orders, or at least make it look like she was. Peel apart the layers of the scene, expose every grisly clue. Put the pieces together. Rely on Blackwood's brain and candour to get things processed, fast. Lean on Jake for his computer genius and mad World Wide Web setup. Solve the case. Catch the killer. Pump fresh Mahoney blood into her father's legacy.

The rest was just icing on the cake.

Now this. A partner. Some young rookie who looked like a Calvin Klein model. She bet Calvin's name was branded on Parker's tight athletic-cut boxers. *Dammit.* Why was she thinking about his boxers?

"Stella. You with us?" Sutton's voice snapped her from the trainwreck of her meandering thoughts.

"Yeah. Here, boss." Stella crossed her arms and leaned back against the wall.

Jake snickered next to her. She elbowed him and shot him a glare. He went back to his typing. She forced herself to focus on Sutton.

"Stella, what did you get from Blackwood?" Sutton looked at her.

She slipped her notebook from her leather jacket pocket and flipped it open. "The skin, on the arms and legs, it was cooked. Open flame. Over several hours. Burns were there pre-mortem."

"Yikes," Jake whispered.

"It was like the skin was broiled. Cooked low and slow, to death," Stella concluded.

"Anything on the symbol?" Sutton asked.

"It's from an album cover. the Devil's Track. Jake found us a copy. I snagged it. Produced by the Poison Sisters. Guy at the store said he'd never heard of the studio. Got the name of the guy who pawned it. I'm gonna pay him a visit," Stella stated.

"Good. Take Parker," Sutton said.

Stella grimaced.

"Jake, find out where the recording studio is. What about the wood?" Sutton asked.

"Standard pine. Sold everywhere," Jake reported.

"Dead end." Sutton looked at Stella. "Are you a witchcraft expert yet?"

"Working on it," Stella said.

"Accelerate your effort." Sutton turned back to the photos. "We need to look more at this location. Where the body was...displayed. Thoughts?"

"Outs—" Stella's words collided with Parker's. They looked at each other.

"Go ahead," Parker said.

"I was just going to say, outside the perimeter of the cemetery. Across the street. Close to the entrance, but distinctly outside of the boundary. And the body was positioned to be facing the cemetery. There's a reason for this," Stella said.

"Good. Parker?" Sutton asked.

"Stella conveyed my thoughts exactly. I think the killer positioned the body specifically, for some reason," Parker said.

Clown. How can he have the same idea as me? Stella sunk harder against the wall, a pout pulling at the corners of her mouth.

"Good. You two think alike. Parker, dig into this. Why outside the cemetery? It's one of the oldest in the city. Look into the history." Sutton walked up to a whiteboard mounted on the front wall of the room. He uncapped a marker and began jotting down notes in neon green. "We track active leads with green. Assign names with blue." He capped the marker and nodded at Parker.

Parker nodded back.

"Jake. Help these two with your searching power," Sutton said.

Jake nodded.

"What else? Blackwood indicate any progress on ID?"

Stella shook her head. "No ID. Body appears to be that of a woman in her late twenties or early thirties. ID is still a mystery. The state of the body isn't helping. Blackwood's pursuing dental records."

"Anything else?" Sutton stroked the green rabbit claw dangling from his belt.

"Toxicology scan is still in progress. Initial results indicate traces of phenolic compounds and alkaloid. Victim might have been on some sort of booze-and-cocaine bender." Stella crossed her arms.

"We need an ID. Then we can look into the victim's history," Sutton said.

"Traces of titanium in the flesh around the abdomen, where the symbol was burned," Stella continued.

"Jake, look into sources of phenolic compounds and alkaloids. And titanium and branding," Sutton said.

Jake nodded.

"Stella, stay in touch with Blackwood. Notify me if anything turns up."

"Got it." Stella nodded.

"OK, team. You might feel stretched thin, but you're all I've got for this case. So get to it," Sutton said.

Stretched thin. Whatever. I'm a Parker heavy.

Sutton grabbed his stack of files and made for the door. "Stella, take Parker with you on the follow-up on that album."

Jake finished his typing, grabbed a chipped mug, and headed for the door.

Stella shot a suspicious glance at Parker, then followed Jake.

Chapter 26

The Hood

The sun cast a blood-orange hue over the horizon. The lights of the downtown core glimmered in the distance. Night was descending fast. There wasn't much more time to follow leads before they'd have to pack it in for the night, and Stella would have to go back to her lonely apartment.

She pressed hard on the gas pedal, shoving away the empty hole pulsing in the pit of her gut at the thought of another evening alone in her apartment, surrounded by memories of a past she couldn't go back to.

"So, how long have you been in homicide?" Parker asked from the passenger side.

Fuck. He wanted to make *small* talk. She looked at him. He smiled back at her. "Just over a year." *Get along.* Sutton's words stuck in her mind. *What if she didn't?*

"Really? I would have guessed longer."

"Really?" She raised an eyebrow at him. "You thought I was *older?*" she challenged.

"No." Panic riddled his face. "No. I just...you seem to know what you're doing."

She yanked her Sunfire around a tight right, shooting the car up the main artery of the city, into the deep north end. The lights of the downtown core twinkled behind them. Parker grasped at the side of the door, steadying himself. Stella smirked.

He continued the small talk. "Honestly, I just thought you had more experience than that."

She shrugged. "Runs in the family."

"Homicide?"

"Yeah. Homicide." She shot him a look. "My dad was a detective. Now I'm a detective. That's it."

"Huh. That's cool. No one in my family is in law enforcement. I'm the first one. My mom worries." He chuckled. "Guess I'll always be her little boy." He looked over at her. His face flushed. "Sounds silly, I know. But my mom was always worried about all of us."

"All of you?" *Dammit, Stella, don't engage him. Don't encourage his small talk.*

"Big family. Eight of us. I'm smack in the middle. Well, almost. Third youngest. Five boys and three girls. Kept my mom on her toes. Dad was away a lot. On business. Always said us damn kids kept him on the road working late nights. Just so we could eat." Parker smiled.

Stella took a hard left, off the freeway. They rolled down a quiet, dark street. Houses that looked ready to be bulldozed lined both sides of the street. A single streetlight buzzed, blinking on and off. The others were dark, either burnt out, or not ready to make an attempt to shine light on the forgotten street.

"Geez. This is a dark part of town," Parker said.

"Guy at the music shop said the pawner seemed nervous. Jumpy. And he mumbled a lot. I'm guessing he's living day to day, trying to feed his habit."

"Drugs," Parker concluded.

Very good. Want a golden star? "Yeah. Drugs." How sheltered has this golden boy been? Looked after by mom and dad. A big loving family. *Jeepers.*

Stella slid her Sunfire up along a curb and put it in park. "That one." She pointed to a faded-blue house. Large chunks of exposed siding glared through sections of paint that had chipped away entirely. The lawn looked dead. A couple sections of grass miraculously poked through the otherwise brown, lifeless patch of where a lawn used to be. The mailbox looked ready to topple right over, hanging on by the few remaining splinters of the wooden post that hadn't split.

Stella opened the door, got out, and slammed it behind her. She scanned the street. No movement. Only silence.

Parker emerged from the car.

"C'mon. Let's get this over with." Stella nodded at the house and made her way up the walk.

A bottle clanked in the distance.

Chapter 27

Satanic Pawner

Stella pounded on the door. Several chips of paint fell away. A dog barked in the distance.

"Wonder if he's home," Parker pondered aloud.

Stella shot him a glare.

Shuffling came from behind the door. It creaked open.

A wiry man, about five foot nine, clad in a coffee-stained robe, looked at them with a hazy expression.

"Cletus Dynkin?" Stella asked.

The man, presumably Cletus, stared at them. "Look, I don't want no trouble. I got no money. Whoever sent you, tell them I'll have it by Friday."

"Detective Mahoney." Stella flashed her badge. "This is...my partner." Stella choked on the ill-tasting words. "Detective Parker."

Parker flashed his badge.

"We're not here to bother you, Cletus. We just need to ask you a few questions about an album you pawned at Hot Wax," Stella said.

Cletus' eyes widened. "Devil's Track." He gulped.

"Yeah. That's the one," Stella said. "How about we come in for a moment, Cletus. You can tell us all about it."

Cletus looked uncertain. "Well. Uh...sure. OK." He shuffled away, leaving the door open.

Stella nodded at Parker, then followed Cletus. A perfume of booze and weed drifted from the small front room. Their sitting options were limited. The first choice was a floral-patterned couch, split open in several spots, cotton innards spilling out, and a spring poking through one of the cushions. The other option was a pair of wooden chairs looking ready to cave in.

Cletus plopped down on the couch.

Stella took a wooden chair. Parker took the other.

"So, Cletus..." Stella slid her notebook from the pocket in her leather coat and flipped it open. "You pawned a single copy of the *Devil's Track* at Hot Wax. Along with a stack of eleven other CDs. For fifty percent commission upon sale." Stella looked at Cletus. "Is that correct?"

Cletus glanced at the ceiling, mumbling something. He looked back at Stella. "Uh, yeah. I think so."

"You remember the *Devil's Track*?" Stella asked.

Cletus nodded. His lips trembled. "Yes. I do." He stared right at her, his words suddenly crisp. "You don't forget something like that."

"Where did you get the album?" Parker asked.

Who asked him to speak? Stella shot him a sideways glance.

"Well, I...can't say...really." Cletus' lips trembled worse.

Stella nudged Parker. "Easy," she whispered.

She looked back at Cletus. "What was on that album?"

Cletus' eyes went wide. "Evil. Total evil. Chants. Of Satanic extremes." His voice rose with a terrifying edge. He raised his arms, his fingers grasped at the stuffy air. The bulb in a lamp perched in the corner blazed from a soft glow to a bright blast.

Stella squinted. "Was it music?"

"No. Words...evil," Cletus hissed.

Parker elbowed her lightly. "We need to know where he got it."

"I *know*." She glared at Parker.

"Where did the album come from?" Stella asked.

Cletus narrowed his eyes. "The depths of *hell*." The bulb blazed bright, then went out with a zap. Cletus snapped his gaze to the corner. "Extinguish all light. *Purge,*" he said to the extinguished bulb.

Stella sighed. "Where did *you* get the album?"

Cletus snapped his gaze back on her. "A woman. One of *them*."

"One of who?" Parker asked.

"Them," Cletus said.

Parker leaned in toward Cletus. "Listen, Cletus, I can see you have it rough around here. Maybe your life isn't going as you planned."

Cletus leaned in toward Parker. "No."

Parker continued, "You could do some *good*. Help us. That album may have gotten into the wrong hands. We might be able to stop them."

"Stop them," Cletus repeated.

"Yes. Think hard. Can you remember who you got that album from?" Parker asked.

Cletus closed his eyes. His lips pursed into a thin line. "A woman. One of them. Hair like fire. Blue eyes...like ice. Black cloak..." He snapped his eyes open and started choking.

Stella looked around. She grabbed a glass of what appeared to be water and handed it to Cletus.

Cletus took it, swallowed a gulp. His choking eased.

"What woman? What cloak?" Stella asked.

Cletus stared vacantly across the room. Stella turned and followed his gaze. Cletus gazed into the blazed-out lightbulb. His lips moved. He whispered, "Leviathan. Baphomet. Samael Lilith."

Chapter 28

Demon Accusations

Viviana walked quickly down the dirt path, the clear stream trickling, leading her back home. The little house at the end of the forest came into view. It wasn't the same. It was a different house. Different than the one at the end of the birch forest. Different than the one that had burned into a charred carcass.

It looked similar. It was small. It was at the end of a forest. A pine forest. It looked cozy, inviting, homey, just like the other one had. But it wasn't.

As soon as Viviana reached the walkway leading up to the front door of the house, it stretched its icy hands toward her, gripping her hard, filling her with a freezing-cold energy. It didn't feel at all like the other house.

The first time she'd walked into it, following Damaris, listening to her sister rant on and on about how perfect it was, a slight chill had crept through her. The house felt off. Her instincts told her that her father had been justified to send their aunt away. But she'd ignored her feelings, her inclinations, her inner guide. She was eager to please Damaris. Damaris had been extra friendly for some reason. Maybe it was the new town, welcoming them like a new beginning. Maybe it was the hope that finally they would find what they were looking for. That they might be coming to the end of this long, exhausting journey.

As time went on and Damaris fleshed out their plans for their stay in this city, the house got colder. Its pull on Viviana got stronger. At the same time, the darkness within Damaris intensified. Her aura grew darker. Her eyes transuded something bad. Her essence smelled of rot.

It was as if the house and Damaris were attached, somehow. Breathing together. Rotting together.

Viviana took a deep breath and walked up to the front door. She paused. *It will be fine. You're cleansed.*

She opened the door and walked in before she could change her mind.

Damaris sat on the couch in the centre of the main room, holding a silver goblet, leaning in a strange pose, off kilter. A half-empty bottle of cacao wine, Damaris' poison, sat on the table in the centre of a ring of candles. An ominous orange glow lit the room. All the curtains were pulled shut, warding off the warmth of the forest surrounding them. Keeping out the world.

"Where have you been?" Damaris slurred in a sickly tone.

The icy hand of the house reached down into Viviana. "I just went for a walk. It's a lovely day out." She forced a smile over her quivering lips.

Damaris glared. The demon inside glimmered through her pupils. "A walk." She snorted, then took a loud gulp of her wine. The scarlet liquid dribbled down her lips. "I needed you."

Viviana gulped. "I'm sorry. I didn't know."

"You didn't know," Damaris spat. Scarlet sprays dotted the table, sizzling out one of the candles. "You should have known. I will always need you after a sacrifice."

"Yes. I-I should have known," Viviana sputtered. Was Damaris serious about this *cycle of purge?* Viviana slipped her hand into the folds of her cloak and clutched her straw doll. What would her mother tell her to do? She'd always been the one to deal with Damaris' mood swings.

"Yes. You should have." Damaris glared, titling to the other side. Everything about her was off.

Viviana wracked her brain, seeking her next words. "Yes. I should have." She walked up to Damaris, knelt down at her feet, and looked up at her with pleading eyes. "I should have. I should have known. I should have been here. I'm sorry." She gulped, hoping this was what Damaris wanted.

The evil glimmer in Damaris' eyes flickered. Her expression softened. She took a long sip of her wine. "Well, you're here now."

"I am." Viviana grabbed the bottle of cacao wine and took Damaris' goblet. She filled the silver cup with red wine and handed it back to Damaris. "I am here. I will do what you need."

Damaris' lips pulled back into a smile, mostly a happy smile, with only the slightest tinge of sickness to it. She appeared to be coming around.

The icy hand of the house retreated, pulling out of Viviana, leaving behind a slight chill.

"What do you need?" Viviana asked.

Damaris sighed. She leaned back into the couch, her hair falling softly over her shoulders. Her expression turned to despair. Her black lips pouted. "I wanted it to be perfect."

Viviana sat up on her heels. "I thought it was." It had to be. She didn't know exactly what this idea of perfection was that seemed to be so clear in her sister's mind. The vision of perfection that Damaris clung to was impossible. Its grip was pulling them down a dark path.

Chapter 29

Electric Ave

The goat glared at Stella from the centre of the five-pointed star. Its evil eyes pierced into her. She could swear she could feel it looking into her soul. She turned the album over, concealing the front cover. She couldn't look at it for another second.

She shot back the rest of the bourbon she'd been nursing and summoned the bartender for a refill. Up at the bar, on a cracked wooden stool, she could case the entire joint. The room was long and rectangular, nestled in the basement. The electronic beat from the dance bar above pelted out a steady rhythm through the ceiling. The thin crowd trickling through the joint looked as second rate as the bar itself. Weekdays brought out those who drowned themselves in alcohol more often than the weekend party or social. Stella didn't come down to Electric Avenue often. The strip of nightclubs and dance bars, lit up in neon pinks and purples, attracted the youth of the city. The vibrant lights attracted mobs like moths on the weekends when the university students and young working class needed to blow off steam. Stella wouldn't be caught up in that if her life depended on it. But on a slow weeknight, she could hide in the basement of *Three Cheers* and soothe herself with a few high-ball specials.

After they gave up on getting anything useful from Cletus, she'd dropped Parker at HQ. She finally had time to grab a copy of today's paper from a late-night convenience store. Her heart pattered as she'd scoured it for information on the murder at The Cecil. Her shoulders dropped several notches when she found a small article buried far from the front page titled *Drug Dealer Dead, Another Night at The Cecil*. She was going to have to find a better way to deal with cold case killers.

As she headed home, her Sunfire somehow made its way to the electric strip instead of her lonely apartment. Usually when she needed to clear her head she went for a late-night run. Tonight, a shot of bourbon called to her.

The bartender returned with her drink. As he set it down, he winked at her. She gave him a sly smile. He had luscious-looking sandy-blond hair. But he looked slick. His smile was too perfect. She couldn't decide if she'd rather fuck him or put him in a chokehold.

She took a long swig of bourbon, then turned the album over. The goat, or whatever the fuck it was, was freaking her out. The *Devil's Track.* The slimeball at the record shop said he only listened for a couple minutes. Chanting. Deep. Dark. It wasn't music, he said. It creeped him out, he said.

Then there was Cletus. Sure, he was obviously a druggie. Who knows what he'd been flying high on when she and Parker paid him a visit. But he had seemed far too creeped out by the album. It bothered her. His reaction when she mentioned the album was severe. He'd said the same weird shit as the grease boy in the record shop. Chanting. Dark. Deep.

Coincidence? Unlikely.

Sipping more bourbon, she stared into the evil eyes of the goat.

Where did Cletus get this strange album filled with chanting? All they had to go on was a woman in a dark cloak. What the flying fuck were they supposed to do with that?

Stella shot back the bourbon, slapped a bill on the counter, and turned from the bar. She couldn't wait for Jake to dig up more on this album. Grease Boy and Cletus had to be blowing smoke up her ass. She was gonna find out what was on this freaky album, before any more time ticked away on the investigation clock.

Chapter 30

Satanic Sounds

Stella dropped her car keys into her father's chipped red glass bowl. She slid off her leather coat and draped it over the side of the couch. Removing the *Devil's Track* from the case, she walked over to the CD player and slid it in. She paused, staring at the play button.

Grease Ball record store clerk and a high-as-a-kite druggie. They both had to be over-reacting, right? She could still see the fear etched into both their faces. She shook off the image. She took a deep breath and pushed play.

A deep thrumming echoed through her small apartment. She shuffled over to the couch and plunked into the cavern worn into the middle. The thrumming deepened, vibrating through her. An uneasy energy trickled through her insides. She shifted on the couch.

C'mon, Stella. Stop making this into something it's not.

The thrumming morphed into a voice. A low, deep, female vocal. She couldn't make out the lyrics. She thrust herself from the comfort of the couch and walked over to the CD player. She cranked it to full volume.

The voice flowed from the speakers, vibrating through the room. Another language. Contorted words. Stella's brain buzzed. The language morphed into her own. Her mind seized, grasping the meaning of the words worming into every part of her.

In the name of Satan
The Ruler of the World
I summon your forces
May you bestow your infernal power upon us
Open wide the gates of hell
Come forth from the abyss

Satan

Lucifer

Leviathan

Baphomet

Samael Lilith

The voice grew louder. Stella backed away from the player, walking backward. Her feet shuffled, pulling her from the controls. The words wrapped around her brain. Her arms twitched.

Her heel bumped against the wall on the other side of the room. She turned. She looked at the wall. Right into the vortex of the murder collage plastering the blue paint. Right into the core of evil. Human manifestations of Satan—walking the earth, torturing and killing other humans—stared at her from the photos she had hunted down, clipped, and pasted, in a sadistic scrapbook.

The room swayed around her. She grasped the wall with her palms. Her fingers grazed the face of a sergeant with a polished exterior and rotting insides. The one who caused her father's death. An image of a hot brand searing Sergeant Tomlinson's flesh shimmered over his photograph tacked to the wall. Stella's hand squeezed as if she were holding the branding iron to his flesh. His eyes plunged into her soul. She fell to her knees.

Her mouth moved. A whisper slipped from her lips. "Leviathan. Samael Lilith." She repeated the words over and over. She couldn't stop.

Crawling on all fours, Stella reached the CD player. She pulled herself up, grasping a CD-lined shelf. She pressed the stop button.

The room fell silent.

She crumpled to the floor. Curling into a ball, she wrapped her arms around herself and closed her eyes. Her cheek sunk into the fuzzy carpet.

The quiet of the room washed through her. Her mind cleared. She lay on the floor, trying not to think of the words thrumming through her mind.

Chapter 31

Satanic Hangover

The alarm clock on Stella's nightstand buzzed. She groaned, rolled over, and slapped it off.

She pulled the quilt down to her neck and opened her eyes. How did she get to bed? Parts of the evening flashed through her mind. The grease ball at the music shop. The burned body in the morgue. Parker. Bloody hell. What was she supposed to do with a new partner? Cletus, the drug-infused pawner. The album.

She'd come back to her apartment and listened to the album. After her stop at *Three Cheers*. How many bourbons did she have? She swore she'd capped it at two. Did she have a drink when she got home?

She slid out of bed, slipping her feet into black, fuzzy slippers. The back of her skull thrummed. She rubbed the base of her neck and shuffled to the main room. Mentally retracing the steps from the night before, she looked for evidence. Her keys sat in the chipped red glass bowl. No sight of any bottles or glasses. Her leather coat hung on the side of the tattered couch.

The album cover. It lay on the floor, directly beneath her murder collage. The five-pointed star seemed to pulse.

Her mind clicked. She came home. She listened to the album. No drinks.

The veins in her temples throbbed. Her mouth was parched. Two bourbons earlier, at the bar. Why did she feel like she'd had more? Many more.

She walked to the kitchen and filled a glass with cold tap water. As she chugged it back, she looked at the album out of the corner of her eye. She put the glass on the counter and walked across the room.

She stared down at the album. The five-pointed star pulsed back at her again. She closed her eyes and rubbed small circles into her temples.

The voice. The deep voice slithering through her apartment from the CD player speakers. She couldn't explain it. It was like nothing she'd ever heard. It had reached into her. It was like imaginary fingers had wrapped around her brain.

Stella shook her head and snapped her eyes open.

What was she thinking. Must be lack of sleep. What time had she gone to bed?

She bent over and picked up the album. As she stood, her gaze caught on a photo. The face of a rotten sergeant stared her down.

Her phone beeped from the bedroom. She sprinted across the room, dropping the album on the glass coffee table. Five rings in, she reached her murder phone.

"Mahoney here."

"Good morning, partner," Parker's too-perfect voice chirped through the phone.

Bloody hell. "What's up?"

"Need a ride to HQ? I just picked up fresh bagels and coffee," Parker said.

She could see his clean-cut, good-boy face, charm seeping from every pore. "No."

"All right. Meet you there."

Whatever. Stella pushed the off button and stared at the phone. A partner was the last thing she needed.

Chapter 32

Ceremony and Witchcraft

A deep-purple haze glowed over the horizon. The stars were still out. The sun wouldn't be up for another couple of hours. Stella pulled her Sunfire into the empty lot of HQ. Her boots clanked as she stomped through the tall glass doors and down the main hallway. Not even Pegs was here yet.

A light in the far corner of the clutter of cubicles caught her attention. She dropped her leather coat over her chair and walked toward the shining light.

"Jakey? What're you doing here?" She leaned over and tousled his soft locks.

Jake halted his typing and looked up groggily. "Stella." He slid his thick black glasses down his nose and rubbed his eyes. Holding his glasses in his hand, he looked at her. His dark eyes had a sweet innocence to them. She couldn't recall ever seeing him without his glasses on.

"Did you go home?" she asked.

"Is it morning?" He looked at the small radio clock on his desk.

"Yeah. Sun's not up yet, but it's morning," Stella said.

"Geez. I got lost. Down a rabbit hole. There's a lot to know about witchcraft." Jake put his glasses back on and leaned toward the computer screen.

Stella pulled up a chair from the desk next to Jake's, sat down, and rested her boot on her knee. "Tell me."

"OK. So, there's all this stuff, like you see in horror flicks. Witch hunts. Hangings. Burnings. It all happened. Europe. Even here. Started out east. But..." Jake grabbed a mug perched on his desk and took a swig. He scowled. "Eck. Homicide coffee. Cheap and cold." He plunked the mug back down.

"Go on. The witches," Stella said.

"Sorry. My brain is fried." He cleared his throat. "So, all that crazy stuff happened. These men, designated witch hunters, would decide who was a witch.

Based on all kinds of weird stuff. The way these women acted around animals. Markings they had. Arbitrary things. These hunters decided who would die." Jake shook his head. A lock of his hair broke loose and slipped over his right lens. He brushed it away.

"So? You're saying witchcraft was real?" she asked.

"Yes. No. Well, both. There were people, primarily women, who formed covens. Sure, you can call it witchcraft. But it's no different than any other religion. I mean when you get to its core. They believed in higher spirits. But they didn't worship Satan. That's a falsehood." Jake clicked on the keyboard, scanning the screen.

"Falsehood?" Stella chuckled.

"Shut up." He smirked. "They believed in higher spirits. They held ceremonies. It wasn't that different than other religions. Church services. Believing in their chosen God." Jake shook his head.

"What about magic? Spells?" Stella asked.

"Another false...lie." He chuckled. The dimple on his right cheek made an appearance. "It all comes down to energies. Constructive and destructive. Positive and negative. They're not the only ones to believe in energies. Even scientists have studied the concept of energies and how they impact the ions that compose the human body." Jake turned and looked at her. "Witchcraft is just a term used to label a set of spiritual beliefs."

Stella leaned back in the chair. Her foot shook against her knee. "So where does that leave us? This staged burning at the stake. It's as if the victim was tagged as a witch. I mean, the symbol of Satan burned into the abdomen. And the slow burning. Like the killer wanted to torture the victim. Specifically leaving the stake intact. To make a statement. So, what? The killer is delusional, really believes this victim is evil. A witch who worships Satan. Or, the killer is out for revenge. Uses an old way of torturing. Burning the evil." Stella leaned forward, resting her elbows on her knees. "I dunno..."

"What about the album? Anything on that?" Jake asked.

"Yeah. The greasy record store clerk and a high-as-a-kite druggie were both telling the truth when they said there's some creepy shit on that album," Stella said.

"You listened to it?" Jake asked.

"Only part of it. Couldn't take it anymore. It was like all the energy inside of me was turning bad. Rotting."

"Wow." Jake stared, mouth open.

"Yeah. Cletus, the guy who pawned the album, said he got it from a woman with hair like fire, eyes like ice, and a black cloak. Said the woman was one of 'them.'" She shook her head. "He was all spaced out when we dropped in on him. We shouldn't take him seriously." She bit her lower lip and rubbed her chin.

"But?"

"I can't shake this feeling that he was telling the truth. What he said about the album was spot on. Maybe he *did* get it from some woman in a cloak. As fucked up as that sounds." She paused. "Maybe..."

"Maybe what?" Jake asked.

"Maybe the killer thinks he's a witch hunter. Declaring his victims as evil. Burning them. Hanging them from stakes."

Jake turned and typed madly on the keyboard. The screen lit up with bright text. "Here. The most famous witch hunters. Matthew Hopkins. Sebastian Michaelis. Nicholas Remy. The list goes on. They all wore black robes." He adjusted his glasses. "Maybe whoever is dishing out Satanic albums is hunting witches. Or...what he...or *she* thinks are witches."

"You said there'd been witch hunts here in Canada?" Stella asked.

"Yes. The highest profile hunts were out east. Looks like covens migrated west, all across Canada. High level of activity in the prairies." Jake adjusted his glasses.

"Anything local?"

"Give me some time. If there was, I'll find it." He grabbed a thick folder filled with printouts. "Your reading material. To become a witchcraft expert."

"Jakey. You're a star. I'll go make you a fresh pot of homicide coffee." She grabbed the folder, patted Jake on the shoulder, and walked away.

Chapter 33

Church Seed

The fresh pot of homicide coffee that Stella had perked wafted through the stuffy war room. The fluorescent tubing electrified her eyes as she stared at the cream-coloured crime scene wall. She hoped the folder thick with information on witchcraft would give her some answers.

"Morning, Stella," Sutton greeted as he walked through the door and snapped a stack of folders onto the long table lining the centre of the room.

It's Detective Mahoney. "Morning, boss." She'd love to shove a snarky retort down his throat, but she held back. She was groggy from her late-night listening to Satanic chants.

Jake joined them. "Morning." He beelined for the corner where his computer was perched. "Stella." He smiled at her, pouring himself a fresh cup of cheap coffee.

"You're welcome. It's even hot. Still cheap though," she said.

"Thank you." He took a long sip.

"Morning, everyone," Parker said with too much cheer in his voice as he walked through the door.

Sutton scanned his team. "Geez. Jake. Stella. You two look like you were up all night." He looked at Parker. "You should take a note from the new guy. Don't burn yourselves out before the case has even started."

Stella glared. First at Parker, then at Sutton. "Someone has to solve this thing."

"You've solved it?" Sutton clasped his hands together.

Jake jumped in, "No. But we're getting somewhere."

"Really?" Sutton asked.

"Really," Stella said. "Parker and I went and saw Cletus last night. The guy who pawned the Satanic album. Said he got it from a woman in a dark cloak. That she was one of 'them.' It's probably a stretch, but she *could* be connected to the murder. Whoever did this could think they're a witch hunter."

"You got a name for me?" Sutton asked.

"No." Stella stared at Sutton.

All they had was a theory. No name. No real lead. This witch hunter thing sounded cuckoo as she said it out loud. Was her mind cluttered with witch-infused heavy metal lyrics?

Sutton grimaced, then looked at Parker. "Anything new?"

Parker shook his head.

Stella smirked. Fucking clown, getting enough sleep. Did this rookie think detectives got a solid eight hours of shut eye?

"Jake?"

"I've exhausted the searches on the Poison Sisters. Can't find any recording studio by that name." Jake studied his notes.

"Leave it for now. What else?" Sutton asked.

"Phenolic compounds are used for fermentation," Jake said. "Stella could be right; the victim could have been drinking."

"The alkaloids. Bet it was cocaine," Stella said. "Our vic was probably on some sort of booze-and-drug bender. Or hiding a new habit."

"Are there other sources of alkaloids?" Sutton looked at Jake.

"Lots of things. Things ingested by humans, mostly plants. Drugs. Nicotine. Caffeine. Not enough in the victim's bloodstream to come to a conclusive source," Jake said.

"What about the titanium? Anything on that?" Sutton asked.

"Not typically used in branding. There's only a half-dozen places that make brands in the city. Not sure if any of them use titanium." He shook his head. "It's strange. It's one of the purest metals. In fact, it's used to purify other metals."

"Purify?" Stella asked.

"Yeah. It's mixed with other metals to increase their purity," Jake answered.

"The victim was branded with a Satanic symbol. Tagged as evil." Stella crossed her arms and leaned against the back wall. "Maybe this is some sort of *purification* thing."

Sutton looked at her.

"If this killer thinks they're hunting evil, maybe they're trying to rid the earth of it." Stella bit her bottom lip.

"Speculation." Sutton opened a folder and pulled out a few photos. "We've got an ID on the victim." He punctured a photo of a young woman with a bright-blue tack. "Madeleine Martin. Thirty years old." He secured a second photo with a sunshine-yellow tack. "She led The Church of Life. Started in the spring of last year." He poked a cherry-red tack through a third photo. "Single. No kids. Her church was her family."

Stella walked across the room and stared at Madeleine. The same stick poking holes in her theory sent a shard of pain through her gut. What? This didn't make sense. A minister could be boozing and drugging it up. But, would they be considered a witch? "A minister?"

"Yeah," Sutton said.

"But she was branded with a Satanic mark. Tagged as evil." Stella looked at the photo of the victim, wracking her brain to make sense of why the killer would choose her.

"According to your theory," Sutton said.

His hot breath hit her neck. He was standing far too close to her. She turned and walked to the back of the room.

"Parker. Stella. Find out everything you can about this Madeleine," Sutton ordered.

"Seems clean cut." Parker flipped through the files.

Stella shot Sutton a look.

"Seems." Sutton returned her stare. "Looks can be deceiving. We're not throwing any theories out, yet. You two do your job. Poke holes in what you have, or prove it right."

Stella's stomach settled. He wasn't extinguishing her investigative path. Yet. She had to find out why a clean-cut minister of God would have alcohol and cocaine in her system. And why she would be branded with the symbol of Satan.

"She had no family. Lives alone. Find out who her friends were. What she did at church and in her free time. I want progress by end of day. And a full report," Sutton said. "And follow up on those custom brand shops. Find out if any of them use titanium or sold one with this strange symbol burned into our victims."

Dammit. She'd have to spend all day with super boy. Getting along.

Sutton looked at her, then Jake. "Follow your threads of speculation. Turn them into something concrete."

Chapter 34

Minister and Metal

Jake stopped typing and looked up at Stella. "Stop hovering. You're in my personal space."

She tousled his hair. "Yeah, I am."

"This is gonna cost you, you know." His dimple appeared as he smiled.

"What? Doing your job?" She scowled.

"I'm spending way more time on your searches. You're not the only detective I work with. You're not the only one solving murders around here." He grinned.

"Yeah, but I'm the detective working on the highest-profile case. Should take precedence." She smirked.

"You? Only you? What about that clean-cut, handsome partner of yours?" he asked.

Partner. Yeah. More like pain in the ass. "He's not that helpful. Just a rookie."

"Rookie? Aren't you a rookie?" He looked at her, raising an eyebrow.

"Whatever. He just got here. Doesn't know the city." Or anything.

"So, show him. Get him up to speed. He might surprise you. Two is better than one," Jake said.

"I don't have time to hold his hand. I need to solve this case." She rolled her eyes.

"Stella: The hard to get along with. Doesn't play well with others. Too aggressive. Doesn't want help. After one year as a homicide detective, she was kicked off the force. No one would work with her," Jake said.

She punched him in the arm. "Shut up."

"Ow." He recoiled.

The computer blipped. He looked at the screen.

"What's it say?" Stella leaned in over him.

"There's a service in forty-five minutes at The Church of Life."

"The victim's church?" Stella peered at the screen.

"Yeah." Jake jotted on a slip of paper with a pen, then handed it to her. "Here's the address. And here's the list of custom brand shops." He slid her a second piece of paper.

"You rock." She turned to leave.

"You'll take Parker with you, right?" Jake called after her.

"Sure," she responded without looking back.

Chapter 35

The Church of Life

The chapel was a humble building resembling a small house. Stella hung out at the back of the sanctuary. It was small, quaint, yet had a godly air about it. Triangular stained-glass windows cast a rainbow of colours over the floor and the wooden pews that had seen better days. Music echoed from a series of pipes lining the left side of the back wall. A petite woman played the organ perched alongside the pipes.

The whole place has some sort of enlightened aura about it. Like something spiritual lived here.

Stella sidled into an empty pew at the back and scanned the thin crowd. A woman walked up the few stairs leading to the stage at the front and began the service. She was softspoken, her demeanour gentle as she explained the purpose of the service was to support each other in the loss of their spiritual guide, their friend.

Stella listened to the words as the woman repeated the message that their leader had taught them: *"The purging of evil will guide us to the light."*

Purge. Evil.

Madeleine. A woman who was thought to be a ray of sunshine, a golden example, the most wholesome human being. At least, according to the half-dozen members of the congregation Stella had been able to talk to before the service began. She'd even questioned the organist, the woman leading the service, and the janitor. Nothing came up. Madeleine was a shining example of a pure person.

Why would she be branded with the symbol of Satan?

Tagged as evil?

If she was consuming alcohol and cocaine, did someone know about it?

Was there someone who disagreed with her message of purging evil to reach the light?

The whole thing didn't add up.

A vibration against her hip snapped her from her thoughts. Her phone. Probably Parker, wondering how her progress was coming on the branding shops she was supposed to be visiting. She'd convinced him to divide them up and go their separate ways in order to speed up the process. The church service was her little secret. She'd told him the next one was tomorrow. She'd have to come clean, of course, at the next team meeting. She wanted a little more time to go solo on this investigation. To stave off the requirement to get along with others.

She sighed.

Why did Sutton have to throw this whole partner thing at her right now, when the first real case finally came her way?

The sparse members dotting the pews stood and started singing along with the organ. Stella stood, silently scanning each singer, looking for any indication of something off. Someone not enjoying the service. Someone who might not have loved Madeleine as much as everyone else seemed to. The scene was perfect. Nothing was out of the ordinary.

Stella silently prayed for a clue to fall from the heavens into her lap.

Chapter 36

Tweed and Derby

A soft glow cast a dim hue over Stella's apartment. A streetlight outside flickered, then burned strong. She sat on the couch, in the middle of the main living area. Staring at the walls. One of them lined with the music belonging to her father. One of them lined with her own collection. Albeit more modern, still infused with passion and guitar masters.

She turned on the couch, resting her chin on the side of the sofa. She scanned the printouts, heavy with the history of witchcraft, scattered over the coffee table. How long had she been at this? She stretched over the couch, resting her head on the arm. Her phone vibrated, bouncing on the table. She ignored it. It was probably Parker, for the millionth time. After watching the service at The Church of Life, she'd checked out the list of brand shops, then sped back to her apartment. The shop staff had never seen the strange symbol before, nor had they made any titanium brands. The words from the service pulsed through the back of her mind as she'd read and reread the files on witchcraft. *The purging of evil will guide us to the light.* It was weird. They seemed connected to the underlying theme of all the articles Jake had given her, somehow. She had yet to develop a concrete lead.

Her eyes wandered until she was staring at the wall behind her. The one covered in a meticulously organized, grisly account of the worst murders in the country over the last twenty years. In the centre of the gruesome collage, a pictorial account of the last three cases her father had worked on lined up in sequence. The cases had been the core of his life, at the end. They were now the core of hers. Despite the cases she worked on here, now, in the present, these three had a hold on her. The first two had been solved. Both killers had been killed. One by their own hand. The other, by the hand of a hotshot criminal profiler who busted in on the struggle between her father and the killer. The weirdest part of it all was that the killers knew each other. A sadistic stepfather-and-son duo. One passing on his sick tendencies to the other.

The third had the strongest hold on her. It was the last one her father had worked on, before his own life ended.

Following her gut, as everyone had told her to do—Sutton, Blackwood, even her father through the words he had written in the guide to life he'd left behind for her—she knew there was something wrong with how that last case of her father's was conducted. He'd been called out east, to Toronto, to help on a case that mirrored one he'd been on sixteen years earlier. It had never been solved. Suddenly a body was left, in a park. The display was elaborate and identical to those left behind when the case went cold.

Stella had read and reread everything she could get her hands on. Case files. Medical examiner notes. All of it. Her father had been the one to find the killer. He'd gone alone to a gothic mansion up on a hill, with a knife, and gutted his prey. After stopping the killer, he'd fled the scene, bleeding to death. He hadn't lived to see the next sunrise.

Many questions had been raised. Accusations flew, belting insanities at her father's actions. Yet, no one could argue that he'd stopped a killer. Girls stopped vanishing. Those in the depths of the gothic mansion prison were freed.

Some said her father died because he took unjustified risks. That idea did not settle within her. The more she dug up, the more she believed his actions were justified. And necessary. For his mission was not to save himself. His mission was to save those girls, at all costs.

Others pointed the finger at the sergeant in charge. *Tomlinson.* It was clear he'd had a hidden agenda. It was printed in the paper. He'd been taking money from the killer himself. He'd swayed the investigation off course for the sake of saving his indulgent lifestyle. It was clear, to her, that he was the reason her father had died.

Stella let out an exasperated sigh. She turned, leaned back into the tattered couch, and sunk into the soft tweed of her father's coat. She had kept it. All these years. She couldn't look at it often. But every once in a while, she couldn't stop herself from putting it on. The smell of him, *Blue Jeans* cologne and Maker's Mark, drifted from the tightly woven material. She took a deep breath now, taking in his essence. Letting it become part of her. She ran her hand down the scarlet stain, left the last day he wore it.

She looked at the glass coffee table, stained with splashes of bourbon and littered with Captain Chow's takeout boxes. In the centre, a knife sat. Not just any knife. A special knife. A knife for hunting large game. The blade of the knife glimmered. The ivory handle, carved with intricate symbols, gave off a heavy vibe. It was the kind of knife that had killed her father. It was the kind of knife Stella had to snoop around in the underground market to find. It was the perfect knife to slide into the sorry excuse of a sergeant who had no morals, no ethics, and no guts

.

She leaned over, reached for a bottle of Maker's Mark, and poured herself a splash. She shot it back, then poured another.

A dull ache throbbed in her gut. Sliding the knife into the gutless Tomlinson would dissolve that ache. Forever. It had to.

She'd solve this case. She'd elevate her father's legacy.

Then she'd fly across the country and put an end to the pain within. Once and for all. It was the only way.

Chapter 37

It Continues

The walls of the basement swelled with the heat from the ring of candles. The flames flickered, their small orange glows melding in a single red-yellow haze. The basement seethed with a sinister vibe.

Viviana clenched her jaw and willed herself to face the human hanging in the centre of the sacrificial circle. The second purge of the cycle. The cycle seemed to be driven by her sister's energy. For a brief time between kills, she'd be on some sort of high, drowning herself in hallucinations, drinking her cacao wine and reliving the purging ceremony. After the second kill, the high intensified, morphing Damaris into the dominant woman she was, and beyond. She became savage and beastly. Something other than a woman. What would happen after the third kill?

Viviana shuddered. She couldn't think about that right now. She had to focus on the current kill. She opened her eyes and looked at the man hanging from his bound wrists in the centre of the circle. Blood trickled down his arms, excreting from the open wounds raggedly cut into his wrists from the tight binds holding him captive. Sweat poured down his face, infused with heat from the flames and fear from his pores. His cries suffocated in the cloth shoved into his mouth and tied around his head.

She was supposed to believe this man was the spawn of Satan, purging people wrongly from the earth. The resemblance was there, to the man who had ignited the little house at the edge of the forest that she loved so much. The same age. The same build. The same features. Yet, Viviana couldn't help but question the rightness of forcing someone else's actions onto another human shell that looked the same from the outside. She couldn't help but be pulled by the energy within, the higher spirits whispering in her ears, guiding her away from *this*.

"It is time," Damaris' deep voice boomed from the bottom of the staircase.

Viviana jumped. She spun around and looked at her sister. A yellow-brown tinge bled over the whites of her eyes. A sour odour seethed from the folds of her cloak. Damaris was the darker version of herself at this moment, as she always was during a kill. Damaris took on this demeanour. It wasn't simply a mood change. It was more than that. It was as if Damaris was a different being.

Damaris walked over and stared at the sweating man as she pulled a glove over each of her hands. "It is time. For your purge. You are the one, the man, who unrightly took our coven leaders. It is your turn to be removed." She walked over to the fireplace on the far wall, glowing with an orange-red heat. She picked up a long metal rod, the emblem of Satan moulded in a smooth circle of metal at the end. The brand that Dami had fashioned herself from an ancient looking pendant that she'd brought home one day. She had buzzed with excitement, telling Viviana that the pendant was titanium, and the key to purifying the earth. As Viviana watched Dami melt it down over hot coals, she'd bit her lip against the urge to ask where it had come from. As Dami pressed the hot metal with a custom mold, Viviana had cowered back in fear. Now, Dami's sick yellow stare crawled over the room as she held the metal emblem over the searing coals.

A chill prickled the back of Viviana's neck. She didn't want to watch, but she was too terrified to confront the being her sister had morphed into.

Damaris walked up to the man as she clutched the metal rod. "You will pay," she spat as she pushed the blazing emblem into his exposed abdomen.

The room filled with the odour of rancid cooking meat. Viviana forced back a gag. The man's skin smoked. His muffled cries intensified. Tears streaked his face.

Cold clutched at Viviana's gut. The walls closed in around her. The sour odour seeping from Damaris wove down Viviana's nostrils, mixing with the smell of hot flesh, rotting her insides.

She wanted to look away. She wanted to turn, run up the stairs and into the arms of the forest. She pictured it, her feet hitting the pathway with soft thuds, the fresh pine soothing her senses, the soft moss-covered stone sitting vacant, waiting for her to take the head seat in her natural sanctuary.

"Viviana. Open your eyes and see," Damaris demanded.

Viviana snapped her eyes open and stared at the smoke swirling from the man's reddened skin. If she ran to the forest, her sister would never forgive her. She would feel the wrath of the version of Damaris that stood before her now, broiling human flesh. Her disloyalty to her sister would be the same as her turning her back on her coven, her leader, her father.

Her gut clenched. The walls of the room reached around her. Damaris' outline hovered over her. Damaris' dark hair hanging like a thick raven fan melded into her cloak, enlarging her stature, making her seem like a Satanic god hovering over the room, hovering over Viviana.

Viviana shivered. She swallowed as she watched the man burn.

Devil's Hold

Chapter 38

Murder No. 2

Parker clutched the holy-shit handle as Stella took a sharp right. She loved how her Sunfire cornered.

"Gonna get us there in one piece?" Parker asked. Worry lines riddled his forehead.

"Can it. Boss said to hurry," Stella said.

"Yeah, but he needs his detectives *alive* when they arrive to investigate a dead body."

"Whatever." Stella cranked the volume on the CD player. Guitar wails echoed to the background of pouring rain. The introduction erupted into a pounding fast-paced riff, driven by a mad drumbeat. *Raining Blood* by Slayer seemed more than appropriate on the way to a murder scene.

"You ever tried listening to something more soothing?" Parker yelled over the metal madness.

"This *is* soothing."

"Yeah? On what planet?" Parker shot her a look from across the car.

"Planet Earth. They've done studies. Heavy metal eases anger," Stella retorted.

The metal god screeched his final words of blood and horror. The soothing sounds of rain eased through the car. The silence between tracks followed.

"Well, I'm not sure it's working for you," Parker said as he finally released the handle in the roof of the car.

"You're funny," Stella said.

She pulled off the main road onto a side street. A parking lot came into view, housing Sutton's shiny blue truck and Blackwood's brown-and-black Jeep, along with a shiny black SUV emblazoned with the CST lettering.

"These guys really like to announce their presence, don't they?" Stella remarked.

"Can't argue with you on that point." Parker met her gaze.

Stella rolled her eyes, then opened the door. "Let's move."

She paused, scanning the horizon, looking for the scene. Wondering if it would be as spectacular as the last one. She reviewed Sutton's orders. He'd said to grab Parker and get there, pronto. That there was *another one.* And it was likely linked to the one across from the Queen's Park Cemetery.

The sun was low in the sky. Dawn was approaching. She spotted movement, narrowed her eyes. A bright light flashed as a photo was shot. She spotted a techie.

"There." Stella pointed.

Parker snapped his gaze in the direction of her finger. "Yeah. Must be them."

They walked in silence toward the bustle across a park. The only vehicles in the parking lot belonged to homicide-related personnel. The only movement came from the direction of the flashing cameras as the scene they were about to be exposed to was recorded. Forever.

They approached the top of a grassy hill. Sparse glints of green leapt out from the hillside, catching the first rays of sun as it peeked behind the treeline. Four techies scattered in different directions of the park, snapping photos. Sutton stood beside Blackwood. They were both looking up at the scene. Another body. On display. Hung in the air, looming over them, but facing away.

"It does look the same," Parker offered.

Stella remained silent, taking it in. The tingles in her gut told her this was definitely the work of the same killer. But she didn't need any sort of special instinct to know that. It was obvious. Same stake. Same hanging figure. Stella clenched her jaw. This time, the body wasn't facing a cemetery.

"Parker. Stella. Good hustle," Sutton greeted them. He looked up. "As you can see, this appears to be the work of our killer."

Parker looked up at the body. "It's even more...grisly, up close." He whistled.

"Humdinger," Blackwood said. "Medical Examiner Terra Blackwood." She nodded at Parker.

"Detective Gavin Parker. Mahoney's partner," Parker said.

Blackwood raised an eyebrow, then shot a glance at Stella.

Stella grimaced, silently sharing her thrill with her new partner.

"I'm nearly done what I can do here. I'll let you two have a scan. I'd like to get the body removed so I can finish processing," Blackwood said.

"Sounds good," Parker said.

Clown. Show-off. Looking obedient for the boss. "Sure thing," Stella chimed in.

"Have a quick scan. I'm gonna confirm the perimeter." Sutton strode off toward one of the techies.

"Same smooth-looking wood. Not burned," Parker said.

"Yeah," Stella said. It was. Light and not a char or burn at all.

Parker walked around to the front of the body. Stella followed. Her gut tingled. Fresh adrenaline coursed through her. The arms. The legs. They were broiled almost identically to the first victim. Reddish-pink bunches of contorted flesh riddled the arms and legs in sick, distorted protrusions. The same style of dark cloth wrapped around the lifeless body. This time, the abdomen was completely exposed. The cloth covering the body had a clear opening, right in the centre of the stomach. The same symbol—a snake forming a circle, housing a five-pointed star, a savage animal face with evil eyes at the core—was burned right into the flesh. The symbol looked like it had been burned with a hot iron brand, sizzling the flesh, imprinting the message forever. Had it been burned before or after the victim had passed on from this world? Would they be able to determine that?

"Same burning. Same symbol," Parker said.

"Yeah," Stella whispered, mesmerized by the symbol. The skin bubbled. Moved. "It moved."

"What?" Parker asked.

"The skin. It moved," Stella spoke quietly, in a trance, fixated on the bubbling, fleshy symbol. "Where the symbol is."

Parker sidled up next to her. They both stared at the symbol. Waiting.

A contour rippled through the skin. Something moved. *Underneath* the burnt flesh.

"Oh my god. It *did* move," Parker stated.

Didn't believe me? Clown. "Just like I said," Stella said, sarcasm dripping from her words.

The skin moved again. Something was definitely alive underneath.

Stella looked up the hill. Blackwood was on her way back. "Blackwood, come quick."

Blackwood ran down the hill, halting next to Stella.

"Look," Stella said.

The flesh rippled again.

"What?" Blackwood asked.

"*Leviathan.*" The words slipped from Stella's mouth before she could think.

"What did you say?" Blackwood looked concerned.

Stella shook her head. "I...I don't know."

The flesh protruded in a sudden jolt. Something was still moving, underneath.

Blackwood snapped on a fresh set of gloves, then unzipped a pouch on the side of her pants. She retrieved a shiny silver tool, then reached it out toward the branded flesh. Where the flesh was rippling, she made a small incision. Something slithered, sliding a black, sleek body through the slit.

"Holy cow," Parker said.

Stella stared in fascination. Fresh excitement rippled through her as she watched the live thing pushing its way through the slit in the flesh of the dead body.

It slithered, its slippery body protruding from the innards of the victim. It broke free and dropped to the ground with a soft thud. Black scales shimmered. White markings curved the long body in a symmetrical pattern. It coiled into itself. Blackwood bent down and picked it up with her gloved hands. She held up the long snake, wet with the internal fluids of the dead body. Mucous dripped down its black scales.

"Humdinger," Blackwood said.

"Leviathan. Sea snake," Stella whispered. The words *Samael Lilith* pulsed in her mind.

"What?" Parker asked.

"It's a sea snake. The symbol, the brand, it has a letter at each of the five points. The letters spell *Leviathan* in Hebrew. Leviathan means sea snake."

Blackwood stared at her, then back at the snake.

"Jake told me. He researched the symbol." Stella clenched her jaw. Jake *had* told her about Leviathan. How did she know *this* snake was a sea snake? The chants from the album echoed in her mind.

Parker leaned in, inspecting the reptile. "You're right. It's a Turtle-Headed Sea Snake."

Blackwood raised an eyebrow.

"Parents wouldn't let me have a dog. I got into reptiles."

Blackwood pulled a plastic bag from another pocket in her pants, placed the reptile inside, and secured the bag. She poked a pair of tiny holes in the plastic. "I'll take a look at this guy, then get him to a good home. I've got to get this body tagged, bagged, and en route." Blackwood returned her attention to the body as she waved over a couple of the crime scene techs.

"OK. So, we've got the same burned skin. The same symbol. The same clothing. But a snake inside the body? Underneath the brand?" Parker said.

Stella looked down the hill, across the park. "And we're not across from a cemetery."

She walked down the hill. Parker followed. At the bottom of the hill, an expanse of grass rolled out over a vast open area. Dark blotches of dead grass dotted the landscape.

"What are you thinking?" Parker asked.

"What used to be here?"

Parker shrugged. "Don't know. I'm new in town."

"We need to find out." Stella clenched her jaw, examining the patches of dead grass. Her gut told her that something used to be here. Before. And that whatever it was, it meant something.

She needed to find out. And she needed to know what the hell *Samael Lilith* meant.

Chapter 39

Snake Man

Parker toppled into the passenger-side door as Stella took a hard right. She let off the gas and eased her Sunfire into a spot next to a black Trans Am. A menacing bass line jolted the entire car. A rambling cadence made everything seem off kilter. Strange lyrics of kissing craniums with aluminum baseball bats came to a halt as she turned off the car.

Parker shook his head, opened the door, and got out.

"Show-off," Parker muttered.

"What?" Stella spun on her heel and glared at Parker.

He sighed. "I think you like to show off. Blasting death metal. Driving like a maniac. I think it's all a show."

She rolled her eyes. "Whatever. It's *not* death metal. It's thrash-funk. Experimental. Interesting." She crossed her arms, standing her ground.

"You know, I think we'd be good partners. If you'd just chill out a bit. Take a foot off the gas." He stood, expressionless.

She hated that she couldn't read him. He was always so calm. Composed.

"I can't believe I wanted to work with you. I must be insane." He threw up his arms.

What? "What? I thought Sutton assigned you." What was he talking about? No one wanted to work with her.

"I asked for the transfer. I requested you as partner. I was impressed by your record," he said.

"Didn't you read the part about how I don't work well with others?" Fuck Sutton for putting it on her record.

"Yeah. I did. Thought I could influence you. I must have been delusional." He slammed the car door. "Let's get this done."

Cold shot through her gut. He was polite. He put up with her attitude. Did what she said. He knew the type of sea snake slithering from the last victim's gut, leading them here. *Dammit.* He was useful. She couldn't start to like him.

She shook it off. A ray of sun shot a glint off the Trans Am parked next to her. She squinted. A pair of fuzzy dice hung from the rear-view mirror. She walked to the back of the car. The licence plate said *SN8KMAN.*

"Hey. Get a load of this," she called after Parker.

He turned and walked toward her. An unenthusiastic look washed over his face. It was the first time she could read him, and it didn't feel good.

He chuckled when he saw the licence plate. "Think it belongs to Hue?" He pointed to the sign over the store directly in front of Stella's Sunfire. *Hue's House of Reptiles* flashed in neon green.

"Let's find out." She walked toward the reptile house.

Bells jingled as she opened the door. Purple neon lights lined the ceiling, casting a nightclub vibe over the room. Techno music pumped through the space. A cloud of *Drakkar Noir* permeated the place. On the far side of the room, a separate area, dark, lined with glass cages, glowed soft red.

"It's like a nightclub in here," Parker said.

Were they cool? Had he vented and moved on? Why did she care? She hated having a partner. "It's weird. Looks like the reptiles are back there."

She headed for the glowing red room. Inside, rows of glass cages lined the back wall. Red pot lights cast a soft hue over the room. The techno beat was muffled from the main space. "Guess the reptiles need it quiet and dark." Stella looked in the row of cages in front of her. Beady black eyes inspected her from scaly bodies. "Kind of gives me the creeps."

"They're harmless. And yeah, these species do need dark and quiet." Parker leaned over, looking into a cage housing a small dragon-like lizard. "Always wanted one of these. Bearded Dragon."

Stella walked up beside Parker.

"Dad wouldn't allow pets. We probably couldn't afford it anyways." He shrugged.

"Why don't you get one now?" Why did she care?

"Not sure. Maybe I have commitment issues."

She chuckled.

"What can I do for you folks?" a voice broke their banter. A man, dressed in a silk shirt, matching tie, and cheap-looking shiny suit, walked into the red room. "I'm Hue. Welcome to my house of reptiles."

Slick, Trans-Am-driving sleaze ball. "I'm Detective Mahoney. This is my partner, Detective Parker." The words slid way too easily off her tongue. "We're looking for a snake." She slipped a photo from the pocket in her leather coat.

Hue inspected the photo. "Turtle-Headed Sea Snake. That one's a beaut." He clicked his tongue.

"You carry it?" Parker asked.

"Sure do. Only place in town. Well...except Tom. He used to. He doesn't anymore. This is the place to purchase top-quality exotic pets. Hue has your back." Hue shot them a slick smile, revealing a gold cap.

God. Was this guy for real?

"Tom?" Stella asked.

"Yeah. Tom's Top Reptile Emporium. His selection isn't as good as mine," Hue said.

Parker jotted in his notebook.

"The sea snake?" Stella pointed at the photo.

"Oh yeah. Right this way." Hue led them to the back of the red room over to a doorway. "In the snake pit." He pointed at a sign over the doorway. *Snake Pit* pulsed in red.

Seriously? Did anyone buy this guy's shit? Stella followed Hue into the snake pit. A dark-blue glow illuminated the room. Stella squinted as her eyes adjusted. Snakes. Everywhere. An entire wall of glass-housed snakes slithered and hissed, inspecting them with beady eyes.

Hue led them to a far corner. "I only have three left. Imported from Australia. Rare find."

Stella stared at three small black snakes, entwined with each other behind a glass case. Their obsidian scales shimmered. Symmetrical stripes lined their backs, bright white against black bodies. A yellowish light glowed over them from above. Several crickets jumped erratically around the snakes.

"We got them mid-meal. These little ones are only a few months old. I had a fresh a batch arrive a couple weeks ago. Sold three of them right away. Just have these three left." Hue looked at his prized snakes with admiration.

Maybe the snakes were his favourite in the house of reptiles. Might explain his licence plate.

"How many did you want?" Hue asked.

"We're not here to make a purchase. We need the sales records of the Turtle-Headed Sea Snake," Parker said.

Suspicion hijacked Hue's face. "What?"

"We're investigating a situation. One of these snakes was found at a crime scene. We need to know who purchased the other three snakes," Parker said.

"This is fishy. I don't have to give you private information of my clientele," Hue said.

"That mud turtle, in the other room. You got proper paperwork for selling those?" Parker asked.

Hue hesitated.

"You do realize that the sale of a number of types of small turtles is illegal due to the risk of salmonella poisoning?" Parker continued, staring sternly at Hue. "It would be a shame if the SPCA paid a visit and found your inventory less than legal. Now what would that do to business? I bet Tom would love it."

Stella stood, shocked at this side of Parker she hadn't seen before. Now this...*this* she might be able to work with.

"Fine. I'll get you the sales records," Hue said. He turned and left the snake pit.

"Nice work, Parker," Stella said.

"Thanks. Let's get those sales records. Might get us a suspect." Parker left the snake pit.

Stella looked at the sea snakes, slithering over each other, white markings melding with shimmering dark bodies. Why had she frozen? Why didn't Hue succumb to her pressure? Where had this feisty side of Parker come from? What was happening?

Chapter 40

Missing Snake

Stella left the red glow of the snake pit and re-entered the purple nightclub vibe of the main room of Hue's House of Reptiles. Parker was at the front counter, talking to Hue. The techno beat pumped obnoxiously.

"Got anything?" Stella asked as she sidled up next to Parker.

"Yeah. Two names." Parker showed her the open page of his notebook. John Jansen and Kim Karson were scribed in neat penmanship on the paper. God, he was clean cut. Too perfect. She berated herself for starting to like him.

"Thought you sold three." Stella glared at Hue.

"I did. Or, I could have sworn I did. My inventory indicates that six were delivered. Three left in the pit. I could have sworn I sold three. Only two sales records here."

He hit the arrow key on his computer keyboard frantically. His eyes jittered over the screen.

Hue scrambled with the keyboard. "Look, if I sold the snake, the record would be here. It's a foolproof system. The customer info has to be entered to make the sale."

"So, what? A missing snake? Did it slither right out of your snake pit?" Stella looked right at Hue.

"The cages are secure. They have to be opened from the top. The latch has to be released. From the outside."

Parker looked at Hue. "I suggest you get your inventory in order." He snapped a card onto the counter. "Call me when you do." He looked at Stella. "Let's go."

Stella shot Hue a glare then followed Parker. What were they turning into? Bad cop and bad cop? The bells jingled behind her as she walked out of Hue's House of Reptiles.

Chapter 41

Slew of Partners

Stella stepped on the gas hard. Her Sunfire shot out of the parking lot, the tires spitting gravel.

"Hey. Chill out," Parker said.

"Whatever." Stella increased the speed. "What do you make of this snake thing?"

"Only three options. Sales record got lost. Snake slithered away. Or someone stole it," Parker said. "Hue seemed pretty confident in his inventory system and security."

"And you believe that slimeball?" Stella raised her eyebrow.

"Did you see how worried he was when I mentioned the proper paperwork? I think the slimeball exterior is a show. I think he does have his reptile house and his snake pit in order. I think he's on top of the inventory and sales. Needs to be, to stay ahead of Tom. He knows the proper import process. I think he's cutting corners. But not in inventory. He can't afford to lose an expensive reptile," Parker said.

It made sense. "So. What? How does someone steal a snake?"

"The sea snake isn't very big. Someone could easily slide it into a bag. And back in that dark pit, if Hue was busy with another customer, he wouldn't have noticed," Parker said.

"Dammit. We should have asked for security footage." Stella clenched her jaw.

"Nah. There weren't any cameras in the pit. Only in the main room," Parker said.

Observant fucker. Why did he have to be useful?

"We'll get Jake to run the names. Maybe one will pan out," Stella said.

"Yeah."

Dammit. He was beginning to feel like a partner. Stella summoned the images of the last few chumps Sutton had thrown at her. Chaz. Stupid blond-haired, blue-eyed mamma's boy. Cringed at Stella's harsh comments. Rick. Too-tanned, too-muscular jock. Fast in a chase. Slow between the ears. Told Sutton that she needed sensitivity training. And Brad. Dark-haired, dark-eyed, wiry thing. Had some good ideas. But weak as fuck in a physical encounter. It wasn't her fault Sutton threw her a series of duds.

She snuck a glance at Parker through the corner of her eye. This one. Annoying. Too perfect. *Nah.* He wouldn't last. Time to up his dose of Aggressive Stella. If he wasn't holding her back, she would have gutted Hue and walked away with a real lead.

Chapter 42

Floral Spice

Damaris stood in the centre of the small room, silver goblet raised in her right hand, her amulet adorned knife raised in her left. "To the perfect purge," she declared, then sat on the edge of the couch. "This one was perfect, Viv. It was *perfect*." Her voice trickled like a giggling schoolgirl. Only, instead of talking about the cute boy she had a crush on, she was babbling on about how perfect her sacrifice of a human being had been. "You should have some wine. Celebrate our accomplishments with me." She filled her own cup, then filled a second goblet with deep-scarlet liquid. Spice and heat wafted from the cup.

Damaris handed the cup to Viviana. Viviana walked over and took it. She perched herself on the edge of a chair, facing Damaris.

"Well, go on, take a sip. Finalize our toast," Damaris said.

Viviana hesitantly brought the goblet to her lips. She took a sip. Spice hit her tongue; heat slid down her throat. She was wary of drinking the hallucinogenic cocktail. She saw what it did to her sister. Then again, her sister consumed a lot—and her sister *saw* things with or without the wine.

"See? It's nice. Right?" Damaris smiled. Her real smile. The one Viviana loved. The one Viviana remembered from their childhood.

"Yes." Viviana smiled back. Nervous fingers tickled her insides. She didn't know how long this would last. The appearance of her sister, her real sister, the one who showed real human emotions, occurred less and less often. After a kill, her real sister was vibrant and present. A day or two after, her real sister faded and the darkness within her seeped out.

Damaris patted the cushion beside her. "Come and sit with me, Viv. I miss you. You seem...so distant lately."

Viviana's stomach clenched. She stood and walked over to the couch, sitting next to Dami. Her shoulders clenched and her internal guide screamed a warning.

"You seem so tense." Damaris put down her goblet and wrapped her arms around Viviana, rubbing circles over Viviana's back with her palm. "You can relax. The cycle is going well. We've had two successful purges. The final one is sure to be *perfect*."

Viviana knew it wouldn't be. Optimism flooded from Damaris after each of the first two kills. Between kills, it had dwindled, fizzled out, turned to a dark pessimism. She could see it happening again.

Viviana wanted to believe her sister, that things would work out, that things would be perfect. But they never were. And she was struggling to understand what this demented perfection was.

Damaris slid her arms away from Viviana and took a long swig of wine. Lavender exuded from Damaris, weaving a spice-infused bouquet around Viviana. The optimism pouring from Damaris filled the room with an uplifting aura, lifting Viviana with it. She took a deep breath. She exhaled, letting everything go. Her worry. Her anxiety. The looming image of what Damaris could become again in a day's time. She let it all go.

Could she stop it from coming again? She doubted it. What would she do when faced with the next terrifying commands from the dark version of Damaris as her scarlet lips parted? She didn't know.

Right now, right here, she was in this room filled with the floral essence of what her sister once was, and what her sister had transformed back into now. She wanted to be here. She wanted to be *here* and present in this moment.

She looked at her sister, took a sip of the wine, and nodded her head, listening to the trickling songbird chatter pouring from her sister's mouth.

Chapter 43

Team Meeting

The fluorescent lighting burned Stella's eyes. The hot, stale, coffee-infused room closed in on her. The clock on the front wall ticked, echoing through her ears. She stared at the two murder scenes, plastered in a rough collage across the cream-coloured crime scene wall.

"Stella." Jake walked through the door. "How'd it go at the reptile house? What was that guy's name again? What was he like?"

Stella looked away from the photos of burned bodies and ran her hands through her hair. "Hue. He's a slimeball. His house of reptiles looks like a freaking dance club."

"Really?" Jake sat behind the computer in the corner and booted it up. It hummed. "Parker dropped the two names off. Didn't give me any details."

"Did they come up?" Stella walked over to Jake.

"Yeah. Both middle-aged men, wives, kids. Seems they bought the snakes for their kids. Tim. And Tina. Respectively. I got their info, if you want to follow up. But it seems like a dead end," Jake said.

"There's a missing snake." Stella poured herself a fresh cup of stale, lukewarm coffee.

"Missing?" Jake looked up from the computer.

"Yeah. Hue acquired six. Three were gone. Only two sales records," Stella said.

"Hmmm. Escaped?" Jake asked.

"Or stolen," Stella said. "Killer could have taken it. Stay off Hue's sketchy sales records. And Tom's was a bust."

"Tom?" Jake asked.

"Hue mentioned this other shop. Run by Tom. Said he may have had the same snake at some point. Turns out he didn't." One missing snake. One missing lead.

Parker and Sutton walked in.

"Team." Sutton nodded, slapped a folder on the table, and walked up to the crime scene wall.

Parker hung out in the corner.

"Two bodies. Strikingly similar. Tell me you've gotten somewhere," Sutton said.

"Tracked the snake down," Parker said.

Sutton stared at the photos on the wall. "The snake that was in the belly of the body?"

"Turtle-Headed Sea Snake," Parker said. "Only sold at one store in town. Shipment of six came in. Three gone. Two sales records."

"Both look like dead ends," Jake added.

Dammit. Super boys stealing the show. All my thunder. Stella grimaced.

"You said three snakes, but only two sales records?" Sutton asked.

Stella jumped at her chance. "Could have escaped. Or been stolen."

Sutton stroked the green rabbit claw dangling from his belt. "If it escaped, then how did it slither into our body here?" He walked up to the crime scene wall and looked at the photo of the victim. "What do you think, Stella?"

"I think it was stolen. By the killer." *Back in the spotlight.*

"But no way to follow up on that." Sutton grimaced.

"No," Stella said, clenching her jaw.

Sutton turned back to the crime scene photos. "Just got an ID on the second body." He walked over to the centre table and opened the folder. "Willard Posner. Thirty-two. Started the *Seed of Love* Church in the spring, three years ago. Single. No family."

Sounds exactly the same as Madeleine. But male.

"Same drill as with the first victim. Scour the congregation," Sutton said.

"Nothing came up on Madeleine. No social life. No family. Only her congregation. They all loved her," Parker said.

He wasn't ratting her out. She'd filled him in on the service. Told him she found out about it after they split ways. "Yeah, but we must have missed something. I mean, both of these people were church leaders. Both churches started in the spring. What's the size of the congregation at the *Seed of Love*?" Stella walked toward Sutton.

Sutton scanned the file. "Eighty-six."

Stella placed her palms on the table. "Both small congregations. There's a pattern here. We need to find out why."

"I agree." Sutton nodded.

Good. Still in control. Still on top here. She nodded at Sutton.

"Jake. What you got?" Sutton asked.

"I looked into the location of the second scene. The direction the body was facing, down the hill, there used to be a burial ground there. It was one of the city's oldest cemeteries. Over 15,000 buried. It was moved to the St. Mary's Cemetery in 1897," Jake said. A curly lock fell over his eye.

"Intriguing. Good work," Sutton said.

"It was Stella's idea. She asked me to look into it," Jake said.

"Good work, Stella. What do you make of it, both bodies facing a cemetery?" Sutton stared at her. The green rabbit claw swung back and forth.

She fought the urge to state her name as *Detective Mahoney*. "Two religious leaders. First one apparently had a clean slate. Yet, she had alcohol and cocaine in her bloodstream."

"The cocaine is speculation only at this point. Source of the alkaloid traces is undetermined," Sutton corrected her.

"OK. *Maybe* she had coke in her system. She had alcohol. What if these prime leaders were being called out? Tagged as evil. Branded with the symbol of Satan. Second vic was stuffed with a snake. Leviathan." Stella's gut blazed as she spouted the theory that seemed to naturally flow from within.

"What does this have to do with facing a cemetery?" Sutton asked. Skepticism flooded his face.

The words from newspaper articles pulsed in her mind. "Witches weren't allowed in cemeteries. If these victims are tagged as evil, maybe the killer is putting them in the same category as a witch." Stella rubbed her chin.

"The staged burning at the stake," Parker said.

Maybe she wasn't crazy. Straightlaced Parker seemed to buy her theory. A wild metal man flashed through her mind. Or, her metal obsession was filling her mind with lyrics of burning witches.

"OK. Let's get moving. I want progress. If this theory has any hold, show me. Before sundown." Sutton grabbed the folder and walked out the door.

"Jake, I need some searches," Stella said.

"Sure thing." Jake powered off the computer and led the way, Stella close behind and Parker in tow.

Chapter 44

Service of Purge

Organ music vibrated through the chapel. Candles glowed with soft orange flames along both side walls. Several dozen people sat in polished wooden pews scattered through the main room of the church.

Stella recoiled. She hovered at the back of the church.

"You just going to cower back here, or are you going to sit?" Parker said as he approached from behind her.

"Don't usually spend much time in churches," Stella said.

"Your parents never took you?" Parker asked.

"No. Told you, my dad was a detective. Didn't have time for church. I guess. My mom isn't into organized religion. She's more of a free spirit." Stella caught herself before she could say anything else. *Dammit.* How did super boy get her talking about her family?

"My parents were strict about it. As much as my dad worked to put food on the table for all us hungry kids, Sunday morning was for church," Parker whispered.

Stella rolled her eyes. She didn't want a family history.

"C'mon." Parker nudged her elbow, then led the way to an open bench at the back.

She slid in next to him. "So how long do these things last, anyways?"

"The service?" Parker asked.

"Yeah." *Dingbat.*

"Usually an hour. Most, anyways. Depends on what kind of church it is. This one, being non-denominational, your guess is as good as mine. But my bet's on an hour," Parker said.

An hour? They couldn't spare an hour. The clock was ticking. Time was running out. She didn't want another body. Or did she? As tragic as it would be, it would give them more information. It was taking far too long for them to pull apart the lives of the victims and put together the patterns. With a third body, it would be confirmed they were dealing with a serial killer. And patterns would have to fly off the scene.

The organ music suddenly rose in volume. Everyone stood in unison. Parker followed suit. He nudged her shoulder. "Stand. It's polite."

She sighed, then stood, reluctantly. She placed her palms on the back of the pew in front of her and leaned on it. The service-goers started singing in time to the chords vibrating from the pipes lining the back wall of the church. An odour of incense wafted over them as a woman in a long white dress walked up the aisle holding an incense stick in her hand. Puffs of lavender-and-spice-infused smoke swirled around her. Drowsiness washed over Stella. The woman reached the front. Everyone sat down. Stella fumbled to find her seat.

The woman began speaking, her voice like a stream of sunshine. "Welcome. Old friends. And new." She looked right at Stella.

"Today, we will have a fresh service. However, before we embark on a new message from the spirit above, we must pay tribute to our fallen friend, Willard. Let us remember his words: *'We must purge the evil within ourselves to flourish.'* We know Willard had done just that. He had cleansed every drop of evil within his being, a long time ago. Willard lived pure. He lived right. He was clear of anything putrid. Anything toxic. Anything evil. Willard is thriving now, in the afterlife. In his afterlife. He is among the spirits above, among the innocent souls of our other departed friends." The woman stopped. She looked up. Bells chimed behind her. Clouds of lavender and spice spiralled up to the ceiling.

Purge. Stella shuffled in her seat. She slipped her hand into the pocket of her leather coat, searching for her notebook. She slid it out and flipped it open, scanning pages.

Purge.

There it was. In the message of Madeleine Martin. 'The purging of evil will guide us to the light.' It had been her message to her congregation.

Was purging a common theme in these places? Was it simply too common to mean something? Or did the act of *purging* the members of their congregation of evil mean something? Link the two churches together? Through the killer's eyes?

The killer could be tagging these holy leaders as evil. Maybe the killer was offended by their similar messages. If Madeleine was on a booze-and-drug train, maybe the killer knew about it. The killer could be using the titanium to purify the evil out of his victims while branding them with the symbol of evil.

As the hour ticked by at a much-too-slow pace, Stella stewed over the meaning of a *purge*.

When the woman finally made her way back down the centre aisle, Stella couldn't wait to pump some circulation through her limbs. Sitting still for a full hour wasn't her forte.

"Finally," she whispered to Parker.

"Sssh," he hushed her.

She glared at him.

"We should stick around. Talk to the organist," he said.

Stella looked up at the front of the church. An older woman sat at the organ in a perfectly pressed, prim-and-proper, navy-blue suit. Her silver hair, secured in a tight bun, rested at the nape of her neck. "She looks, like, a hundred years old," Stella hissed.

"She would have heard every word of every service that Willard gave," Parker said.

"*If* she can hear." Stella smirked. Still, it wasn't a bad idea. Of all the members of the congregation, she had likely been to every single service, clinging to every word of the evil-purging Willard.

"C'mon." Parker stood and walked up the main aisle.

Stella followed.

The woman behind the organ concluded the final chords of the song, then folded the sheet music perched up on the instrument.

She saw them approach. "Hello. Can I help you?" Her voice wavered.

Geez. She *did* look a hundred years old.

Parker responded, "Hello, ma'am. I'm Detective Parker. This is my partner, Detective Mahoney."

She did love the ring of it. Detective Mahoney. Maybe Parker could give Sutton some lessons on how to address her.

"Detectives? Oh my." The woman sat up on the bench and placed her hand over her heart. "Are you here about Willard?"

"Yes, ma'am. Could we ask you a few questions?" Parker said.

Get to the point. His politeness grated on her nerves. At this pace, they'd only get one interview in before sundown. And Sutton would be hovering over them for a report on their progress.

"Well, of course. But I really don't know what help I can be," the woman said.

"Do you come to every service?" Parker asked.

"Yes. I do. I play the organ for every service held here," the woman said.

"How long have you been part of this church?" Parker asked.

Oh my god. Get to the point. Who hated Willard? What were his secrets? What's with all this purging?

"Since Willard started it. I loved his services right from the start. His messages really resonated with me. They're..." she hesitated, "I'm sorry...they were so powerful. I can't believe he was taken from us. It doesn't make any sense." She shook her head, looking down at her hands.

"Was there anyone who might have wanted to hurt Willard?" Parker asked.

The woman's eyes grew wide. "No. It's so absurd. You can ask anyone in this congregation. Willard was the sweetest man. He was kind. Gentle. Shy. Except when he was up there on the podium." The woman looked to the centre of the front stage, beaming.

"What do you mean?" Stella jumped in.

"Well, when Willard got up there and started a service, it was like his shyness melted away. He came to life. He was much more...fierce. Alive. Passionate." She smiled wide.

"This...purge." Stella looked at her notebook. "We must purge the evil within..." She looked at the woman. "Was that Willard's message?"

"Well, yes. But it's a little taken out of context here," the woman said.

"Really? It sounds rather harsh. Not something a kind, gentle man would say. That we all have to purge what is within us. Wouldn't you say?" Stella loomed over the woman.

"Well...this is all...Willard didn't mean any harm. He was doing good. For everyone." The woman blinked several times. "This is all...overwhelming."

Parker glared at Stella. He stepped toward the woman. "Yes. I am sure it is. Sorry, my partner here didn't mean to overwhelm you. We just care about what happened to Willard. Are you okay?"

The woman looked at Parker and smiled. "Yes, dear. Don't you worry. I'm just fine."

"We want to find out what happened to Willard. If you think of anything, anything at all, that might help us figure out who was involved, please call me." Parker handed a card to the woman.

She took it.

"This is my direct number." He smiled at the woman. "We want to find out what happened to your wonderful Willard. If anything odd pops into your mind, please, call me." He stepped back.

The woman smiled. "Oh yes, I will. I promise."

Stella rolled her eyes and turned away. Super Boy does it again. What a slop fest.

Chapter 45

Human Messages

Stella stared at the two photos pierced with brightly coloured tacks. Madeleine Martin. Leader of *The Church of Life*. Willard Posner. Leader of the *Seed of Life*. One female. One male. One thirty years old. The other thirty-two. They both started churches. Both in the spring. Years apart. They both led congregations of less than a hundred. Small, devoted followings. Both single. Both lived alone. Neither of them seemed to have any friends. All they had was their congregation.

Nothing provided a concrete link with an opening down a clear path. No one stood out as a suspect. Yet, the situations were too eerily similar. They both ended up broiled and hung from a stake facing a cemetery.

Stella tapped her foot. She clenched her jaw. She wanted to see something in this.

The pit of her belly was vacant of tingles, pulses, imaginary pins. Nothing. That instinct everyone seemed to think she had, inherited somehow from a father she barely knew, didn't seem alive in her right now. It seemed dead. Or maybe it had never existed.

She sighed. What was she missing?

She shuffled closer to the photos. The symbol of Satan burned into the flesh of the bodies with purifying titanium. A snake sealed within the flesh of the second victim. *Like a message.*

The door swung open. A gush of cool air pierced the stuffy, stale space.

"Can you come to my desk?" Jake asked.

She abandoned the murder collages and followed Jake through the empty clutter of cubicles. Were they the only two who pushed on into the night? Didn't anyone care about murder anymore? And where was Super Boy? Home getting his beauty sleep, she supposed.

Jake tapped at the keyboard attached to the black screen smeared in cryptic neon-green letters. "I kept thinking of why someone would be outside a cemetery. Looking in. I dug through the witchcraft data again and launched more searches. Your theory holds." He stared at the foreign neon language.

She sighed. "What are you talking about?"

"Your theory. That the murders have to do with witchcraft. I know you've been wavering on it." He looked at her.

How could he know that? He didn't know her *that* well. Did he? "Jake, we need *proof*. Till then, that's all it is. A *theory*." She crossed her arms and tapped the toe of her boot.

"Listen. Like I said before, there were burnings of people accused of being witches. They were killed other ways, too. Hangings. Other terrible forms. The point is, they weren't allowed in the cemeteries. Back when people accused of being a witch were sentenced to death, their bodies weren't to be buried on sacred ground. It was believed they worshipped Satan. That their souls weren't worthy of a burial within a cemetery boundary."

She looked at him. "The killer is tagging the victims as witches, then."

"Precisely. I mean, we know they weren't. But they *did* believe in their own version of higher spirits. So, the killer deemed them to be witches, burned them, hung them from a stake, and pointed them facing the very cemeteries they weren't allowed in." Jake smiled; his dimple appeared.

The pit of Stella's belly tingled, coming back to life. "The pile of printouts you gave me, it's all there. Witches, from the view of the hunter, worship Satan. When, in fact, witchcraft is a religion, a belief in spiritual enlightenment. Both the victims had messages of purging evil." She shook her head. "I don't know...maybe the killer simply had it out for religious leaders."

"No. Let's go with your theory. Why would these holy leaders be tagged as evil?" Jake adjusted his thick glasses, wrinkles riddling his pale forehead.

The tingles in Stella's gut sprouted, reaching through her arms. "A message."

"What?"

"Before you came in and got me...the victims. The *victims* are the *messages*. From the killer." She rubbed her chin. "Look through the eyes of the killer. The killer *saw* them as witches. For some reason. The killer sees this victim type as the representation of evil."

"Human messages," Jake said.

"Yeah. Leviathan. Symbol of evil. Literally sealed within the human body." Stella's brain buzzed. "Like when messages used to be sealed with hot wax and a signature stamp."

"Right. In fact, at the time of the surge in witch hunts, that is precisely how messages were sealed, for delivery," Jake said.

"The killer is sealing human messages. With the symbol of Satan."

"Yikes," Jake said. His dimple deepened.

The tingles in Stella's gut dissipated. Cold chilled her insides. "It just...it still doesn't quite add up. I mean, why? The victims were ministers. Holy leaders. Maybe the killer was offended by their messages of purging. Maybe the killer knew about the alcohol and drugs. I don't know...it just doesn't seem to be enough to kill over."

"Yeah." Jake pursed his lips. "We need to keep digging. What else should I look for?"

"Samael Lilith." Stella clenched her jaw.

"What?"

"The words. Samael Lilith. I need to know what they mean."

Jake started typing. "Where'd you hear that?"

"I think when I listened to the album." She bit her lip.

"You think?"

"Yeah. I mean...I keep hearing them. I think it started after I listened to that *Devil's Track* thing." She rubbed her chin.

Neon green flashed over a black screen. Jake adjusted his glasses and leaned toward it.

"Samael, the accuser. Lilith, banished from the garden of Eden." Jake scratched his head.

"Accuser. Banished." Stella clenched her jaw, looking past the screen. "We need to twist this around. The killer tagged the victims as evil. Branded them with the symbol of Satan. Purified them with clean metal. Banished them from the cemetery. Like they are witches." She swallowed. "The victims are ministers. Who sees religious leaders as evil?"

"Accuser…" Jake said.

"Maybe the killers see the ministers as accusers. You know, their message of purging evil? This killer is sick. Evil. Maybe he feels accused by what the ministers represent." Stella stood to leave. "I gotta go. Gotta get back to the printouts. And the album."

Jake looked at her with concern. "Be careful."

Chapter 46

Flaming Stella

A city haze clouded the midnight sky. The bulbous moon glowed on high volume. Skyscrapers lining the edge of downtown reflected off the dark river snaking along the pathway. Stella walked briskly. The chilly air bit at her cheeks. She nodded at a woman wrapped in a filthy quilt settling in on the riverbank for the night, next to a rusty shopping cart piled high with odd belongings.

The woman smiled back. Her eyes seeped experience. Acceptance.

Stella continued walking, looking at the reflection of the city landscape shimmering on the surface of the dark water.

Things had been bubbling. They weren't getting anywhere on the murder investigation. She was contorting her theory into a twisted mess. Making it fit. No physical evidence. No suspects. Dead end after dead end was leaving her feeling at her own wit's end.

Parker. She snorted. Parker was no help. He was constantly dazzling Sutton with his bright ideas. Sometimes seconds before Stella was about to spout the same brainwave. He was the clean-cut, bright-eyed rookie that she didn't need. Especially not as partner. He was too nice. He was too helpful. He was...too much. And that fucking cologne. Why did he have to wear the same damn cologne that triggered memories of her father? She'd verified—it *was* Versace. It was *Blue Jeans*. She'd sprayed the familiar odour in a mist through her tiny bathroom from the bottle she'd found in her father's apartment. Why the fuck did this too-good, too-smart, hot young rookie have to smell like her father? Hell. Why was he so smart? Why was he so *easy* to work with? Why was he so...good to look at.

A bubble of rage broiled in her belly. No. She didn't want these thoughts.

She took a deep breath. Sutton. She sighed. Sutton was no help. He was pushing her to her limits with his fucking *belief* in her Mahoney instincts. If he was so right, then why hadn't she solved the case yet? So what, they were only two bodies in, the second one a fresh file. So what, the clues were cryptic? So what, there wasn't an ounce of physical evidence left behind that didn't belong to the victims? Not a drop of saliva, a tiny strand of hair, even a partial print. Nothing.

If her instincts were so strong, then why hadn't she solved this?

Because. You need more. More clues. More info. Some sort of trace of who this killer is.

She knew it. But she didn't want to believe it. The worst cases her father had solved had left him with a stack of several bodies before a clear break came through. She knew that.

Yet something in her pounded her with unrealistic expectations that she would somehow solve something so intricate with only two bodies on the stack.

Stella clenched her fists and stomped her boots against the path. Sweat drizzled down her back. Heat flushed her arms and legs despite the chill air.

Two bodies. Broiled and hung.

Right now, she was on fire. Heat blazing through her, stomping her way down a dark path. To where? She didn't know. She had to find a way to cool the fuck down. Her mind whirled. She couldn't see straight.

She came to the Centre Street bridge. She passed by the intricately carved statues at the start of the bridge. Her heels clicked along the pathway. She walked to the middle and stopped. The Bow River trickled beneath her, glimmering under the glow of the moon. Geese honked their warnings to each other, huddled on the rocky bank.

She took a long, deep breath. The air stung her throat and chilled her lungs. She exhaled slowly. The tall buildings of downtown lined up in a row on the left side of the river, forming a landscape of twinkling glass architecture. Even on the wrong side of downtown this city was pretty. She loved it. She understood why her father stayed, even when her mother yanked her away. She couldn't blame her mom, really. The warmth of the sunny coast with soft sand beaches had been a lovely place to grow up. The restlessness that surfaced within Stella after the move wasn't her mother's doing. Nor could either of them have predicted it. There was something dark within her. Something that stirred when she was moved away from her father. She understood. She knew her father believed his own darkness was bad for her. But she had her own darkness within. It was there. With or without him. It pulsed and morphed. It grew within her. It pulled her back here, to the place her father loved. To the place that knew him better than she did. Here, now, on her own journey, in this place, she knew she was at home.

She had to figure out how to move forward, before she spiralled out of control—if she hadn't already.

Chapter 47

Satanic Pull

Stella stared at the plastic case in her trembling hand. The evil eyes of the goat-like creature bored into her soul. A strange vibe rushed into her pores.

It had been a long day. Two bodies into this gruesome case and she needed to sleep. Even a few hours in a deep, peaceful rest would revive her. Give her a fresh wave to ride for the day.

She'd come home, intending to curl up in her bed, rest her head on pillows, slip a set of earphones on, and push play on her portable CD player. Heavy metal had always calmed her. Ever since the first time she'd listened to a metal track, the day she found out her father was dead.

She'd stared at her mother, saying nothing. When her body jolted back to life, she'd run out of the house, down the beach, and along the line of rundown shops dotting the boardwalk. She found herself perusing rows upon rows of used albums, polished and tagged, in Sam's Swap Shop. With only a few dollars in her pocket, she'd walked away with a cassette in a cracked case dripping in dramatic blood-red letters—*Skid Row.*

Back home, after convincing her mother to leave her in peace to rest, she'd curled up under the covers in her bed, slipped the tape into her Walkman, and pressed play. Something about the entire thing pulled her into a peaceful state. The rough, guttural guitar riffs. The pumping percussion. The raw edge to it all. The voice. Sonorous yet edgy. A power metal angel. The sound seeping from her headphones soothed her to sleep. *Piece of Me* quickly became her favourite track to fall asleep to.

Ten years later, she still had to put on a heavy metal album every night.

She'd intended to follow the routine tonight, seeking to get a few hours of much-needed rest.

As soon as she'd walked into the door of her apartment, something pulled her against her will across the room. Next thing she knew, she was standing here holding the *Devil's Track.*

Ever since she'd listened to it after her visit with the slimeball Hot Wax clerk and the drugged-out Cletus, the deep chanting had been humming in the back of her mind. She'd been too afraid to play it again. Now, she couldn't resist. It had a pull on her. She had to hear it.

She slowly opened the case and slid the CD into the player.

Bells tolled. Deep chanting wove through the room. Dark voices wove into her pores and seethed through her veins. Vibrations shook her being. She stood frozen, eyes wide open, in a trance.

Words slipped from her mouth in whispers, "Leviathan. Baphomet. Samael Lilith."

Chapter 48

Showdown

*B*ang. *Bang.* A sharp knock on the front door jolted Stella. She jumped, splashing liquid over her arm. She looked down at the glass in her hand, half full of bourbon. In her other hand, she held her hunting knife in a white-knuckled grip. Her veins ran icy with cold. Her gut tingled with sharp pricks.

What the hell had happened?

She stared at the epicentre of the elaborate collage of serial killers plastered on the wall. Tomlinson, in his pressed sergeant's uniform, sneered back at her. The word *Baphomet* pulsed in her mind like a red neon sign.

When had she poured the bourbon? Why was she holding her knife? Why was she staring at Tomlinson?

Bang. Bang. Another knock on the door. *Dammit.*

Bang. Bang. "Stella. Are you there?"

Sutton. She'd know that patronizing voice anywhere.

Double dammit.

"Please. If you are there, I need to talk to you," Sutton said from the other side of the door. "I need to know you're OK, Stella. *Detective Mahoney,*" Sutton's voice pleaded like she'd never heard before.

Bloody Hell. He even called her Detective Mahoney.

She shuffled over to the coffee table, set down the glass of bourbon and the hunting knife. She made her way to the door, wiping the sticky alcohol off her arm with the bottom of her wrinkled t-shirt. She pulled her hair back into a loose ponytail and answered the door.

"Stella." Sutton scanned her, head to toe. "Are you okay? You didn't show up all day. I called. Many times." He pushed past her and made his way into the main room. He looked around. "What the fuck?"

She slammed the door. "You can't just barge in here. This is my apartment." She walked into the main room.

Sutton looked around, seeking the source of the strange dark voice. "What the…" He walked over to the CD player. "What the *hell* are you listening to? This is even worse than your death metal."

"I *don't* listen to death metal. And what's so bad about death metal, anyways?" She walked over to the coffee table and retrieved her bourbon. She took a big swig.

Sutton found the CD controls and stopped the devilish trance. He saw the album cover on the CD player and picked it up. He walked over to her. "This is the album you found, from the symbol on the bodies, isn't it?" He looked at her.

"Yeah. So?" she said, dipping her lips deep into the golden liquid.

"Why are you listening to this?" Sutton asked. Real concern washed over his face. Had she ever seen him concerned for her before?

"Research," she said.

"You were supposed to be focusing on leads. Besides…" he paused, "It's creepy as shit. There's something not right about that. It's like it reaches into you. Are you sure you're okay?"

She'd never said she was okay. But of course she was. She didn't need him here.

He reached down and put the album on the table. He halted, staring at the knife.

Fuck. She should have put it in her bedroom.

"What the hell, Stella?" He straightened and stared at her. "Why do you have what looks like a hunting knife on your coffee table?"

She shrugged, pulling at the scarf around her neck, holding the glass of bourbon into her chest.

"You need to talk to me. Now," he said. "Your theory is right. We need you. You have to come in and finish off this case." He paused. "Tell me you're okay."

She sighed. "Yeah. I'm fine. Seriously." She rolled her eyes. "Fine, I'll come in."

"What have you been doing in here?" He eyeballed the glass of bourbon.

She plunked the glass onto the coffee table. "Oh for fuck's sake. I haven't been here drinking all day." Had she? "I just had a couple bourbons. Take the edge off." Is that what her father used to say? "It's no big deal. Seriously. I was just reviewing everything. On the case. Looking for a fresh perspective." Tomlinson's face flashed through her mind. Or, reviewing the details of the case I'm secretly working on. The one in which a killer dies.

Sutton paused, contemplating her explanation. "Really?"

"Yeah. Really." Did he buy it?

He looked around the room. "That's quite the collection you have." He nodded at the racks of CDs. He turned, seeing the rows of LPs. "Wow." He walked over to it.

"They were my dad's." Why was she sharing anything with him? She needed to get him out of here. Now.

He walked over to the rows upon rows of LPs, scanning the titles. "Yeah. He did love his blues. And his old rock. I didn't realize how extensive his collection was."

She walked up behind him.

He turned. "Listen…" He stopped. He'd spotted the wall. The wall of murder. How could he have missed it? It was gruesome. Looming. It seemed to eat up the entire apartment. "What the…" He walked over to the murder wall. He stood, mouth open, taking in the series of collages recapturing the series of dead bodies left by the sickest people to walk the earth.

"It's research." She shot over to the coffee table, grabbed the glass and slammed back the bourbon. She set the glass down with a loud clink, then walked up behind Sutton.

He continued to look at the murder wall. "I don't even know what to say. This is crazy. Why are you looking into all these cases? These are all closed, or cold."

"Research. I told you." She swallowed. "Learning from the past. These cases were the most serious in the country."

Sutton didn't speak. He just stood, looking at the wall.

What the fuck was she going to do? She had to distract him. Before he…

"Fuck me," Sutton whispered.

He saw it.

"Stella. Tell me this isn't the last case your father worked on."

He knew it was. There was no other human vampire that had glammed himself up like that. He'd been one of a kind.

She gulped.

He turned, looking down at her. "Stella. That knife. It looks like the one your father had. On that last case." He gritted his teeth, trying to find his words. "Don't tell me you are stewing over what happened. Don't tell me you have some sort of plan to do something with all that anger and hurt that is so obviously inside of you." His blue eyes pierced into her.

A series of images flashed through her mind.

Her hunting knife. In her hand. Sliding into the man that killed her father. Hot blood seeping over her fingers, from the sliced-open flesh.

"Stella. Are you listening to me?" Sutton's voice forced its way into her thoughts.

She stared at him. "No. Of course not."

He looked back at the murder collage. He found the centre set of photos. "This *is* the killer in the last case your father worked on." He slid his gaze along the wall. "Tomlinson," he whispered. He scanned the photos. He spun. He faced her. "You've got it out for Tomlinson."

"He *sabotaged* that investigation," she spat out. "My dad..." she sputtered as hot tears sprung down her face. "He had no choice. Tomlinson fucked up the whole thing." She shook her head. Shaking, she fell to her knees. She buried her face in the scarf clinging to her neck. Her hot tears soaked the material.

Sutton knelt down in front of her, put his hands on her shoulders, and spoke softly. "You're right. Tomlinson did conduct a shady investigation. Hell. He didn't conduct an investigation at all."

Stella sniffed. Thick tears mixed with mucous clogged her throat. She sat back onto the rug, rubbing her eyes with her scarf. "I know. It was *his* fault. Fucking dick of a sergeant."

Sutton chuckled. "OK. I can't argue with that. But it wasn't Tomlinson's fault your father died."

"Yeah, it was." She sniffed loudly.

"No. It wasn't." He stared at her.

She met his gaze.

"Your father had a strong instinct. Your father respected the rules. The protocol. Your father saw a lot of bodies. Young people. It stuck with him." He paused, then sighed. "Your father *chose* to go against the lead of the investigation. Stella, he *chose* to go after that killer. He *chose* to take matters into his own hands. To go off the books. To go rogue. He knew what he was doing. No one forced him. He could have found a way to work with the system."

Stella's lower lip quivered. Her tears halted. "But he didn't *want* to. He wanted to stop the killer. Before any more girls died."

"Yes. He did." Sutton sat down across from her.

Stella took a deep breath and wiped her face with her scarf.

She looked at Sutton. "So now what?"

"You stop thinking about Tomlinson. You stop playing with that knife. You finish off this case." He smiled. He unlatched the rabbit foot from his belt and dangled it in front of her face. "You tap into that Mahoney instinct you have, and you find the killer who's branding victims and burning them."

The images invading her mind suddenly vanished into thin air. All she could think about was the woman in the black cloak.

Chapter 49

Pulsing Eye

Lightning flashed the All-Seeing Eye to life. It flickered on, off, then on again, staring Viviana down. She cowered into the corner, bringing her knees to her chest, pulling the sides of her cloak around her. What had she done?

A voice boomed through her mind, vibrating her very core, questioning her intentions. There were no clear words, only vibrations, like thoughts, whirling through her mind.

Where was she? Was this real?

She stared at the eye shimmering above her. Its dark inner core blinked with the flashes of light.

It looked like the eye her father had told her of. The eye that watched everything. The eye that could see the good and the bad within every seed. Within every human.

Yet, it didn't *feel* like the same eye. It hovered over her. Wrong. Off kilter. Like her sister.

This couldn't be the same eye.

The deep vibrations of the pseudo voice buzzed into a clear set of words.

"What are you seeking?"

The same words her father used to ask her, every time she asked him for guidance. Every time she asked him to read to her from the purple book etched in gold. Every time confusion wracked her as she tried to understand the principles of spiritual enlightenment.

She looked up at the flashing eye now. Whether it was real or not, whether it was the same eye or not, she had to answer it.

She swallowed, parted her lips, and forced the words out. "I am seeking truth." She pushed herself onto her feet, crouching on the floor. "I am seeking the light."

She stood up, her cloak falling around her. Her fire-red hair fell behind her head as she looked up at the blinking eye. "I am seeking spiritual enlightenment."

The eye flashed. It vanished. The lightning stopped. The room dimmed.

Was this real?

Her mind whirled. She looked around the room. A small flame burned bright in the corner across the space. She walked toward it. The rough patch of flesh branded into her arm itched. The flame called to her. She walked closer. The itch morphed into a slight burn. The flame flickered. It pulled her in. She kept walking, toward the heat, the fire, the flame. The slight burn heightened to a searing pain. She clutched her arm. She shook her head. *No. It wasn't real.* No one was burning her now. She pulled back her cloak and inspected her skin. No burning. No heat. No fire.

Only the distorted contours of ruined flesh, a forever reminder of the day her sister saved her from the burning ruins of their childhood home. The little house on the edge of the forest. A brand, burned into her flesh, to remind her every day that they ran from the house while their parents burned.

The flame in the corner of the room flickered. She walked up to it, bent over, and blew it out. A sliver of smoke snaked its way into her nostrils, weaving the smell of ashes into her nose.

She ran her fingers over her distorted flesh, feeling the rough contours, the remnants of the past. The itch was gone. It no longer burned. It wasn't real. No one was burning her now.

She'd answered the All-Seeing Eye. She'd faced the flame. What was left?

Damaris' dark eyes crept through her mind. Damaris. The dominant woman.

Something pulsed within Viviana. When she was outside of the grasp of the off-kilter replica of their childhood home, out of reach of Damaris' commands, she could picture herself resisting the demands of both of them. As soon as she re-entered their grasp, she followed their lead.

She was at a loss of what to do.

She wanted to plunge herself deep into the light aura of the path she had sought before Damaris had steered them down a series of sacrifices. Could she get back to the split in the road before it all began?

She took a deep breath, looked around, and realized where she was. In the basement. Had she wandered down here seeking truth without even realizing it?

The basement was still. Nothing stirred. She needed to face Damaris. Doubt churned in her stomach, telling her she didn't know what she was truly up against.

Witch/Hunt

Chapter 50

Satanic Beast

A silver glow from the full moon filtered through the windows of the little house on the edge of the forest. Orange-red flames danced from the wicks of a ring of candles on the small wooden table, blending yellow-orange streaks into the silver hue. It gave the room a warm feeling.

Nothing inside of Viviana was warm. As the house took its hold upon her, she froze in its icy grasp. In sync, the demon within Damaris seared hot pokers through her eyes and her words.

Viviana teetered between her little purple-and-gold book and the demands of her sister. One of them led to spiritual enlightenment. Did she want that if it meant she'd be alone? The other led somewhere unknown, down a path of murder. Would it be dark? Or would it be salvaged by the love of the open arms of the only family she had left?

She sat on the edge of the couch, staring into the circle of mini flames. An itch crawled over her rough patch of skin, migrating over her entire arm. Her fingers twitched, wanting to respond. She willed them not to.

A set of twisted horns sat on the table, the orange hue of the small flames dancing over the smooth charcoal-tainted bone. Remnants of a rare beast, beautiful and strong, now detached and vacant. A piece of a carcass, torn from the head of the magnificent beast they had birthed from. Would she, herself, be a carcass, a skeleton of what she could be?

Viviana stared at the horns. Images of the man she'd purchased them from shimmered through her thoughts. *Torrence.* A beastly bulk of a man. His stare violated every part of her the minute she'd entered his shop full of dead animal heads. Some thought of them as trophies. She could only think of them as empty carcasses.

Her sister had insisted they have the twisted horns of Baphomet. The Goat of Mendes. The ultimate symbol of evil. The one that Damaris seemed to worship. The perfect prop for the final sacrifice in the cycle. Viviana couldn't argue with her. She was too terrified to disobey.

She could still feel the words slipping from her lips as she gave her full name to the grisly Torrence. Her real name. Her family name. Why had she done it? It was as though she had lost control over her actions. She knew something deep within her was desperate for someone to stop the next kill.

Viviana never thought it would go this far. She didn't think they would *kill* anybody. As the cycle of purge continued, the ball in the pit of her belly grew. The All-Seeing Eye invaded her thoughts every moment. It pulsed in her mind, staring her down, looking into her soul.

"Viv. You up there?" Damaris called from the basement.

Viviana sat in silence. A bottle of cacao wine sat, nearly empty, next to the horns. How much had Damaris had today? Was the hallucinogenic cocktail responsible for the things her sister claimed she saw? *No.* Viviana shook her head. Damaris had spoken of things Viviana couldn't see far before she started drinking the wine. It may have enhanced the visions, pushed her over the edge. But it wasn't the source of the demon inside of her.

"Viv," Damaris' voice seethed.

"Yeah. I'm coming."

"Hurry. We need to start," Damaris called.

Which version of Damaris would be down there in the basement waiting for her?

With every sacrifice, the demon within Damaris seemed to grow. It seemed to *feed* upon the sacrifices, devouring each sacrifice of human life like it was a satisfying meal. The demon took over Damaris, one sacrifice at a time. Changing her. Possessing her.

Viviana grabbed the scarlet-stained glass set next to the wine, filled it halfway, and chugged it back. The spice and heat hit her throat. She swallowed it down, hoping it would give just enough of what she saw in Damaris to help her get through this night.

What would happen next time? *Stop it.* She couldn't think about that now. She had to get through this night.

She tilted the bottle, emptying the last drops into the glass. She shot it back, set the glass down, and picked up the horns. Running her fingers along the bone, she wondered what role this piece of a beast would play in the evening's ceremony.

"Viviana. It's time," Damaris' voice, soaked in fury and evil, called up the stairs.

Viviana stood and carried the horns to the stairs. She descended, walking toward the ceremony. Walking toward the command of her demonic leader.

Chapter 51

Demonic Loyalty

The basement glowed with bright reds and oranges, the flames from a ring of tall candles reaching hot fingers over the walls and the ceiling. Heat swelled through the claustrophobic space. The concrete wall morphed into the walls of her childhood bedroom, engulfed in flames, closing in on her, ready to take her. For a moment, Viviana forgot where she was. The walls of the basement snapped her back to reality.

Viviana looked across the room. A chill ran through her.

Damaris stood facing the circle, her long, dark cloak hanging around her tall frame, making her look unearthly.

Damaris turned. Her raven locks fell around her shoulders, her hood pulled halfway over her head. Sweat glistened over her reddened skin. Her eyes were no longer hers. A red glow bled over the rich, dark colour. A yellow tinge tainted the white. Was it the glow from the candles? Or was it something else? How long did the cacao wine take to spill its effects into a human brain? Viviana couldn't tell. Her gut told her to trust what she saw.

Damaris walked toward her, reaching out her hands. The house clawed its icy hand down Viviana's insides, groping the pit of her belly. She raised the horns toward Damaris. Damaris took them, holding her stare.

Something jolted inside Viviana. The icy hand squeezed harder.

Muffled cries came from behind Damaris. Viviana refused to let her gaze find the inside of the sacrificial circle. She knew who was in there. She didn't want to see it. To make it real.

Damaris spoke in a smooth, deep voice, "It is time. For the purge of perfection."

Viviana swallowed. What was perfection? The All-Seeing Eye hovered in her mind, a single, dark eye, looking into her. Beckoning her to follow its gaze.

"Come," Damaris said. She turned and walked toward the candles.

Viviana followed. The muffled cries intensified. The flames soaked the air with heat. The room swelled. The concrete walls took a deep breath, swelling with the heat, pulling Viviana from all sides. Ice crusted over the pit of her gut, sliding icicle fingers around her instincts, numbing them.

As she reached the circle, the cries seared her ears. The source of the cries came into view. This time, there were two. *Two.* Damaris insisted that for the sacrifice to be perfect, it must reflect the events it was intended to imitate. The events it was intended to avenge. It had to create the fantasy growing in Damaris' mind to perfection. The fantasy that seemed to be driving her mad. From the outside looking in, Viviana wished she could see this dark dream that morphed in her sister's mind.

The cries from the centre of the sacrificial circle poked the pits of her ears until she could no longer avoid the source. Until she could no longer avoid looking at the people, the humans, who uttered these desperate pleas in their weakened states. Two people hung in the centre of the ring of candles. Sweat poured down their faces, coating their bare chests with a slick sheet, slithering down their exposed legs. Blood trickled over their arms—tied above their heads—from the open flesh of their wrists sawed by tight binds. Their mouths gagged, their cries simmered to meek muffles. Their fear present in their wide, wild eyes.

One man and one woman. To represent the pair that led the purge of their parents.

Viviana's brain wrenched. She desperately wanted to understand this. To comprehend how these two people were symbols of the hunters who burned their mother and father. What did Damaris see? Was her view of the world so distorted that she actually saw the hunters from that night?

Viviana wanted to see what Damaris saw. She wanted to follow her sister, to carry on the ways of the coven, to do what her family needed from her. To be loyal.

"It is time." Damaris held up the horns, facing them toward the victims. "It is time you answer for the people you purged. It is time for *you* to be purged." Damaris lowered the horns and set them on the floor, facing the circle. She picked up a candle and walked toward the man. The man squirmed, screamed, and fought. His movements were minimized by the binds holding him. His screams were muted by the gag choking him.

Damaris' lips stretched into a sadistic grin.

Viviana's stomach roiled. Icy bile clawed up her throat.

Damaris held the flame to the man's chest. The sweat coating his skin sizzled, evaporating in puffs of steam. The heat reddened his flesh until a foul odour of cooked meat wafted through the air.

Viviana gagged. She closed her eyes and searched for the image of her natural sanctuary. A flash of a moss-covered rock. A flicker of a trickling stream. The stench of hot raw meat. The images wouldn't materialize. The energy of her natural sanctuary was too far from the rotten aura of this sacrificial basement. The house erected a cold ice wall between them and the forest.

"Viviana. Open your eyes," a deep voice invaded the space between her and her sister.

Hot, sour breath hit Viviana's face. She opened her eyes. Damaris stood, her face a mere inch away.

"It is your time to show your loyalty to your coven. To your family," Damaris said. "Produce your weapon for sacrifice."

The house descended upon her, coating Viviana with a sheet of ice. It had her. Damaris had her. The eyes of a demon, staring at her now, red shimmers in a yellowing hue, the sign that her sister was no longer present. Had Satan himself descended upon them? Had Damaris morphed into a being with no traces of good?

Viviana looked at her sister's gloved hands. She slipped her own shaking hand into the folds of her cloak and pulled out her knife. She held it up. The red flames shot glimmers off the crystal amulet. Her heart pattered. The blade had shed no blood except her own, for her own sacrifices, for the justified purpose of seeking true spiritual enlightenment. To show loyalty to her father and the purple-and-gold book he'd taught her from. To show loyalty to the All-Seeing Eye.

"You must pierce him. Through his heart," Damaris' deep demon voice commanded.

The blade shook in Viviana's hands. She hoped Dami was too far gone to notice they were bare. Orange light shot off the blade in all directions.

Damaris leaned her face into Viviana's. Hot puffs of foul breath shot from Damaris' nostrils. Her eyes narrowed into slits of yellow. "You must pierce him. You must purge his Satanic blood. Now. It is your calling. You must prove your loyalty to your coven. To your family. To *me*." The dark words pierced Viviana through her heart, her gut, and her soul.

She turned to the man. She shuffled up to him. She pointed her knife to his chest, poking the tip into his broiled skin. A droplet of blood burst from the hole, pierced by the tip of the blade, and trickled down his sweat-coated body. His chest heaved.

She looked into his eyes.

"The time is now. Show your loyalty," Damaris screeched.

The All-Seeing Eye flashed across the room. Viviana's hands trembled, cutting jagged slices into the man's chest.

"Show your loyalty or forever be *banished*," Damaris yelled.

The flames flickered madly. Flashes of red shot through the room.

"Now. Purge. *Now*," Damaris screamed.

Viviana closed her eyes, raised the knife over her head, and plunged it straight into the man. Flesh ripped. Hot blood gushed over her hands.

Her eyes sprang open. She jolted back, her blood-soaked hands slipping from the knife. The blade stuck in the man's heart. Blood trickled over the daisy protectors engraved in the ivory blade, coating their protection with evil intentions.

He gasped, desperately drawing in air.

The woman cried. Tears poured down her face. Thick liquid seeped from her nostrils.

Damaris licked her lips, staring at the knife, the blood, the purge in progress.

The All-Seeing Eye pulsed over Viviana. Her vision blurred. The flames licked at her. The flesh on her arm seared with heat. She fell to her knees, crumpling into her cloak.

Damaris pulled the knife from the man's chest. Blood sprayed over the blade. She knelt and handed the knife to Viviana, presenting it with both open palms.

Viviana took it in her bloody, trembling hands. She stared at the red-streaked blade.

Damaris spoke as she stroked Viviana's arm. "You have shown your loyalty. The clan opens its arms to you. Forever."

Damaris stood and walked over to the gasping man.

Why was he still breathing? Why couldn't he slip away before Damaris could torture him further?

Viviana looked up. The blood seeping from the gash in his chest taunted her. How long would it take him to die?

Damaris picked up a candle and held it up to the open wound. The smell of burnt copper took over the room. Viviana looked into the man's eyes. The hopelessness there seized her heart. He spoke to her with his eyes, pleading for death, seeking relief. All hope lost. All desire to live vanished. A desperate calling to end the pain. The only thing that mattered now.

The room spun around Viviana. She stared at the crystal amulet, seeking guidance. Her desperation mirrored the man's. She needed release from the shards of ice piercing her insides. From the flames of pain poking her flesh. Had her path been chosen?

Chapter 52

Double Purge

The sun had departed for the evening. The dark sky hung over the horizon. Stella mourned the abandoned boxes of Captain Chow's takeout growing cold on the countertop in her cluttered kitchen. Her heart sank the moment her murder phone had buzzed. She wanted another body. It was the only way to get more information. It was the only way to catch this killer. But why couldn't the body have been left after she'd gorged on Peking duck and Hot Palace chicken?

She wolfed down the dry granola bar she'd grabbed from the one box of anything edible in her kitchen cupboards. How could people live on nuts and seeds?

She washed the dry clumps down with a swig of cold coffee as she pulled her Sunfire into a spot next to Sutton's glossy blue Chevy. A massive archway declared the entrance to the *Union Cemetery,* the city's oldest home for the dead. She stepped out of the car and slid on her leather coat. The tall trees hovered over her like dark, ghostly figures. The stars quivered in their midnight backdrop.

Stella scanned the familiar lineup of vehicles. Sutton. Blackwood. CST. Parker. His cherry-red Corvette annoyed her. He'd declined a ride. Said he was safer driving himself. *Fucking clown.*

She walked toward bright flashes of light coming from within the depths of the cemetery. Muffled voices stretched through the silence. A cemetery. At night. With a full moon. She shuddered. Even she had to admit this whole thing was creepy.

She pulled her coat around her chest and walked toward the light and the noise.

Two bodies hung from the dark night sky, looming over them from a perch. Stella froze. Her breath caught in her throat. A twisted horn from the head of a beast impaled each body, piercing clean through the flesh and bone from back to front, then shooting into the dark sky.

"Baphomet," the whisper slipped from Stella's lips.

Two stakes rooted into the ground, at least eight feet tall, speared into the blanket of stars overhead. Flakes of charred wood fluttered from the spears, finding their way to rest on the ground.

The skin of the bodies was more than broiled. This time, it had been charred, well done. Overcooked. No reddish-pink contours of flesh. Instead, the darkened skin clung to bones in crispy flakes, barely concealing fresh meat underneath.

"Stella. Good hustle." Sutton startled her.

She hadn't even realized she'd closed the gap between her and the team. She'd been in a trance, staring up at the charred bodies as her feet transported her across the cemetery.

"It's *Mahoney,*" she hissed.

His eyes widened in surprise. "Fine. Mahoney." His lips pulled into a thin line. "Good hustle. It's getting worse. I need your full attention. Can you do that? Focus. On the scene."

"Yeah." She swallowed. Had her agitation over the way he addressed her grown into full anger?

"Good. Parker's over there with Blackwood. Get caught up. Work *with* him," Sutton said.

"Yeah." She walked toward Parker and Blackwood. Toward the bodies. The adrenaline-infused energy shooting through her morphed into a cold chill. Sweat trickled down her back. Heat swelled underneath her leather coat. Cold washed through her gut.

Blackwood caught her eye as she approached. "Mahoney. I'll give you a quick recap."

Parker nodded.

"Thanks," Stella said as she sidled in next to Blackwood.

"I'm sure you've noticed the state of the skin and the wood. Charred beyond what we saw on the first two victims. This time, two victims, each impaled with some sort of animal horn. We were just taking a look at the abdomen." Blackwood lifted the familiar dark cloth with a gloved hand. "As you can see, the stomach of the victim was not burnt like the rest of the skin. It was branded with the same symbol. Appears only the heat from the hot iron hit the skin. Nothing further. It's the same on the other body."

"Baphomet," Stella said.

"What?" Parker asked.

"Baphomet. The beast in the centre of the pentagram. Baphomet. The Goat of Mendes. The horns belong to a goat."

"Humdinger." Blackwood looked at Stella. "You're getting deep into this witchcraft thing."

Stella's brain buzzed. Her gut tingled. "Jake gave me a lot of reading material. Whoever did this isn't tagging the victims as witches. The killer is the witch."

"What?" Parker asked.

Was he on repeat? Like a parrot. "This is a tribute to the beast in the centre of the symbol. Our killer worships Baphomet. Our killer is a witch. The evil kind. And they're progressing." Stella clenched her jaw.

"Progressing?" Parker asked.

"The scenes are getting more elaborate. The killer is escalating. Elevating his creations as he, or she, gains experience," Blackwood said.

"This is a purge," Stella said.

"Ridding the world of evil." Parker rubbed the back of his neck.

"Yeah. For some reason, this killer thinks these victims are evil. Killing them off is purging them from the world," Stella said.

Parker's eyes lit up. "Hey, idea."

Oh fuck. What brilliant thought did Clown Boy have now? "Yeah?"

"Who would a witch see as evil?" Parker said.

Good point. "A witch hunter."

"Precisely. What if these victims are witch hunters, through the eyes of the killer? The witch, or killer, deems them as evil because they hunt his kind." Parker smiled.

Damn. Not bad. "You might be on to something," Stella said.

"Really?"

"Yeah. Really." Stella swallowed back the tinge of admiration crawling up her throat. "Ministers. Religious leaders. Tagged as evil. Someone could be pissed off at these righteous leaders for their message of purging evil. Or purging the hypocritical leaders hiding booze-and-drug addictions. Or...if the killer is a witch, or at least thinks they are, they could see religious icons as the enemy." Stella crossed her arms and stared at the bodies.

"I'm on board with your theory." Parker nodded.

Dammit. He was becoming far too likeable. "Well, that makes one." Stella glanced over at Sutton, deep in conversation with a techie.

"Let's get this scene processed. Be meticulous. Find something to turn your theory into truth." Blackwood grabbed her pack and went to work.

Chapter 53

Taxidermy

The door had been painted black in some previous decade. Now it was a series of crumbling wooden panels, barely holding together. The sign over the door declared it led to Torrence's Trophy Emporium.

An icy breeze clawed across Stella's face. She shivered as she pulled her long leather coat tighter around her chest.

"Fall is in the air," Parker said.

"Summer doesn't last long here," Stella said. She looked at the door. "Ready?"

"I'm right creeped out and we haven't even gone in yet," Parker said.

Stella rolled her eyes. "C'mon. Let's meet Torrence." She adjusted her Glock in her belt, then turned the knob.

A barrage of dead beasts assaulted them. Row upon row of heads lined every wall. There wasn't a square inch of space left. The lower rows housed deer, foxes, and coyotes. As the rows climbed, so did the size and presence of the animals displayed. Massive antlers sprouted from stags, and wild cats bore teeth. The highest row displayed the most savage beasts. Captured, killed, decapitated, and made into another trinket in a grisly collection. At the top in the very centre, a monstrous grizzly head was mounted. Its savage eyes stared them down, questioning its fate. Rough black fur, polished and groomed, removed all remnants of the life it had led in the wild.

"Geez." Parker whistled. "Not sure I want to meet this Torrence."

"The sooner we do, the sooner we can get out of here." Stella shuddered under the watching eyes of dead animals.

The head of the savage goat caught her eye. Its eyes narrowed into an evil stare. The eyes. Just like the ones on the goat burned into the flesh of each of the victims. Its twisted horns shot from its head.

"Look." Stella pointed at the goat staring her down.

"Jeez. That's it," Parker said.

Shuffling from behind the wall grabbed their attention. A man walked through a doorway at the far-left end of the main trophy wall. His hair, long and scraggly, hung around his broad shoulders. He wore a beaver-fur hat and a red-checkered hunting jacket. His boots clomped heavily against the creaky wooden floor.

"Can I help you folks?" the man asked. The bushy handlebars of his thick moustache twitched over his rough, porous skin.

"Torrence Sims?" Stella asked the man.

"Who's asking?" the hunting man challenged.

Stella flashed her badge. "Detective Mahoney." She nodded at Parker. "My partner, Detective Parker."

The man complied. "Fine. Yeah. I'm Torrence. What right do you have to barge onto my property?" Torrence scowled.

Stella eyeballed the large hunting rifle leaning against the wall in the corner, behind Torrence.

Parker stepped in. "Mr. Sims. We just want to ask you a couple of questions. About your...products." Parker looked up at the trophy wall.

Torrence stepped closer, leaning over a thin wooden counter separating him from them. "I got all the right permits. For the stuffing and selling. And for the *kills.*" Torrence leaned farther over the counter. His sadistic smile pulled his bushy handlebars apart.

"I'm sure you do," Parker said. He stepped closer to the counter. "We're trying to locate a pair of horns. Just like the ones on that goat head." Parker pointed up at the wall.

Torrence leaned his six-foot-four frame over the counter. "That one's a prize. The Markhor. Don't see a magnificent animal like that too often. And not around here." He slapped the counter. "Best time to get a set of those horns is when the beast is about five or six years old. Perfect time for the kill. The horns are in tiptop shape. Freshly grown, fully mature. Not battered by activities of the wild. The need to survive." Torrence's dark eyes took on a tint of evil.

Who is this guy? Stella didn't like it. She didn't like the vibe he gave off. She didn't like his savage odour. "You ever kill one?" She stepped toward the counter and stared Torrence in the eye.

"Yeah. Sure. I've killed everything a man can kill. Within the limits of the law, of course." He smirked.

Stella nearly choked on the wave of testosterone seeping from Torrence. She held his gaze. "You ever sell a set of those horns?"

"Now, sweetie, you listen here. I rarely take the weapons off a magnificent beast. Even after it's dead." He leaned toward Stella. "I keep them intact. I only sell the full trophy."

Stella gagged back a burst of bile. This guy was too much. "It's Detective Mahoney." She cleared her throat. "So, you only sell the whole head?"

"Yeah, sweetie. The whole head. The trophy. Cleaned and groomed." Torrence sneered.

"It's *Detective Mahoney*," Stella spat the words out.

Parker nudged her. "Mr. Sims. Would you have sales records for any purchases of the Markhor trophy?"

Torrence looked at Parker and smiled. "You get it, boy. It's a trophy." He slapped his palms on the wooden counter. "As for sales records, well, now, I'm not sure I have to share that kind of information."

Stella got half a word out before Parker nudged her again.

Parker slipped his hand back into his corduroy jacket pocket and retrieved the required warrant. "Of course, Mr. Sims. The records of your clients are your business. Unfortunately, a set of horns belonging to this rare animal have been found at a crime scene. Due to the circumstances around the scene, we require the names of anyone who has purchased a Markhor trophy from you." Parker set the paper on the counter.

"How do you know whoever left these horns got them from me?" Torrence's eyes grew wild.

Parker jumped in. "Your collection is rather rare. Impressive." Parker paused.

Torrence relaxed his shoulders and his face. "Yeah. It is."

"You are the only taxidermist in the area who sells such a rare collection. Including this magnificent beast." Parker looked back up at the goat head on the wall.

Torrence pondered the situation. His mouth twisted, pulling the bushy handlebars along with it.

Stella slapped her hand on the search warrant. "Do you not see this? It's a search warrant. You have no choice." Her hand slid underneath her leather jacket, finding her Glock.

Torrence scowled and stretched to full height. "Listen, *sweetie*. I don't care what it is. This is *my* property. You can't just barge in here and tell me what to do." He shot a glance out of the corner of his eye at the hunting rifle in the corner.

Parker jumped in, "Stop." He cleared his throat. He shot Stella a warning look. He turned and faced Torrence. "Listen, Mr. Sims. All we need is a copy of the sales records. Only for the Markhor. We'll be out of your hair. Your business will continue as usual," Parker said. "Nobody wants any trouble, now do we?" He glanced from Torrence to Stella, then back at Torrence.

Torrence sighed. "Fine. I don't want any trouble." He eyeballed Stella, smirked, then turned and walked down the counter. "I only had two of those. As you can see, one of them's still here." He pushed the button on a small computer. It hummed to life. He typed on the keyboard. "Other one. Not my usual clientele. Quite a looker." He paused and smirked. "Young woman. Just screaming for it. Real flirtatious, too." He licked his upper lip, then continued typing.

Stella's stomach roiled. *What a sicko.* She stared at him as he scanned the computer screen. Parker stood close to her, looking ready to pounce if she attacked Torrence again. *Clown.* He was really getting under her skin. His too-perfect air was getting too macho for her. Whose investigation did he think this was?

"Here." Torrence motioned them over. He turned the screen so they could see it.

Viviana Celeste.

Stella flipped open her notebook and jotted down the name.

"You remember that woman?" Parker asked.

"Oh yeah. Like I said, she was looking for it," Torrence said, his eyes lit up.

Looking for what? Jackass. Stella calmed her voice. "What did she look like?"

"Oh, long hair. Fire red. Shiny. Beautiful blue eyes. Curves." Torrence cupped his hands and hovered them around his chest. "Knockers to die for. Big enough to really give 'em a good squeeze. Even with hunting hands." He spread his fingers and raised his large, calloused hands. "*Real* fresh. Barely a woman."

Parker chuckled. "You think she was eighteen?"

"Maybe. Not more than twenty," Torrence said.

Better be part of the cop show. Stella forced a smile.

"Go on," Parker said, leaning over the counter, egging on Torrence.

"She was a bit weird. Friendly. But, kind of...distant. Wore a long, dark cloak."

Stella's attention piqued. There it was again, the cloak. Fire-red hair. Blue eyes. Young woman. Same description that drugged out Cletus gave them. This had to be the same woman. Was she the killer?

He shook his head. "She was persistent she needed the horns removed, undamaged."

"Thought you didn't do that." Stella continued scribbling in her notebook.

"Made an exception." Torrence narrowed his eyes.

"Thank you for your time and your co-operation." Parker slid a card onto the counter. "If you think of any more details you want to share, give me a call."

Parker nudged Stella's elbow, pushing her toward the tattered black door.

Stella took a final look at Torrence. He stared back at her with a sickly smile and shot her a wink. Fury broiled in the pit of her belly. She'd love to put Torrence in his place. Too bad she had Super Boy here to manage her. That had to end. Soon.

Chapter 54

Purge Re-Creation

The cold air in the morgue soothed Stella. The dim lighting took her energy down a notch. She walked across the room toward the bright light in the corner where Blackwood stood. The army-green collar of Blackwood's turtleneck clung to her, poking up from her white lab coat. Her hair fanned over her shoulders, the single silver streak shining under the bright light.

Blackwood looked up from her work, large plastic goggles amplifying her eyes. "Detective Mahoney. Here we are again."

"Yeah." Stella nodded.

"Real humdinger. Two in one," Blackwood said.

"Any IDs?" Stella asked.

"Not yet. It appears we have a male and a female. Likely close in age. Late twenties, early thirties." Blackwood slid the goggles down her nose, letting them dangle from the thick black elastic around her neck.

One man. One woman. Were they the same ages as Madeleine and Willard? Stella flipped open her notebook.

"As you know, they're both charred. The burning was much more severe than our first two victims. Identifying them could take a while." Blackwood opened a notebook and flipped the pages. "You ready for some grisly skin facts?"

"Shoot."

"Burning fact one. The burning has escalated from third-degree to fourth-degree. Thus, the charred appearance. Burning fact two. Both victims have heat damage to their internal organs. Conclusion, COD for the woman is burning. She cooked, like the first two victims."

Stella pictured the woman's skin burning, reddening, blistering as she writhed and screamed in pain.

Stella clenched her jaw. "What about the man?"

"Another humdinger. There's a stab wound, just above his heart. Deep enough to cause significant bleeding. If left long enough, he could have bled out. COD for the man is a toss up between bleeding and burning," Blackwood said.

Stella saw the man hanging and helpless, watching a blade pierce into his flesh, his eyes wide with fear. Was the killer aiming for his heart? Had their method of purge changed?

"What about the horns?" Stella asked. "They were pierced right through them."

"They were. Postmortem. The level of bleeding from the wounds and the skin tissue lodged on the horns indicates the victims were dead several hours before the horns pierced the bodies." Blackwood grabbed a fresh pair of latex gloves.

Stella could still see the woman, the horns of a beast savagely piercing through her dead flesh, part of some demented ritual forced upon the dead. The dead animal. And the dead woman.

"I need to show you something." Blackwood snapped the gloves on and walked over to two steel slabs side by side.

Stella followed. An odour of charcoal and copper wafted from the tables. The man and the woman, unrecognizable as human, lay side by side. Stella clenched her jaw and scanned the bodies. The only flesh that was recognizable was the red-pink skin over each abdomen, pulled into distorted contours, branded with the symbol of Satan. The five-pointed stars seemed to spin, pulling her in. The goat eyes stared her down, evil orbs of red flesh.

"I know, it's grisly. It's difficult to clean these two up," Blackwood said.

Stella snapped her gaze from the symbols.

"Burning fact three. Their hands aren't burned. Burning fact four. They have deep cuts in their wrists." Blackwood turned one of the hands over. It appeared to belong to the woman. A dark slit cut into her wrist, the edges rough.

It all came together in Stella's mind in a flash. The man and the woman, both hanging by their wrists, blood trickling down their arms from the binds digging deep slashes into their skin as they writhed in pain and struggled for their freedom. The killer, standing over them, slowly burning their skin, burning away their supposed sins. The hot brand searing their flesh, steaming from the cooked flesh, burning the Satanic symbol into them forever, marking them as evil.

"It's rough. Like they were bound," Stella said.

"That's for you to figure out," Blackwood said. "And of course, the skin around the abdomens suffered less burning. The brands are the same as before."

Same symbol. More severe burning. Bound at the wrists. Were the other two? The stab wound. That was new. Why?

"I found a partial print near the heart on the man," Blackwood said.

"Really?" Stella clenched her jaw.

"Don't get too excited. I've tried lifting it. It might not be enough. I'll get it into processing. The skin is so charred, it's difficult to process anything. Other than this partial print, there's nothing. No fibres. No blood. No fluids."

"Meticulous." Stella said.

"Yeah."

"Why the stab wound? Why the horns?" Stella pondered.

"That's your realm. The why. I'm just here to feed you fun-filled corpse facts." Blackwood made a meek attempt to smile.

The stab. Maybe things escalated. The horns. Those were postmortem. Planned. Another symbol. The moment Stella had seen the two victims hanging, each pierced by a horn, the word *Baphomet* had flashed through her mind. It continued to pulse, thrumming in her brain like a signal that could not be ignored. Those who put Baphomet on a pedestal were those who worshipped Satan. Stella's entire being screamed to her that the killer she was hunting was a witch. A witch gone rogue. If only she could find the physical evidence that would lead her to the witch.

"Look at this." Blackwood flipped open her notebook and pointed at an entry. "Full toxicology scan, for both victims. Same traces of phenolic compounds. Stronger traces of alkaloids. And, traces of PEA. Phenethylamine. Cacao mucilage is the source."

Stella raised an eyebrow and pulled at her chin.

Blackwood lowered her plastic goggles. "As you pointed out, alkaloids are present in cocaine. They come from the cacao plant. Alkaloids are also in the cacao plant, from which cacao mucilage can be extracted."

"Cacao wine." The words slipped involuntarily from Stella's lips. Her brain caught up, flashing images of the words written in the pages of witchcraft she'd been consuming. "Part of a witchcraft ceremony. Made by fermenting cacao."

"That's your realm. I found multiple puncture marks on these two new victims. They were injected with something. If it was this cacao wine, a small amount would have an extreme effect. A tiny shot would be enough for a wild ride. They could have been injected with a small amount, then perhaps forced to drink more. They had much higher traces than the previous victims."

"Drugged. Taken. Tied up. That's why there were no signs of struggle," Stella concluded.

"Again, that's your realm." Blackwood scanned her notebook. "Skin. Stab. Horns. Liquid." She looked up from the book. "That's all I have. I'll keep working. This is one hell of a job."

Stella snapped her notebook shut. "So much evidence, yet no lead to an actual suspect."

"Reminds me of cases I worked with your dad," Blackwood said.

"Really?"

"Yeah. There were a couple of cases in a row; the clues, they were strange and complex. None of them seemed to go together. And then all of a sudden, they would. Your dad, he'd ask his team so many questions, looking at it from every angle, until it clicked." Blackwood smiled.

Until it clicked. Could she do it? Like her dad had? Anxious tendrils pulled at her gut. She rubbed her clenched jawline with her hand.

Blackwood chuckled.

"What?" Stella asked.

"Your dad. He used to do that. Although he'd be rubbing his five-o'clock shadow."

Stella smiled. Maybe she could make it click. Maybe there was enough of her father in her to make it click.

"OK. Keep me posted," Stella said.

"Will do," Blackwood said. "Oh wait. There was one more thing."

Stella turned.

Blackwood walked over to a counter and searched through the pockets in her pack. She escalated her search, opening the pack and rummaging through the contents. "Dammit." She looked at Stella. "I had one more thing—I jotted it down, in my notebook."

"Lost notebook?" Stella asked.

"Yeah. It's a smaller one I always take on scene with me. I always put it in the same pouch in my pack. It's not here. I don't know where it would be. I've been so engrossed in processing these two." She pointed at the charred bodies. "I hadn't even gone through it yet." She paused. Concern washed over her face. "Unless...I dropped it at the scene." She furrowed her dark eyebrows. She twirled the silver strand of hair around her finger. "Double dammit. I have to go look for it." She pulled off the gloves, dropped them in a trash bin, then pulled off her lab coat.

"I'll go with you," Stella said.

"No. We can't let this investigation slow down. I'll get the print processed. You go make something click here. I can't leave that book, if I did drop it, exposed like that." Blackwood pursed her lips, then pulled on an army-green jacket full of zippers. "C'mon. I'll walk you out."

Chapter 55

Witch's Spell

A purple glow encased the entire room. The room was small, yet the openness it exuded made Stella feel like she had all the space in the world. An uplifting aura washed through her as she stood staring at the wiry, dark-haired man behind the counter. *Witch's Spell.* The one store in the city that claimed to sell cacao wine. Jake was a computer genius. He'd agreed to keep this between them, for now. Something throbbed in Stella's gut when Blackwood had told her about the traces of cacao. Phenolic compounds and cacao mucilage had to add up to cacao wine. The drink used in the ceremony to reach spiritual opening.

"Cacao spirit." His voice a mere whisper, the dark eyes of the man behind the counter probed her.

Time seemed to expand. "What?" Her voice seemed far away.

"Most of my clients who are interested in cacao wine buy it already formed. I ferment it myself, here, and sell it in ornate bottles. I have the appropriate licence, of course."

"Of course." She nodded.

"Cacao spirit. I had a woman come in here several times, recently, searching for cacao in its raw and natural form. She was seeking to create her own cocktail. She was intending to infuse it with spirit. To access higher dimensions." His steady gaze focused straight ahead, as if the woman he spoke of was in the room with them.

"Why do you think this woman is the one I am seeking?" Stella asked, although the tingles in her belly were telling her that the witch she was hunting had been standing in this very spot, not so long ago.

"You are asking about someone who has purchased cacao wine. That the use of this wine may be connected to some kind of purging ceremony—witchcraft, even." He paused, his eyes taking on a darker shade. "As I said, most of my clients simply want to consume a wine that is like a dessert. They know nothing of ceremony. This client, the one seeking the cacao spirit, had an aura of ceremony with her every movement. Her words. Her attire."

"Attire? What was she wearing?" Stella's veins buzzed with adrenaline.

"A black cloak. With a hood," the wiry man answered.

"What did she look like?"

"Long, fire-red hair, escaping from her hood. Striking blue eyes."

It had to be the same woman.

"Her aura was one of spiritual enlightenment, from her core. It was cloaked in worry, as if there were other intentions misguiding her. Yet, her being was clean and bright. That is why I agreed to sell her the pure cacao." He steepled his long fingers together and leaned his elbows on the glass counter. Glimmers from purple and blue gems beneath the glass cast colours on his pale skin.

"Do you have a sales record?" she asked, even though she already knew the answer.

"She's been in three times. All cash transactions." His lips pursed into a thin line.

He could be lying, but Stella doubted it. If this was the woman she was after, why would there be a name or a sales record?

"I did warn her to be careful. Cacao can create feelings of excitement and euphoria. For a long time, it has been used for shamanic journeying and can take the consumer into a world of lucid dreams. It triggers the release of endorphins and opium-like neurochemicals. Thus, it can become addictive."

Bells chimed. A portly woman entered the shop.

"Excuse me for a moment." The man walked around the counter to greet his new customer.

Stella pondered her next move. A fire-haired woman with blue eyes in a cloak—matched the description given by drugged out Cletus and sicko Torrence. Homemade cacao wine. A mixture that had been used to drug victims. No name. This had to be the Viviana Celeste that bought the goat horns. She wondered if Jake was making any progress on the search. She checked her phone. Nothing. No calls from Parker either. How long could she play this solo game?

Chapter 56

Missing Flask

Two corpses, their flesh burned, branded with the symbol of Satan, and hanging from stakes clung to Viviana's mind. The horns of a magnificent beast, construed as a Satanic symbol piercing through human flesh shimmered through her thoughts. Their faces stared at her, following her as she slithered away from them like the evil entity she was. The All-Seeing Eye hovered over her, watching her every move. She could sense it. She could feel its piercing stare right through the core of her soul.

Her hand had steamed with the heat from the gush of blood that poured from the man's chest, over her knife, staining the daisy protectors engraved along the ivory handle. She'd stained those precious protectors with her own hand. She'd slain the man with her own hand. Dan. His name was Dan. He hadn't even had a chance to bring life into this world. Had he been any different from her own father?

She halted her pacing across the small living room and stared out a window. The tall firs loomed from the edge of the forest over the house. An eerie shimmer of silver wove through the denim sky, reaching down over the house.

The house.

She'd followed every anger-laced command from Damaris' lips. They'd left two bodies across from the old cemetery. They'd made a stealth departure and rushed home. The moment she'd stepped into the house after the last purge, it had reached deep inside of her, coating her within an icy cage.

She'd tried to settle in, but the house traced icicle fingers through her insides while Damaris perched off kilter on the couch drinking glass after glass of cacao wine.

Damaris.

She'd avoided her stare for a while now. Every time she looked into Damaris' eyes, she could swear the red glow in the centre of her pupils brightened. Every time she got close enough to Damaris, she could smell her sour breath and the rotten odour seeping from her pores.

She hardly recognized her sister.

Her sister had claimed that the sacrifice still wasn't perfect. That they needed more practice before they could commit the ultimate purge. The one that would extinguish from the earth the couple that killed their parents. Vivian didn't want to move to another town only to repeat the horrifying sequence of sacrifices. She doubted they would ever find their parents' killers, or that Dami would ever stop burning people alive.

She knew it was never going to be perfect.

Damaris, the dominant woman, her sister, had transformed into a serial killer.

She couldn't ignore the signs any longer. The hints that revealed themselves when they played in the forest as children had been easy to ignore, explain away, dismiss. Or at least, they had been at the time.

Now, Viviana wished she'd listened to her instincts. Told someone. Done something. Sought guidance from the higher spirits.

But she was just a child back then.

Something inside of her told her to turn around. She did.

Damaris leaned over the table, picking up each empty bottle, seeking more wine.

"Need another bottle." Damaris got up and shuffled heavily into the kitchen.

Bottles clanked and bags ruffled as Damaris searched the kitchen for more of her hallucinogenic cocktail. This was the most Viviana had seen her drink in one day. She was afraid to try and stop her.

Damaris hovered in the doorway to the kitchen. Her hair dishevelled into rough clumps, dark circles around her eyes, her voice plunged an octave or two. "It's gone. There's no more."

Viviana gulped. "Well, we can go get some more. Tomorrow."

"I need more now," Damaris spat the words across the room.

"But, you said we need to stay in for forty-eight hours, after..." Viviana halted.

"After a purge. I know." Damaris licked her black lips, her tongue leaving a trail of thick pinkish saliva. "But I need more wine. You know it's healing for me."

"But, you've had enough today. To ward off the headaches," Viviana blurted, hoping her concern would be welcome. "You'll be fine till tomorrow, then we can go out and get more."

Damaris lurched, narrowing her eyes.

Viviana waited for a reaction.

Damaris stood suddenly and walked back to the couch. She smiled sickly and plunged her hand into the folds of her cloak. "My flask. There might be some left in my flask." She searched around in the hidden pockets, standing, both hands deep into her cloak. "What?" She searched some more. "My flask. It's gone." She stood, eyebrows furrowed, dark-circled eyes searching for an answer.

"Are you sure you didn't take it out when we got back?" Viviana asked.

Damaris stood. She walked through the main room, searching every piece of furniture. Viviana helped her. They migrated to the kitchen, searching the countertops and table and cupboards.

"Wait," Damaris declared. "I know where it is."

"Where?" Viviana asked.

"At the purge," Damaris said.

"Are you sure?" Icicles slid through Viviana. How much wine had Damaris had? How did she know she left it there?

"Yes. When we were performing the ceremony, before we left. I took some. That's the last time I had it. It must have dropped," Damaris said, conviction in her eyes. "We have to go back."

"Dami, no. We can't." They couldn't. The rules didn't allow it. They could be seen. They could get caught. She'd have to face what she'd done.

"We have to," Damaris hissed. "The flask was a gift from our coven leader. A symbol of my progression. If someone else finds it..."

Viviana stood, looking at Damaris. "OK. Let's go. Now. It's dark."

Damaris stood, wrapped her cloak around her and walked to the door.

Viviana followed.

Chapter 57

Night Hunt

The moon hung high in the midnight sky, shining a bright glow over the old cemetery. Stars scattered across the horizon, dimmed by the night lights of the city. The downtown core blazed a bright glow, perched in the centre of the city. The streets were empty.

Viviana rolled the van quietly down the street, to the corner of the cemetery. She scanned the cemetery, the park, the streets. They were empty and silent. They didn't usually come into the city unless they were staging a purge, or seeking their next victim. Viviana didn't like any of it. She didn't like being here now, but she couldn't take any more of Dami's darkening demeanour. She couldn't bear to suffer any more of Dami's wrath. She prayed to the higher spirits that they would find the flask quickly and get out of here.

She pulled the van over to a side street and parked behind a large tree, away from the streetlights dotting the sidewalk. She put the van in park, letting it idle.

Damaris breathed heavily from the passenger side. She hunched over against the door, lost in the folds of her cloak, her dark hair plastered to the side of her face.

Should they leave? Was this too risky? Was Dami in any shape to do this? Her usual stealth form was fading. Viviana contemplated slamming on the gas and taking them back to the house. Maybe Damaris was too deep in her cacao-infused haze to notice. Maybe she'd fall asleep, succumbing to the wine-induced coma slowly taking over her.

Dami stirred, turning her head to look across the van. The dark circles around her eyes had deepened. The sickly yellow in the whites of her eyes had darkened to a brown sludge, like a forgotten pond turning into an abandoned marsh.

"I'll be right back." Dami sneered.

"Are you sure about this?" Viviana asked. The rough skin on her arm itched. Tingles in the pit of her belly burst through her insides. "You look tired."

"We have no choice." Damaris opened the door. "I have to get that flask. You wait here." She jumped from the van and closed the door quietly.

Maybe it would be OK. Dami seemed to be pumped with some sort of second wind, an awakened awareness of being stealthy again.

Viviana scanned the cemetery. The dark-grey headstones forming rows across the perfectly manicured grass cast black shadows, reaching their dark fingers over the grounds. The archway marking the entrance to the cemetery loomed high, casting a massive shadow over the headstones. The place exuded a lonely vibe. Viviana shuddered.

She looked across the street and examined the park where they'd left the bodies. The human sacrifices. The staged burning at the stake. The purge. Viviana shuddered. She couldn't stop thinking about it all.

She looked up the hill dotted with trees. Empty of bodies.

No movement stirred. It would be fine. Dami would go across the street, find the flask, and come back. There was no one around. Nobody would see them. No one would ever know they even existed.

Besides, from here she could see everything. If someone came down the street between the park and the cemetery, they wouldn't see the van. If someone came up from behind, Viviana could crouch down in the driver's seat, hidden in the shadows between the streetlights.

Viviana watched Dami. Dami scanned left and right, then darted across the street, ascending the hill where the bodies had hung, her cloak fluttering behind her, her hood concealing her face. The hill, now empty, emanated a sense of pain and loss. The figures shimmered in and out, hanging from stakes, horns piercing their flesh. Hot blood dribbled over Viviana's hand. She shook it away, but nothing was there.

Viviana swallowed and shook her head.

There was no time for this right now. She had to quiet her mind. She had to stay focused and watch her sister. It was critical to their survival.

Dami, halfway up the hill, scoured the park, looking into the trees. She moved from tree to tree, pushing away branches, searching inside, to no avail. She bent deep into a tree. Maybe she'd found it. Tingles erupted within Viviana.

Movement from the far end of the street snatched Viviana's attention from watching Dami. A black-and-brown Jeep rolled down the street along the park, its bright lights bringing the dark street to life.

Keep going. Keep going. Don't stop. Nothing to see here. We don't exist. Viviana mouthed a silent prayer to the higher spirits.

The Jeep stopped, straight down the hill from where Dami was bent over, looking in the branches of a tree, her cloak concealing her figure, her hood hiding her head and face. The lights on the Jeep went out. A woman jumped down from the driver's side, sturdy boots hitting the pavement with a thud. Her long, dark hair fell behind her shoulders, streaked with a single shock of silver. The woman clicked on a flashlight and walked up the hill.

Oh my god. Oh my stars. Oh please, higher spirits.

Viviana froze. Her fingers clutched the steering wheel. What should she do? She couldn't honk. She couldn't move the van. That would alert this woman. All she could do was wait, hoping Dami would see the light and hide.

The woman walked further up the hill, toward the very spot they'd hung the bodies. The flashlight shone bright along the grassy incline, bringing the dark park to life.

Viviana held her breath. The tingles in her gut turned cold.

Dami continued rifling through the tree, bent over, unaware of the light and the woman.

Viviana gulped in a breath. Her insides roiled. Sweat sprouted down her back. *Dami, please, turn around. Higher spirits, I beg of you, watch over her.*

The woman jolted, flashing the light in Dami's direction. The light bathed Dami, illuminating her cloak.

Dami startled, bolting upright.

The woman stood, staring at Dami, running the flashlight up Dami's cloak to her face.

Dami's eyes narrowed. Her hands plunged into the folds of her cloak.

Viviana kept the van idling, the lights off.

The woman took several steps toward Dami. She slipped something from her belt, but Viviana couldn't make out what it was. A muffled voice echoed through the silence. The woman was speaking, but Viviana couldn't hear what she was saying.

The woman took several more steps toward Dami.

Dami stood still, staring straight at the woman with her evil eyes. Her stare cold, her eyes narrowed.

The woman kept walking up the hill.

Dami lunged, right at the woman, her hand raised high above her head. She landed right on the woman, who landed hard on her back; the object in her hand went flying one way, the flashlight the other way.

Dami brought her knife straight down.

The woman flailed her arms, trying to defend herself.

The blade sliced into the woman's hand. Flesh went flying. Blood shot through the air.

The woman fell back. Dami stood and ran down the hill.

Viviana smashed the van into drive and slammed on the gas. She pulled around the street. She slammed on the brakes. Dami ran to the van.

Dami flung the passenger-side door open and jumped in.

Viviana slammed on the gas again and sped away.

Chapter 58

Flask

The voice of a rock god wailed through her Sunfire as Stella took a hard right, spitting gravel in her wake. She peeled into a spot behind Blackwood's Jeep and jumped from her car, slamming the door behind her. The moon glimmered overhead, casting an eerie white glow, mixing with the red-and-blue flashes from a patrol car and an ambulance.

As she strode toward the grassy hill where the pair of bodies had hung from wooden stakes only days before, she saw three figures at the top. They were walking slowly, the two on the outsides supporting the person in the middle. A silver streak in the dark hair caught Stella's eye. *Blackwood.* She was walking. She was OK.

Stella exhaled the breath she didn't realize she'd been holding and bolted up the hill.

Blackwood looked up as Stella approached.

"Mahoney." Blackwood halted.

"What happened? Are you OK?" Stella's words rushed from her mouth.

"We need to keep moving," said the shorter of the two medical personnel, a redheaded woman with freckles dotting her face.

Blackwood stared at the woman. "I need a minute. This is a *murder* investigation."

"But your finger…" the woman said.

Blackwood cut her off. "My finger can wait."

A thick bandage with spots of blood soaking through wound around Blackwood's hand.

Blackwood slipped her unbandaged hand into her jacket. She pulled out a plastic bag with something inside. She gave it to Stella.

Stella inspected the contents through the clear plastic. "A flask?"

"The woman who attacked me dropped it. You need to get a rush on DNA and prints." Blackwood smirked.

Despite the quickly reddening bandage, Blackwood was still in murder-investigation mode. Stella smiled to herself.

"Woman?" Stella looked back at Blackwood.

"In a dark cloak."

"Hair like fire?"

"Nope. Black. Like a raven."

"What? Two women in cloaks?" She clenched her jaw. "Did you see her face? Could you tell how old she was?"

Blackwood shrugged. "Not for certain. Got a quick glance. Dark eyes. Early twenties...maybe. It all happened so fast."

Stella pulled at her chin. "I've got three accounts of fire hair and blue eyes. Young, twenty at best. We *might* have a pair of killers on the loose."

"We really need to get you to the hospital." The other medical examiner, a skinny young man with blond hair, motioned toward the ambulance. "You might need surgery. Time is of the essence if you don't want to lose mobility in your finger."

"Fine." Blackwood rolled her eyes. "Cloaked woman sliced my finger." She raised her bandaged hand in the air.

Wobbly on her feet, Blackwood stumbled a few steps down the hill. The medical personnel quickly moved to support her.

Stella followed behind. "Your notebook..."

"Found it. Thank the murder gods."

Chapter 59

Rush DNA

The red light flashed through the night sky as Stella watched the ambulance peel away from the park. She silently hoped that Blackwood's finger would be fine. She'd listened to the two medics as they settled Blackwood into the back of the ambulance, assessing her hand. They were seriously concerned she could lose mobility in the finger that was sliced, and potentially the ones on either side. It was her dominant hand.

A shiny blue Chevy whipped around the end of the street and stopped a couple feet from Stella.

Sutton. Good. She needed someone with real authority right about now.

"Stella." Sutton slammed the door on his truck and ran toward her.

"Boss." Maybe she should forgive him for addressing her incorrectly in his haste.

"Where's Blackwood?"

"Just left. In the ambulance. Only damage is to her finger. They're rushing her into surgery." Stella held out the bagged flask. "Said her attacker dropped this. Said it was a woman in a cloak, with *black* hair, and *dark* eyes. Maybe early twenties."

Sutton took the bag and looked at it. "We have a pair of killers?"

"*Maybe.* Hair is easy to color. Could be coloured contact lenses. We need to find out if there's any DNA or fingerprints on this flask. *Now.*"

Sutton nodded.

"Blackwood was processing a partial print. On the body of one of the last victims." Stella clenched her jaw. "Can you put a rush on it? *And* the flask?"

"Done."

Her shoulders relaxed. Maybe Sutton wasn't that bad.

"I'll get the rush." Sutton headed toward his truck, bagged flask in hand. "Check in with Jake on that name search. I'll check on Blackwood."

She walked toward her Sunfire.

"Stella," Sutton called after her. "Good work."

She flung the door of her Sunfire open. *It's Detective Mahoney.* Hell, she'd even settle for *Mahoney*. She goaded herself for warming up to him.

Chapter 60

Satanic Beast

The pair of twisted horns hung on the wall, right next to the triple crime scene collage. Stella stared at them. The Markhor head hanging on Torrence's wall shimmered through her mind. The two dark eyes stared her down, seeping an evil vibe. The twisted contours of the charcoal bone wove into survival weapons, protruding from the crown of the beast. Stella stared into the dark eyes pulsing in her mind. A Satanic representation. A symbol of evil.

Stella's mind whirled with images. Burned bodies mounted on stakes. Squirming snakes slithering from open flesh. *Leviathan.* The symbol of Satan. Powerful twisted horns piercing cooked, bloody skin. *Baphomet.* Worshipped by those who believed in evil.

Stella clenched her jaw, staring the evil dead on. The room blurred around her. She imagined a line shooting around the face of the Markhor, forming a five-pointed star. The star pulsed. The cover of the *Devil's Track* materialized in her mind. A deep voice resonated through her ears, thrumming in her brain, hypnotizing her senses. Whispers grazed her ears. *Leviathan. Baphomet. Samael Lilith.*

"Stella," Jake called from the doorway.

Stella jumped, spun on her heel and stared at Jake standing in the doorway.

"What are you doing?" Jake asked.

"What?" Her voice sounded far away.

"Are you OK?" Jake walked to her.

"Yeah. Fine. Just..." Stella looked back over the photos, her gaze catching the twisted horns. "Just taking another look. Trying to fit it all together."

"I can't find a trace of this woman, Viviana Celeste," Jake said.

"Dammit." Stella clenched her jaw.

"Yeah. I've tapped out all sources." Jake ran his hands through his tousled hair.

"Leviathan. Baphomet," Stella whispered.

Jake stared at her. "Are you sure you're OK?"

Stella jolted. "The Seeker. The Rite of Dedication."

"What?" Jake asked. Concern riddled his face.

"It's a coven name." She rubbed her chin. "That stack of reading you gave me, about witchcraft. The Rite of Dedication is a ceremony used to induct a new member into a coven. The coven becomes the family. The killer *is* the witch. The name from the taxidermist, it's her coven name."

Jake's eyes lit up. "I wonder if I can find anything on local, historical covens." He ran his hands through his curls. "Could take a while. A lot came up when I started searching for witchcraft in Canada."

"We may have two cloaked women. The fire-haired one barely an adult. Dark-haired one in her early twenties." She rubbed her chin and clenched her jaw. "If their spiritual beliefs are ingrained as deeply as they appear, they grew up with it."

"Then we're looking for a recent coven in the vicinity, or the nearby prairies." He smiled. "I knew you'd put this together."

"What?" She clenched her jaw.

"When I met your dad, one thing really struck me. His conviction. He knew what he believed. Nothing would stop him from following it."

"So...what does that have to do with all this?" Stella waved around the room at the grisly photos and Markhor antlers.

"I see the same thing in you. The way you clench your jaw. Rub your chin. And say what you think. It comes from the same place as your father's instinct did." Jake walked over to her and placed a hand on her shoulder. "Stella, you need to let yourself believe it. Whatever is deep inside." He turned and walked out the door.

Tingles pricked the pit of her gut. She'd known the moment she saw the first victim, hanging, burned, that recreating the fantasy of the killer was the only way to find them. She needed a new surge of belief. Now.

Chapter 61

Pounding Pain

The moon's glow flickered then dimmed behind a stretch of charcoal cotton. The room darkened. The walls heaved, closing in on Viviana.

She watched Dami, slick with sweat and writhing in the bed, pulling the covers around her in bunches, kicking her legs. Dami put her hands to her head, running her fingers through her sweat-drenched locks. "The pounding. It won't stop. It has me." Dami poured the words out in a spray of spit.

It. It has me. How many times had Viviana heard these words? Every time the pounding pain assaulted her sister, taking down the dominant woman, bringing her to her knees.

The pain, hammering through Dami's head. It seemed to come during each break, invading the quiet time between purges.

"Viv," Dami cried. Tears streaked her pale cheeks. The yellow tinge and red glow to her eyes was gone. Her eyes were once again the rich dark they'd always been. "Help me. It hurts." Dami grasped clumps of hair in her hands. Her fingers shook.

Viviana picked up a bottle of cacao wine set on a stand next to the bed. She poured the rich red liquid into a silver goblet. Spice rose from the cup, followed by heat. Viviana knelt on the floor next to the bed and brought the cup to Dami's black lips, placing a hand on the back of Dami's head, guiding her to the medicine-filled goblet.

Dami groaned, leaned toward the cup, and took loud gulps. The scarlet liquid drizzled down the sides of her mouth. Her head fell back against the stack of silk pillows—purple, burgundy, rose. She breathed deeply, closing her eyes.

Viviana put the goblet on the nightstand and leaned over Dami. She wiped the sides of Dami's mouth with a white cloth.

Dami opened her eyes, looking around the room like she didn't know where she was.

"Dami. You're OK." Viviana stroked Dami's head with her hand. "Take deep breaths. It will go away."

"Noooo." Dami's rich, dark eyes wandered, then focused on Viviana. "Viv. It has me. It won't let go."

It. It again. Viviana's stomach clenched.

"Take a deep breath." Viviana found Dami's hand with her own and gently squeezed.

Dami took a deep breath. The walls of the room seemed to pull away in sync with Dami's rising chest. Dami exhaled. The walls of the room closed in.

"It won't leave, Viv." Dami's eyes pleaded. A sadness drenched her gaze. A desperation shook her. "It won't go. It's a...sickness. I can't stop it." Tears drizzled down Dami's face. "I want it to stop. It won't. Someone has to stop it. You. You have to stop it." Dami shuddered. Her essence floated over Viviana.

The desperation washed over Viviana like a wave eating up a surfer. It overwhelmed her.

"What...what do you mean?" Viviana asked. She ran her hand along Dami's arm, trickling her fingertips over Dami's hand, over her fingers.

"I can't stop it. The need. To kill," Dami said. She grasped Viviana's hand in her own. "It. It's a sickness. It takes me. I'm not...me. I can't stop it. Dad...he used to teach me...how to temper my cravings. I thought I could do it. I can't. You've seen me, after time...a purge...then time...then this." Dami pulled her hand away and rolled over, facing the wall, curling into a ball, pulling the covers over her.

"Dami. I...I want to help you. I don't know what to do." Viviana sighed. The walls were silent and still. So was Dami. "Dami. I love you."

Dami rolled over. Black circles swelled around her eyes. Her hair stuck to her tear-stained face in clumps. She pulled the covers around her chin. "You. You've seen the sickness surface. I know you have. When it happens, I can't reach you. I have no voice. No control." Dami swallowed hard. She licked her top black lip. "You have to stop me."

Viviana stared at Damaris, the dominant woman, curled beneath the covers, crying for help. She didn't know what it meant, to stop it. She had seen it surface.

She'd seen her sister's eyes turn into sickly yellow, glowing red demonic orbs. She'd seen the power take over her sister as Dami held a flame to innocent flesh. She'd seen the hunger, the craving, the need to commit sacrifices, to declare a purge, to burn people, to brand them, pushing a blazing symbol into their flesh until they'd screamed their throats raw.

It wasn't always that way.

When they were children, she'd seen strange hints in her sister. But their father had always whisked Dami away. Viviana had never seen the outcome when the signs revealed themselves. When the purging began, with each sacrifice Dami became darker, more feral, salivating for the next kill. Between them, she would break. Fall to the bottom of a pit. Viviana would stroke her hair, feed her cacao wine, and soothe her until she rose dominant again.

This was the first time Dami had told her to stop it.

Chapter 62

Third ID

The hot air in the small war room closed in on Stella. The ticking of the clock on the front wall echoed through the room. The odour of stale coffee mixed with detective sweat infused the air. They'd been chasing down bizarre clues all week. They'd been holed up in here every night, reviewing progress—or lack thereof—and delivering reports full of holes to Sutton.

Sutton stood at the front of the room, shuffling papers. Parker leaned in silence against the back wall. Jake typed away in his usual corner.

Stella discreetly sniffed her armpit. *Dammit.* The flare of body odour the room had taken on must be her. Parker always smelled fresh and misted with that damn cologne. Why did he have to be so hard to hate?

"We got IDs. On both," Sutton said as he added new pieces to the crime scene collages. He poked brightly coloured tacks through printed sheets of paper, declaring the identities of the latest two victims.

"Both?" Parker asked like the eager kid in the front row of class.

"Yeah. Married couple. Dan and Dawn Swain. Thirty-two and thirty. Respectively. Started the Church of the Seed in the spring of 1994. No kids. No family." Sutton put the finishing touches on the third and largest row of the gruesome collage.

Willard was thirty-two. Madeleine was thirty. "How large was the congregation?" Stella asked.

Sutton flipped through a folder. "Seventy-five."

Small congregation. "We need to talk to members."

"Yeah. You do. Together. And be friendly." Sutton looked at Stella.

She met Sutton's gaze. *Whatever.* They needed answers. Did these two church leaders also have a message of purging that led them to be targets?

"Before she was attacked, Blackwood was chasing down a partial print. Stella, good work bringing that up." Sutton shot her a glance. "I put a rush on the processing of both the print and the flask that Blackwood found after the attack. They're not a match. Two different people. Related. Neither of them are in the system."

"The same coven." Stella clenched her jaw.

"What?" Sutton asked.

"A coven is like a family to a witch. These killers, they're witches, or think they are. DNA says they're related. They're part of the same coven."

"How does that help us?" Sutton asked.

"I couldn't find the name on the receipt from the taxidermist. I started looking for covens," Jake said. "Nothing so far. Covens didn't exactly register themselves for the world to see."

Sutton nodded. "Keep digging." He looked at Stella. "Stella, did you get anything else from Blackwood before she went hunting for her notebook?"

"Same as the first two victims. Same brand. On the abdomen. Given the much higher degree of burning over the bodies, the symbol was the only thing intact." Stella flipped through her notebook, staring at the page where she'd jotted notes about cacao wine.

"Anything we don't already know?" Sutton's lips pressed into a thin line. The rabbit claw dangling from his belt swung back and forth.

Stella rescanned her notes. "Full tox report was done. Higher traces of phenolic compounds and alkaloids. Also PEA. Phenethylamine. The source of the alkaloids as cacao mucilage. Not cocaine."

"Your drugged-up minister theory doesn't hold," Sutton stated.

"No." Stella swallowed. "It's cacao wine."

"Cacao wine?" Parker asked.

Dammit. Why doesn't he shut up? "It's used in some witchcraft ceremonies. I found a source. No sales record, but a description that matches our red-haired cloaked woman."

Sutton looked at Parker. "You know about this?"

"No," Parker said.

"You followed a lead, alone? You didn't take your partner? Or even keep him in the loop?" Sutton took a few steps toward Stella, glaring at her. The rabbit foot swung out of control.

Parker stepped between them. "I was processing the data from the scene. She was gonna fill me in as soon she got back to HQ."

Sutton looked at Parker, then back at Stella. "This true?"

"The killer, or killers...they're witches. Or think they are," Stella blurted. "The symbol branded on the victims, it's Baphomet. The Goat of Mendes. It's a symbol of worshipping Satan. The wine. It's part of some witchcraft ceremonies." Stella paused as her mind whirled. She needed to get her thoughts together.

"Stella's theory holds," Parker said. "The killer is purging ministers. Religious leaders hunted witches historically."

"The new victims, they had puncture wounds. Multiple. They were injected with this cacao wine. Looks like they were forced to drink it too. That's why there were no signs of struggle. Drugged. Tied up. Burned." Stella bit her bottom lip.

"Purged," Parker concluded.

Sutton eyed them back and forth. He sighed. "Fine. I'll overlook the fact that you deliberately kept your partner out of the know." He looked at Stella. "Seems like the two of you are working as partners despite it. Jake, anything new?"

"Newest crime scene, outside a cemetery perimeter, facing in. Like the others. Accused witches weren't allowed to be buried in cemeteries, so this seems to be symbolic to the killer. The three crime scenes, in three of the oldest cemeteries in the city."

She could always count on Jake. He might be the only friend she had. But why was Parker defending her? She hadn't exactly been nice to him.

"We have more dead church leaders. Burned. Branded. Hung outside of cemeteries." Sutton looked at the photos of the victims. "Stella's theory is the strongest thing we have to go on. The more bodies that pop up, the more this looks like some witchcraft-related burning-at-the-stake shit." Sutton shook his head. "Despite the DNA left behind, we can't find out who they are." He walked to the centre table and picked up a file.

Stella shoved herself from her lean against the back wall and walked up to the series of crime scene photos. "We have three witness descriptions of a woman with fire-red hair in a black cloak. Blackwood was attacked by a dark-haired woman, also wearing a cloak. These women, they have to be the killers."

Sutton walked up to her. "You don't *have* them. You have some crazed hunter killing and stuffing wild animals who told you some hottie came in and bought a pair of goat horns. The name on the sales record leads nowhere. The DNA lead nowhere."

Little fingers of tingles reached through the pit of Stella's belly. She took a deep breath and whirled around to meet Sutton eye to eye. "You're right. That's why we have to *dig*. Deep. We have to put this together. Follow the behavior. They think they're witches. What would witches do?"

Sutton stepped back, pondering the information. The green rabbit claw hanging from his belt swayed back and forth erratically. "No sales record for the wine. The name from the taxidermist went nowhere. DNA isn't in the system." He sighed.

"Follow the name, find the coven, find the witch," Parker said.

"Precisely," Stella said.

Sutton contemplated the path.

"We scour the evidence from the new scene. We talk to the congregation members of the new victims. We'll find these women," Stella pleaded her case, wondering if she was only trying to convince herself.

"Fine. You have twenty-four hours to find this coven name, or we need to take a different path. I can't afford to have anyone else attacked. Make this witchcraft theory into a suspect. Before this supposed witch burns someone else," Sutton said.

Stella found his gaze. She held it for a moment. He didn't look away. He was right. They needed to make this into something real. Now.

Chapter 63

Looking for a Coven

Stella wandered through the clutter of cubicles back to her desk. She needed to get somewhere with all this. Now. But how? Parker had been *useful* and *supportive* back in the war room. Jake had been on the ball, as usual. Sutton was unsettled after the attack on Blackwood. She suspected his superior was breathing down his neck. He was transferring that pressure onto them. She had twenty-four hours to find a witch. What kind of weirdo case was this? The kind she'd wanted. Could she handle it now that she was smack in the middle of it?

The fingers of tingles pulsed in her gut. They reached through her entire belly. As weird as this theory was—and as strange as the path she was leading her team down appeared—it felt *right*. Like she was listening to something inside of her.

She grabbed her leather coat hanging over the back of her chair. The cover of the *Devil's Track* shot through her mind. *The Poison Sisters*. A recording studio that didn't exist. *Viviana Celeste*. If she *was* using her coven name, her ties to her *family* were strong.

Coat in hand, she swung by Parker's desk.

"Parker," she said.

He looked up. "Yeah?"

"We gotta go."

"Got it." He smiled, grabbed his coat, and followed her.

She led Parker over to Jake's desk.

"Jakey. Please tell me you have something."

"I need time. I've found a couple sources on prairie covens. Back in the twenties. Names don't match." Jake pouted. "You need to be patient.

"You heard the boss. I don't have *time* to be patient." She tousled his hair.

He pulled away. "I can't produce information that doesn't exist. I'm getting the impression that most covens stayed under the radar. It makes sense."

"One more thing." She smiled sweetly.

He sighed. "What?"

"Can you dig deeper on the Poison Sisters? Launch a fresh round of searches. Don't assume it's a recording studio."

"What?" Jake raised an eyebrow.

"Two women in cloaks. DNA says they're related. Maybe they're sisters. Maybe the Poison Sisters is a reference to *them.*"

Parker nodded. "Good logic."

"Fine." Jake shooed her away. "Leave me alone. I need to concentrate."

"Call me as soon as you get anything. We're gonna go interview church people." Stella smirked.

Jake turned his head. "Oh? *We?*" He looked at Parker, then turned and went back to his typing. "So you're playing well with others now?"

Stella punched Jake in the shoulder. "Whatever. Call me." She turned, nodded at Parker, then led the way out of HQ, toward the Church of the Seed.

Chapter 64

Newspaper Boy

Stella cranked the knob on the CD player hard to the right, turning the volume of Ozzy's screeching to full. She was amped up, and a good dose of *Paranoid* was in order.

She'd burned half the day with Parker interviewing members of the congregation of the two latest victims. Their twenty-four hours was almost up. They had nothing to show for it.

Viviana Celeste. Poison Sisters. They were chasing covens and recording studios that didn't seem to exist.

Her brain buzzed. A tingle shot through her gut.

She cranked the volume back down. Grabbing the steering wheel hard with her left hand, she fished her phone out of her pocket with her right. She pushed a button and held the phone to her ear.

"Jake here." His voice was breathless through the phone.

"You been running?" She was sure that was impossible. Jake couldn't run a lap if his life depended on it.

"Ha. No."

"You still have access to newspaper archives?"

"Uh...well, I could...but..."

"You still stay in touch with Hammington, don't you?" Neurons fired through her brain.

"Yeah. As much of a pain in the ass as he was when I worked at the paper, he was quite emotional when I left. Guess he liked me after all."

She could see the dimple appearing as she pictured the smile on Jake's face. "Give him something. Prime access to the case we're about to break."

"Won't Sutton bust a lung?"

"Nah. I'll take it. He already hates me."

"He doesn't hate you."

"Call Hammington. Get access," she said, her voice turning stern.

"Fine. What is it I'm looking for?" he said, his voice quivering.

"History. The stack of witchcraft printouts you gave me. Most of them were newspaper articles. Look for Viviana Celeste. Look for the Poison Sisters."

"Guess it's worth a shot."

Chapter 65

House of Fire

Tires squealed as Stella slid her Sunfire into the parking stalls, directly in front of the tall glass doors of HQ. She grabbed her phone, stepped out of the car, and slammed the door shut. She walked briskly to the entrance, punching numbers into her phone.

"Parker here," he answered on the first ring.

"It's Mahoney. You on your way back to HQ?"

"Yeah. Ten minutes."

"Good. We got something."

"Cool." He hung up.

She slid her phone into her pocket and upped her pace. The front desk was empty. Pegs would have gone home hours ago. She made her way through the empty clutter of cubicles, the odour of detective sweat and stale cigarette smoke clinging to the air.

Jake was hunched over his computer, his sky-blue sweater vest bunched at the shoulders. She walked up behind him. "Jakey."

He didn't stop typing. "Stella. Grab a seat."

She pulled a chair over, plunked down, and crossed her booted ankle over her knee. "Show me."

He sat back. A newspaper article appeared on the screen. The headline was blurry.

She leaned over and peered at the screen. "Can't read it."

"Yeah, the scanning and imaging is still rudimentary on this new interface. Doesn't matter. I enhanced the images, pulled apart the article. I found your Viviana Celeste from the sales record you got from Torrence's Trophy Emporium."

"What?" Stella yanked off her coat and hovered next to Jake.

"It was the Poison Sisters and the newspaper archives that did it."

"No way."

"Way. A house was burned down six years ago in Forestville, Quebec. The bodies of Janice and Jaydon Botting were recovered. They started the Coven Celeste. They had two daughters, Damaris and Viviana, who were seventeen and thirteen, respectively, at the time. The girls were presumed dead in the fire, but their bodies were never recovered." Jake took a breath. "The suspected arsonists were Eleanor and Eden Twine, thirty and thirty-two, respectively, at the time. They vanished the night of the fire. Get this. They were the leaders of The Seed of Life Church." He stopped and stared at her.

She leaned toward him. Her brain buzzed. "Church leaders. Mirror images of our victims. So, these girls, they escaped the fire. Survived somehow for years. Now they're purging the mirror image of the church leaders who killed their parents."

Stella sat back, her brain buzzing with the information. "Wow. Just wow."

"I know, right?" Jake exclaimed. His chocolate locks flew wildly around his head. His eyes widened. "There's more."

A swelling sensation swirled around Stella's gut. "Shoot."

Jake typed. Another image appeared on the screen. The Satanic symbol. The five-pointed hexagon. The goat's head. Its evil eyes bored into her soul.

Something inside of her went cold. A haze descended over her mind. That deep voice from the *Devil's Track* pulsed through her mind. Jake was talking. He sounded far away.

"Stella." Jake's face was close to hers.

"Yeah?" She shook her head. What happened?

"You okay?"

"Yeah. Fine. Sorry...what were you saying?" She placed a hand on his arm.

"The symbol. The one on the bodies. The one on the album. It was found etched into the pages of several books that somehow survived the fire. In the basement of the house. Locked away in some chest." He looked at her.

She stared back at him.

"Are you sure you're okay? You look pale. And it was like you left all of a sudden, went somewhere else." Concern hijacked his face.

She sat up and shook her head. "Yeah. I'm fine. The symbol. Etched in books. Got it."

"This all adds up. This house. The church leaders. The symbol," he said.

"They'd be only twenty-three and nineteen now." Stella shook her head. "What they must have done to survive."

"Yeah. And look at this." Jake clicked the keys. A photo appeared. "Viviana and her sister, Damaris. *The Poison Sisters.* That's what they were called by locals in the newspapers. How cruel, they were just kids. The other kids made up stories about them. Look at the younger one. Viviana."

An image of a young girl appeared. Her long, fire hair hung around her face. A sense of knowing in her eyes, a crystal clear blue, like ice. Her expression was dour and mysterious. An aura seeped from the screen. The hood of a cloak settled over her head. The cloak flowed around her shoulders. She stared at them, a piercing stare. A look far beyond her years.

"The woman in the cloak. Purchasing goat horns and cacao wine." Stella clenched her jaw. "Damn. I can't believe it."

"You can't? I can. I knew you would crack this."

"I didn't. We know *who* they are. Not *where* they are."

Jake clicked the keys. "I got something, after I called you." And address flashed across the screen in neon green. "Jaydon Botting had a sister. Only family I could find for the leaders of the Coven Celeste. She moved here, to Calgary, soon after Damaris was born. She died almost a year ago. Looks like her house was abandoned after." Jake clicked more keys. An image appeared.

Stella stared at the image of a small house on the edge of a birch forest, the Rocky Mountains in the background. The house seemed to swell with energy, amplifying its size, making it seem unworldly. Jake's voice muted beside her.

"Stella. Earth to Stella," Jake's voice broke her trance.

She jumped from the chair. "Tell Parker." She sprinted to her desk, grabbed her leather coat and her keys, then darted for the parking lot. Jake's voice called after her, a muted echo in another world.

Chapter 66

Demon Rising

Damaris stood, her back to the ring of flames forming an enclosure around the empty space for sacrifices. A glow seethed from the candle wicks, pulsing into an orange-red essence seeping over Damaris like a Satanic silhouette. Her hood back, her hair fanned around her shoulders in shiny raven waves, melding with her cloak fanning around her body. The pounding pain had subsided, taking with it any sign of weakness. She raised her arms, holding her knife high above her head. The yellow-brown sickly film covered the whites of her eyes. The red glow pulsed from the centre of her pupils. "It is time to bid farewell to our cycle of purge. We must follow the voice of the coven and move to where we are needed." She lowered her knife and turned to face the circle.

Viviana clutched the railing on the stairs, peeking from behind the edge of the wall. Her fingers trembled, grasping the wooden railing until a splinter pierced the tip of her finger. She whimpered, then swallowed back the sound, hoping Damaris hadn't heard her. She slipped her fingertip into her mouth and suckled back the metallic droplets from her skin.

What was she going to do? Her sister was out of control. After the cycle of purge, the trio of sacrifices, Viviana had hope. Damaris had simmered into a soft being. The rich colour of her eyes had returned. The sour odour had vanished, replaced by lavender. Damaris had seemed more like herself than she had been in a long time. It was almost as if Damaris was the sister she knew from before the burning of the little house on the edge of the forest, before they had run into the night, barefoot, over the dirt path, leading them away from the only family they'd ever known. That night had changed Damaris forever. The signs that had been so subtle and so sparse intensified, coming on hard and fast, and much more frequent. Once the killings started, the small bits of behaviour brewed inside of Damaris like a bubbling broth, surfacing as sadistic acts that shocked and horrified Viviana.

"It is time for the next cycle. Perfection must be achieved," Damaris' deep voice rose through the room. Her arms raised again over her head, pointing the blade of her knife toward the ceiling. The flames from the candles flickered and rose, sending red glints off the silver blade. The room pulsed. The walls pulled out, then sank back in.

This house was evil. The moment Viviana laid eyes on its peeling layers of wood and paint, she could smell its rot, feel its icicle fingers reaching inside of her, scraping her insides with cold, sharp shards. She'd brushed it off, telling herself this whirlwind of horrifying events was morphing her mind, making her crazy, making her see and feel things that weren't really there.

But no matter what she told herself, how she tried to ease her mind, clear her thoughts, that inner voice, her inner guide, those higher spirits whispering through her ears told her she was right.

Viviana had seen the first glimmer of red in Damaris' eyes. From that moment, Viviana had smelled the first hint of sour rot trickle from her sister's pores. Viviana had seen the house breathe in unison with Damaris as they chose to meld together and move their souls as one down a dark, demonic path.

"It is time to seek perfection. It is time to seek a new cycle of purge. It is time to achieve the perfect purge," Damaris' deep voice boomed through the basement. The flames flickered and rose, pulsing a red glow around Damaris. The blade of her knife high in the air, perched on the tip of her hands, seemed to hover.

Viviana pulled her finger from her mouth, gulping in air. She froze. Her feet were glued to the wooden stair. The heightened vibe from her sister, from the basement, from the red glow eating up the air, slithered through her, devouring her insides.

She didn't know what was happening. She didn't know what to do. This private ceremony her sister was holding between her, the empty sacrificial circle, and the dark basement was an intense aftermath of a cycle of purge that seemed to be only the beginning.

"It is time!" her sister's dark voice shrieked, reaching high-pitched syllables with a deep, guttural growl to their undertones. "Our leaders, our parents, have burned. Our coven extinguished. We must relight the wick of the candle. We must avenge their death."

Viviana covered her ears with her palms, trying to muffle the shrieking noise. Her sister's words were Satanic. Ungodly. Full of fire and death and burning rage.

She closed her eyes. Her sister rose up in her mind, forming a vision. Flames rose. Blades shimmered. Flesh burned. Her sister's dark lips grasped for words. Damaris' breathing was laboured. Her eyes were desperate. No yellow. No red. No sickness.

In Viviana's vision, blood poured from Damaris as she clutched a knife, the blade piercing into her flesh. The handle stuck out of Damaris' chest, positioned into her heart. Blood slithered over the crystal amulet and down the ivory handle, exposing the soft engraving of daisy protectors.

It was Viviana's own knife.

She flung her eyes open and shook the blood from her hands that wasn't there.

She stared across the room at Damaris, wild and chanting, holding her knife to the ceiling. She quietly crawled up the stairs and away from this terrifying thing her sister had become.

Chapter 67

Poison Sisters

Stella crept down the dirt path weaving through the forest. Her boots sank into the soft trail. The tall firs formed a dark-green roof. The glimmer of the moon, high in the sky, trickled through the boughs of the trees, casting a soft silver glow, lighting her way.

She could see the outline of the house at the edge of the forest. A small dwelling, it looked quaint, yet it was washed in a haze of gloom. The wooden siding peeled away in large strips, as if the house were shedding a new skin, revealing its true nature beneath.

Stella reached the edge of the forest and scanned the house for movement. An orange glow emanated from the small windows. Nothing stirred within. A silence descended from the trees.

Parker couldn't be far. Jake would have filled him in and sent him after her. She thought of Sutton and how he'd pulled her from the gloomy depths of her apartment, from the dark visions of sliding a knife into Tomlinson's gut, and from the hypnotizing hold the *Devil's Track* had on her. She'd turned her theory into real suspects. She could count on him to launch a full tactical assault.

But that would take time. She thought of her father, entering the dark clutches of a gothic mansion alone. He didn't let an innocent victim die at the hands of a killer while waiting for backup. Stella would do the same. She needed to stop the cloaked killers before they burned another victim alive.

She crept up to the house and peered in a window. A ring of candles perched on a centre table around a bottle of wine. A silver goblet sat next to the bottle. Wax clung to the candles in frozen drips, the wicks burned bright. The house may have been abandoned, but it wasn't vacant.

Stella snuck around the house to the back. A pile of chopped wood exuded a fresh pine scent. She walked up to the back door and peered in the window. No lights were on. No movement. No sound.

Stella slipped her gun from its holster and gripped it hard with her right hand. Reaching out with her left hand, she turned the knob on the door. It was open. Returning to a double-handed grip on her gun, she pushed the door open with her boot.

The silhouette of a dark kitchen appeared. Empty. Silent.

Stella stepped inside and closed the door quietly behind her. An archway opened into the next room, glowing with the flames of the ring of candles she'd seen through the front window.

Muffled sound came from behind a door across the kitchen. She walked up and leaned her ear against it. A voice. It sounded like a woman. She couldn't make out the words.

Stella opened the door. It let out a creak. She froze. The voice below continued, uninterrupted. One gentle step at a time, she made her way down the stairs toward the voice.

The basement came into view. A figure in a dark cloak stood facing a stone fireplace glowing from a blanket of hot coals. The glow flickered, stretching red fingers around the room.

Controlling her breathing into soft puffs, she looked at the space.

Over to the left, a ring of candles wove around a stake. Nothing hung from it. It was empty. Yet Stella knew it wouldn't stay that way.

She swallowed, clenched her jaw, then raised her gun at the cloaked figure. "Police. Raise your hands. Turn around. Slowly."

The figure turned. The red glow cast a shadow that stretched out in front of the mystery person. A hood partially concealed the face of a young woman. Dark eyes peered from beneath.

"Raise your hands." Stella positioned her gun at the woman's shoulder.

Arms rose, fingers grasping the hood and sliding it back. Raven hair hung softly over her shoulders.

It was her. The woman. The one in the photo from the newspaper article that Jake had found. The burning house. The missing girls. This was the older sister. *Damaris Celeste.*

The woman narrowed her eyes. The whites were coated with a yellow-brown sludge, the centres glowing red.

What is this?

Bells rang. Chanting trickled through the red-glowing space. Words grasped Stella's ears.

In the name of Satan.

Stella shook her head. *What the fuck?* The Markhor, morphed into a five-pointed star of evil, pulsed in her mind.

The chanting increased in volume, hijacking her thoughts.

Open the gates of hell.

Stella gripped her gun. She scanned the room, seeking the source of the chanting. A CD player and a pair of speakers sat atop a table to the right of the fireplace. The other cloaked woman, the younger sister, was nowhere to be found.

"You have entered my realm," Damaris hissed the words as she walked toward Stella.

"Damaris Celeste, stop where you are."

The chanting from the speakers grew louder.

"Your fate is mine." Damaris took another step.

"Stop. Now." Stella spat her words.

The chanting heightened. Damaris' mouth moved in unison with the words. "Leviathan. Baphomet. Samael Lilith."

The room swayed around Stella. She narrowed her eyes, attempting to focus. Her arms trembled as she tried to hold her gun straight.

In one swift motion, Damaris slid her hand into the folds of her cloak, then thrust her arm up, fingers wrapped around her amethyst-adorned knife. The blade slid into the flesh underneath Stella's arm. Skin tore. Blood flew.

Stella jerked. Her gun dropped, hitting the floor with a clank and sliding behind her. Her mind jolted. She thrust her left elbow up, connecting underneath Damaris' chin with a crunch.

Damaris fell back, pulling the knife down Stella's arm in a zagged tear. Damaris landed hard on the concrete. The knife clinked against the floor beside her.

Pain clawed Stella's arm. She stood tall, pumped her fist a few times, and took stock of the situation.

Damaris crouched. Stella could see the knife on the floor, not far from Damaris. She couldn't see her gun. It was somewhere behind her.

Damaris reached out, grabbed her knife, and rose.

"You. You have entered *my* realm." Damaris swiped her hair from her face. She stared at Stella. The strange red glow in the centre of her pupils turned her gaze demonic.

Stella's brain seized. What was she looking at?

Damaris took several steps forward, closing Stella in. Heat swelled behind Stella as she backed toward the fireplace. Out of the corner of her eye, she spotted a long, cylindrical rod thrusting into the hot coals, a circle of metal at the end glowing orange.

The daunting voices chanted louder, invading her mind, wrapping fingers around her brain, gripping hard. Crushing her own thoughts.

Come forth from the abyss.

The red glow flickered.

Stella stood gun-less. Damaris raised her blade again.

Stella braced, rooting her boots in the ground. She pumped her right hand into a fist, fighting against the searing pain in her arm.

Damaris thrust herself at Stella, cloak flying behind her. She raised her blade, high in the air, aiming straight for Stella.

Stella grabbed the metal rod with both hands.

Damaris reached her arms higher, her shirt sliding up her body, exposing her abdomen.

Stella spun toward Damaris and pressed the blazing metal circle against her stomach.

Smoking flesh sizzled and burnt skin stung the air.

Damaris fell back with a thud onto the concrete floor. She stared down in disbelief at the symbol of Baphomet and the five-pointed star forever burned into her own flesh.

The hot coals flickered in unison. The room swelled. Damaris clutched her knife, curling her knees into her stomach.

Stella dropped the metal rod with a loud clank. She spun, spotted her gun, and lunged for it.

Gripping her gun with both hands, she raised it and walked toward Damaris. "Damaris Celeste," she commanded. "Drop the knife."

"Open the gates of hell," the woman muttered. Her voice became one with those chanting through the room. The sounds of a witch mixed with those of Satanic chants. "Satan. Lucifer. Samael Lilith."

Stella shuddered. The cloaked woman blurred in a haze as the words clouded Stella's mind. A whisper escaped Stella's lips, "Leviathan. Baphomet. Samael Lilith."

The woman rose and slowly approached as Stella was caught in an inexplicable trance. "Yes. Succumb," Damaris said.

The flames blazed in a sudden burst of orange-red heat, clawing long fingers up the walls. The air shimmered, as if the individual particles of hydrogen and oxygen came to life, bubbling from the heat of the room. The walls heaved, as if breathing in the flames.

Stella's mind whirled. She held her gun straight at the woman, squinting through the hot haze. Pain seared her arm. Hot blood soaked her shirt where the blade had slashed.

The flames extinguished in a sudden spark. The room went black. A chill crept through it.

Stella searched the darkness for the outline of the woman. Nothing was visible. Sweat sprouted over Stella's neck, trickling down her back. The sudden chill of the room reached into her, into the pit of her belly. Her gut tingled.

The flames blazed bright again, igniting the room in a yellow glow. The flames dimmed, simmering to a soft orange. The chanting thrummed through her head. Her vision blurred with a red-orange haze. Her hands trembled as her gun wavered.

A *clunk* as her gun hit the floor.

Stella hunched over on all fours.

A pain wrenched her gut.

The chanting violated her mind.

Stella grimaced against the evil voices and the spinning red room, forcing her gaze to search the darkness. Damaris walked toward her, knife raised.

Chapter 68

Kill the Demon

Viviana was upstairs in the bedroom, hiding from Dami, when she heard the loud crash. She suspected that Dami was in another fit, throwing things and pounding her fists. After seeing Dami in the basement, hovering over the fireplace, heating her brand to clean it of the remnants from her last kill, she'd snuck upstairs to get away from the savage vibe. Her throat tightened and her stomach clenched, knowing she had to check on her sister now.

Viviana descended to the main floor, noticing the candles that Dami must have lit, burning an orange glow through the otherwise dark house. That's when she heard it. The evil chanting thrumming from the basement. She was sure it was the *Devil's Track*. How could it be?

She'd walked in on Dami's recording session in the basement. Voices that seemed to come from nowhere joining with Dami's, the chanting crawling up the walls and into the speakers of a rickety old tape deck. A few days later, Dami came rushing in the door with a shiny CD in her hand, letters dripping over the symbol of Baphomet plastered on the front cover, declaring it to be the *Devil's Track*. Dami bragged about her crazy experience in a basement studio, watching her crude recording transfer to the shiny disk, the whole process under the table. Dami had played it over and over, until Viviana slipped it in her pocket and snuck out the back door. Viviana had been *sure* there was only one copy. How many had Dami had made? Had she hidden them from her? She'd gotten rid of the evil recording. She'd dropped it in a garbage can in an alley off Marbank Drive in the middle of the night when Dami was in a cacao-wine-infused sleep.

She crept down the stairs, wondering how much the house, and the evil album, had twisted Dami.

The basement came fully into view as Viviana reached the bottom of the stairs. Red fingers licked the walls. A chill washed through the space, prickling her arms.

Damaris stood beside the stone fireplace aglow from the hot coals within. She hovered over a woman on all fours. Strawberry-blonde locks stuck to the woman's sweat-drizzled face as she looked up at Dami. Dami held her knife high, aiming at the woman. A gun was on the floor, next to the woman's hand.

No. Who was this woman? The glow glinted off a badge on the woman's belt. *Police?* Couldn't be.

But Viviana knew it was. Any number of things could have brought the help Viviana so desperately wanted. The clues she'd left in her plea to stop the killing. She knew the guy in the alleyway off Marbank Drive saw her as she purged the evil album. She paused, looking him in the eyes, hoping he'd pick it up. Maybe even tell someone about the cloaked woman dropping the *Devil's Track* in the middle of the night.

She'd given her family name to the creep she'd bought the goat horns from. The bodies left in the cemetery, each pierced with a horn.

Deep down, she'd wanted someone to piece this together. To find them.

The *All-Seeing Eye* burned bright, staring straight into Viviana's soul. Words dripped from the purple book, the guide given to her by her father. Dami's eyes, clear, without the yellow tinge and the red core, pleading with her. The words slipping from Dami's lips... *Stop me. Stop...It.*

Damaris loomed over the woman. The tip of her blade inches from fresh flesh.

Viviana reached into the folds of her cloak, finding the handle of her knife. In a swift movement, she was upon Damaris, her powerful sister. Damaris spun. The red pupils of her eyes bore into Viviana's heart.

No time. Can't think. The *All-Seeing Eye* pulsed. The words of the purple book pierced her mind.

You, my child, were born with the purest seed within. You must protect it.

Viviana lunged. The tip of her silver blade slid into Damaris' heart. Blood poured over the ivory handle, coating the daisy protectors and the crystal amulet with evil red juice.

A tremendous shock shook Viviana's entire being. She jumped back, holding out her hands, her sister's blood dripping from her fingertips. The slice in Damaris' flesh opened, like a blood-filled mouth, drooling scarlet streams.

Viviana looked at Damaris. Damaris looked at Viviana.

The red glow in the centre of Damaris' eyes vanished; the rich, dark colour returned. The sickly yellow tinge tainting the whites simmered away, leaving a clean, white shine.

"Viv," Damaris gasped. She wrapped her hands around Viviana's knife. Her body quivered.

The icy grasp of the little house at the edge of the forest slid its hand out of Viviana, retreating into the folds of the concrete walls in the sacrificial basement.

Viviana fell to her knees at her sister's feet. "Dami," she cried.

The pit of Viviana's belly flushed with fresh energy. An aura she hadn't felt since her father held her in his arms, reading from the purple book etched in gold. A flood of tears burst from Viviana's eyes in a sudden wave.

"I'm sorry." She wrapped her cloaked arms around Damaris.

Strands of fire-red hair fell from Viviana's hood, around her face. She stared into her sister's eyes. What had she done? Was this real?

Damaris placed her gloved hand on the back of Viviana's head, resting her palm gently. "It's over."

Viviana looked into Damaris' dark eyes. Had she really returned? "It is?" Her tears drenched her hair, sticking strands to her cheeks.

"Yes," Damaris gasped, clutching the ivory handle. She fell to her knees. She leaned her face toward Viviana and rested their foreheads together. Cold puffs of sweet cacao wine and lavender seeped from Damaris, coating Viviana in a luscious aroma. She *was* back.

"But..." Viviana reached out her hand, sliding her fingers over her sister as they both clutched the knife. The crystal amulet, now stained in too much blood, no longer seemed a sign of protection.

Damaris yanked the knife from her body, tearing flesh and spurting blood. She let it slip from her fingers. It fell with a clank onto the concrete floor. She hunched over, grunting and gasping.

"Dami!" Viviana cried. She leaned over her sister, caressing her, stroking her back.

Damaris fell onto her side. She rolled over onto her back. Her dark cloak splayed around her. Her hair fell against the material, melding into a single raven spread. "Viv. You...had to." She smiled. Not a sick, sadistic smile. Not the smile the demon had pasted over her face. The smile Viviana recognized. "I had...to be...stopped."

Viviana shook her head. "But..." she cried, "I could have helped you."

Damaris grabbed Viviana's arm. "No. It...the anger...morphed...into sickness. Inside...me." She swallowed, licking her black lips.

"Dami," Viviana cried, stroking her sister's pallid, smooth cheek. She looked so pale. She felt so cold.

A whirlwind of anxious tingles erupted inside of Viviana. What was she supposed to do? Where was her inner guide now?

"Viv," Dami gasped. Blood-tinged saliva dribbled down the side of her mouth. "Go."

Viviana shook her head. "No. I won't leave you."

A shuffling from the corner ripped Viviana from the moment with her sister. The woman, the *police*, crawled toward the CD player still vibrating with the evil chant.

Damaris wheezed, sucking in a laboured breath of air. She clutched her torn flesh. Her head fell back against the floor.

Viviana gripped her sister's hand. All those times she questioned Damaris" guidance, leadership, *demands,* and still chose to follow what led them to down a dark, devilish path. A path of destruction, a series of sacrifices, guiding Viviana's mind, her hand, to perform acts she thought she was incapable of executing, to this point now where she watched her sister bleed from her heart. From the very gash that she, Viviana, herself, had inflicted.

Viviana closed her eyes. She pictured the purple book etched in gold. She imagined her father reading to her. She saw her natural sanctuary hidden in the forest, her moss-covered rock seat, the trickling creak, the clear sound of her internal guide surging through her. She focused all her energy on summoning her spiritual guide now. The true source of spiritual enlightenment, it had to be there. It couldn't be dead. Not now, when she needed it most.

A glimmer of warmth sparked in her core. It surged through her. Full of tingles and warmth, she let her spiritual guide wrap its arms around her now. She breathed in the aura seeping through her, out of her, into the basement.

A loud crash snapped Viviana back to the basement. She snapped her eyes open.

The policewoman crouched under the red glow of the fireplace, smashing the CD player against the concrete floor. The hypnotizing chant released its hold.

Viviana grabbed her knife, wiped her sister's life juice from its blade, and slipped it into the folds in her cloak. She sprinted swiftly up the stairs and out the back door.

She ran to the edge of the forest, and along the soft dirt dotted with stones, into the welcoming arms of the forest. The tall firs closed their green branches around her, hiding her from the world. Sirens blared through the quiet of the night. Red-and-blue light pierced through the thick fir boughs. She kept running. Away from the little house at the edge of the forest, toward her own destiny.

Chapter 69

Witch Chase

The red haze in the room lifted as Stella narrowed her eyes. The remnants of the CD player scattered in an array of plastic carnage. Damaris lay on the ground, her hair fanned around her head, a pool of blood around her heart. The cloak of the fire-haired woman fluttered behind her as she ran up the stairs.

No.

Stella fought against the buzzing in her brain and the heaviness weighing down her limbs. She forced herself to stand.

One cloaked witch down. One to go.

Stella grabbed her gun and wobbled up the stairs. The pain in her arm intensified, like a hot poker searing her flesh. She burst through the back door of the tiny kitchen and breathed in a crisp breath of fresh air.

A flutter of a black cloak and fire hair from the edge of the forest caught her eye. Stella ran. Fast and hard. Her lungs stung. Her legs burned. She pumped her arms and forced her pace to beyond uncomfortable.

She gained on the woman. *Viviana.* The witch hat had been slipping through her fingers was now within her reach.

She spoke between gasps of air. "Viviana Celeste. Stop. Now. Or I will shoot."

Viviana halted. She turned and faced Stella.

Stella said, "Viviana. It's over."

Viviana's lip trembled. "No. I...my sister. Those people."

Stella paused, gripping her gun hard.

Viviana spun and bolted. Stella burst into a sprint. Stella jumped, thrusting herself through the air, straight at the witch, knocking her down. She landed hard on top of Viviana. Leaves crunched, dirt sprayed, skin tore open.

Stella hoisted herself up and held her gun straight to the back of Viviana's head. She steadied her grip.

"Viviana. It's over."

Noise from behind. Feet pounding down the dirt path.

"Stella. It's Parker. You OK?"

"Yeah. Got it all under control." Stella took a deep breath and let it go.

Chapter 70

The Boss

Stella opened her eyes. The room whirled around her in a bright-white haze. She closed her eyes and took a deep breath. The odour of sterilization stung her nose.

She opened her eyes again and took in her surroundings. White. Clean. Bright. Beeping.

Scanning down her body, her upper right arm bandaged, an IV poking into it, and the rest of her intact. Her arm. The knife. Damaris.

Why had Viviana, the younger sister, slid a knife into Damaris' heart?

Maybe she would never know. The echoes of that damn evil mass still thrummed through her brain. It had hypnotized her. What the hell was that thing?

Movement through the doorway pulled her from her thoughts.

"Stella." Sutton looked at her sheepishly as he walked toward the bed. "I mean, Detective Mahoney." He smiled.

"Boss." She smiled back and rested her head against the pillow. "How much trouble am I in?"

Images of the last twenty-four hours flashed through her mind. The little house on the edge of the forest. Going in alone. Tackling Viviana. Parker showing up. Holding the gun against the back of the witch's head. Blood gushing from her upper arm. Parker cuffing Viviana. The wave of nausea and dizziness that followed. Crumpling into a bed of leaves. The medics. The operation on her arm. How long had she been in here?

Sutton pulled up a chair and sat beside the bed. He pulled something out of his coat pocket, reached over, and handed it to her.

She took it.

A deep-purple rabbit's foot dangled from a string of black leather woven into an intricate pattern. Tingles sprang up her arm and down to her belly.

"Thanks."

"Maybe it's stupid. I know you think mine is gnarly." Sutton chuckled.

"No. It's not." She meant it.

"You have the Mahoney instinct. The way you pieced this case together. You went with your gut, even when you were questioned."

She rested her hand and the rabbit foot in her lap and looked Sutton in the eye. What was the catch? She raised an eyebrow.

"I'm not going to stop questioning. It's my job." He returned her stare.

"Got it." She did get it. She'd never taken the time to think about what it was like for him. "I know I sounded crazy. Witchcraft. Strange brew. Burning at the stake."

"You didn't sound crazy. But I need to poke holes in every theory presented. Point things out so you can prove me wrong. Put a solid case together." He sat back into the chair and rested his palms on his knees. "*I* need *you* to listen to me."

She pursed her lips and looked at the rabbit foot.

"And, I *need* you to keep following that gut. Challenge me."

She looked back at Sutton and smiled. "That I can do."

"Oh, I know you can."

"What will happen to Viviana?" she asked.

"Thanks to you, she's not going anywhere. That partial print matches Viviana's. Seems she was the one who stabbed the last victim through the heart."

Stella shook her head. Viviana was the one who purchased the horns and the cacao powder. She was clearly an equal part in the killings. Why did she turn on her sister?

Sutton continued, "And the descriptions of her, by the taxidermist..."

"Torrence. Creep." She shuddered.

"And the guy at that witchy store..."

"Witch's Spell. It was kind of a cool place."

"She even gave her name to your Torrence creep."

"He was gross." Stella smiled.

"The body of the older sister was recovered. The DNA on the flask matches hers. The house was full of evidence. Solid case."

Parker. He'd been there for her. "Where's Parker?"

"Doing the write-up. Since you're in here."

Her face flushed. "Guess I got out of the paperwork."

"He volunteered." Sutton stood. "You should have taken him with you to the house. But I'm sure you already know that. Jake's the one who got your backup there."

Would it have killed her to wait for Parker?

Sutton slid a folder from under his arm and dropped it on the makeshift dinner table beside her bed. "Some reading material for you. Jake knew you'd be wracking your brain about that album. He said your theory about the impact of certain tones in music was dead on. He called it auditory hypnosis."

Stella's shoulders relaxed against the stack of stiff pillows. Maybe there *was* an explanation.

Sutton looked at her, touching his rabbit claw. He nodded. He stuffed his hand into his jacket pocket and pulled out a portable CD player and set it on the bed. He pulled out a CD case and set it beside the player. The words *Skid Row* dripped down the front in bold lettering.

"What?" Stella whispered, dumbfounded.

"Jake said this was your favourite. He was concerned you wouldn't be able to sleep without some metal."

Jakey. Rockstar.

"Thank you." She looked up at Sutton, face flushed, heart warm.

Chapter 71

On the Beach

The ocean breeze played with Stella's soft, strawberry-blonde hair, tossing it around her shoulders. The sun hung low on the horizon, casting a golden-pink glow over the turquoise water, stretched out like a rippling blanket. Silver diamonds danced over the surface of the water as the sun's rays reached over it. A seagull squealed in the distance.

Stella scanned the vast expanse of amber sand, reaching far in both directions.

She hadn't been here in a long time.

The best memories of her life were made here. She could still see her mother whirling around in the shallow water, her strawberry-blonde hair dancing in the breeze, her blue scarves fluttering around her. She had always seemed so free. Back then.

She could still see her father, on the beach, digging his toes into the sand. Wearing his tweed coat. And his derby. Looking so out of place in a setting like this.

She remembered calling to him from in the water. Saying, 'Daddy, Daddy, watch me swim.'

She remembered his face, looking at her, with so much love. She knew, even then, he didn't know how to be the typical father. The one everyone expected him to be.

She could still hear his voice over the phone. That night. The night he died.

He had sounded so far away. Not just physically. She knew. She could hear it in his voice. She knew she'd never see him again. He'd chosen. To save all those girls. And, she understood. She understood now. And she'd understood then. She couldn't lie to herself anymore.

All these years she'd told herself she could have saved him. She could have convinced him to come home. Right then. Right there. That it was her fault that he had died.

But it wasn't her fault. She knew that now.

Her father had chosen what he knew was right. He wanted to be there for her. But that would have meant turning his back on those other girls. The ones who lived. Because of him. Because he sacrificed himself. For them.

A seagull squealed, bringing her back to the beach. She looked out across the vast ocean rippling under the breeze. A white-capped wave flushed the shoreline. Little birds skittered across the dark, wet sand.

She slid her hands into the pockets of her father's tweed herringbone coat. She'd only ever worn it when she was hiding from the world within the walls of her small apartment, back in the city she now called home. Once again. She looked down at the coat, where the bloodstain had been. The scarlet circle, made by her father's blood. The reminder of his death.

The bloodstain no longer tainted the coat. She'd finally had it removed. Despite the fancy dry cleaning job, the collar of the coat still smelled of Blue Jeans by Versace. It smelled like her father.

She pulled her hand from the pocket, the weight of her knife heavy in her palm. It had been Sutton that had saved her from the visions of sliding her knife into Tomlinson, the man that she had blamed for the death of her father.

She wasn't ready to let go of the knife. It made her feel safe, somehow. She *was* ready to purge her rage and her desire for revenge.

As she dropped the knife back into the pocket, she took a deep breath of the essence of her father still clinging to his coat.

It was time.

She bent down, picked up the small metal urn nestled into the sand at her feet. She walked to edge of the water, slipped off her shoes, and plunged her toes into the chill of the ocean. She walked out far enough, then stopped. She tucked the urn into the crook of her left arm. The last rays of sunshine glinted off glass water. The emptiness of losing her father weighed down her insides.

She slipped her hand into the pocket of the tweed coat and pulled out the little black book filled with her father's handwriting. The book of life lessons he'd left behind. Just for her.

She opened it and flipped through the pages, finding the one that called to her now.

She looked at the page. She read the words aloud, for her, for the birds, for the ocean. For her father.

Always be True to yourself.

Stella. On your journey through life, many people will force their expectations upon you. They will expect you to be a certain way. They will expect you to meet their idea of what they think you should be. Of what they want you to be.

Listen to your heart. You know who you are. You always have. I saw it in your eyes the first moment we met. I saw it in your eyes time after time as you grew. You were an adult far before this world told you that you were.

Stella. You always knew who you were. Be that person. Despite what anyone else tells you.

Love, forever, Dad.

She closed the book and slipped it back into her pocket. Tears trickled down her face. The ocean breeze whipped them away. Sliding the urn into her left hand, she lifted the lid with her right. She turned, aiming the urn to catch the breeze in just the right direction. She swallowed. She closed her eyes. She pictured her father. Wearing the very coat she had on now. His tattered charcoal derby perched on his head. His face rough with a two-day beard. His eyes, knowing all, seeing all, looking at her with love. She opened her eyes and tilted the urn. The ashes slid from the urn, drifting along with ocean breeze as it caught the essence of her father and took it out along the vast, ocean horizon.

Acknowledgments

I have a lot of support from friends, family and readers. Thank you to every single one of you.

A special thank you to Taija Morgan. She has gone above and beyond to make this book, and the entire series all that it is.

A special thank you to Cami Schulte. She has been a star reader for this entire series, and her input has been crucial.

A special thank you to James Hiner for showing me how to tap into my passion and creativity, and how to keep digging deep until the result fits my vision. Thank you for the early feedback on my crazy goat headed cover work. Thank you for all the happy hours, hikes, and winter fires.

Thank you to all of my readers who have found me online and at live events. Your readership is a strong foundation for my creativity and my motivation.

Thank you to all of you who plunged into the depths of Vern's on an icy cold night, danced your hearts out, and grabbed one of the first copies of Final Track to enter the world. Thank you to all of you who stuck around, joined a virtual party when a real one was impossible, and supported the release of Acid Track. Thank you to all of you who rocked out at The Trop and celebrated the release of Back Track with a head bang (or two). Thank you to each of you holding a copy of Devil's Track. Without your support, this writing journey wouldn't be the epic adventure that it's turned into!

About Author

Julie Hiner is an author of heavy metal horror. She spent endless hours during her childhood lost in the pages of books and listening to the metal gods of the 80s. To this day, Julie is a hardcore 80s rocker at heart.

After securing a computer science degree, Julie pursued a career working on large scale network systems. On a break between contracts, Julie followed her dream. She published a work of inspirational non-fiction capturing her journey of facing fear and anxiety by cycling up the mountains of the Tour de France.

Several years ago, she plunged down a fiction writing path. Following her fascination of the dark mind of the serial killer and finding inspiration at a talk given by a local homicide detective, Julie wrote a serial killer novel. She now writes dark crime and horror infused with rock and metal. She has successfully launched an 80s metal murder series, a nostalgic 90s serial killer novella, and had several horror short stories published. She currently runs killersanddemons.com where she serves up toxic cocktails of 80s metal and raw horror.

Also By

Detective Mahoney Series
Final Track
Acid Track
Back Track
Solo Track – Det. Mahoney Side Story
Dead End Track – M.E. Blackwood Story

Other
Owen's Terrarium – Novella by Killers and Demons
The Omens Call – Horror Anthology, Edited by Hiner and Willcocks
Hallowed Killer - in Pulp Harvest by Blood Rites Horror
Corpse Forest - in The Other Side: Horror Anthology by Devil's Rock Publishing
Tuny - in Terrace VI: Forbidden Fruit by The Seventh Terrace
Candy Lady - in October Blood by HawkeHaus

If you enjoyed *Devil's Track* please consider leaving a review.
Come by for a visit @ KillersAndDemons.com.
For review links and tips, check out the review page.

www.ingramcontent.com/pod-product-compliance
Lightning Source LLC
Chambersburg PA
CBHW071432200726
48294CB00002B/607